LUCIANO'S LUCK

Also Available in Large Print
by the same author:

As Jack Higgins
Solo
Day of Judgment

As Harry Patterson
The Valhalla Exchange
To Catch a King

LUCIANO'S LUCK

JACK HIGGINS

G.K.HALL &CO.
Boston, Massachusetts
1982

Library of Congress Cataloging in Publication Data

Higgins, Jack, 1929-
  Luciano's luck.

  "Published in large print by arrangement with Stein
and Day/Publishers"—T.p. verso.
  1. Large type books. I. Title.
[PR6058.I343L8 1982]   823'.914   81-20129
ISBN 0-8161-3304-2   AACR2

Published in Large Print by arrangement with
Stein and Day/Publishers

Set in Compugraphic 18 pt English Times
by Adhanet Elias

FOR SACHA and GEORGE

SICILY — 1943

In July 1943, American forces landed on the southern coast of Sicily and, in an advance of incredible rapidity, reached Palermo in only seven days. That their success was due in no small measure to the cooperation of the Sicilian Mafia acting under the direct orders of Charles Lucky Luciano, then serving a sentence of thirty to fifty years in Great Meadow Penitentiary in New York State, is a matter of historical fact. What is particularly fascinating about this strange episode is that in Sicily to this day, there are those who insist that they saw Luciano in person with the American units during the early part of the invasion. . . .

1

ONE

It was just before evening, when the jeep carrying Harry Carter turned in through the gates of the great Moorish villa called dar el Ouad outside Algiers, and braked to a halt at the ornate, arched entrance.

"Wait for me," Carter told the driver and went up the steps past the sentries.

In the cool, dark hall inside, a young captain in summer uniform sat at a desk working on some papers. The plaque in front of him said, *Captain George Cusak*. He glanced up at Carter, noted the uniform, the crowns on his shoulder, the purple and white ribbon of the Military Cross with a silver rosette for a second award, and stood up.

"What can I do for you, Major?"

Carter produced his pass. "I think you'll find General Eisenhower is expecting me."

The captain examined the pass briefly and nodded. "Ten minutes to go, Major. If you'll take a seat, I'll tell him you're here."

Harry Carter walked out on to the terrace through the open French windows and sat down in one of the wickerwork chairs. After a moment's hesitation he took out an old silver case from his breast pocket and selected a cigarette.

He was forty-two, of medium height, a handsome man with a calm, pleasant face that always seemed about to break into a smile, but never quite made it. And he suited the uniform to perfection, which was surprising for he was the second son of a prosperous Yorkshire mill owner, a scholar by nature, educated at Leeds Grammar School until thirteen and then Winchester. From there he had absconded in 1917, joining the Army under a false age, serving the last eighteen months of the First World War as an infantry private on the Western Front.

Afterwards came Cambridge and a brilliant academic career, which had included spells at Harvard as visiting professor of Greek Archaeology, the University of Florence, and then a return to Cambridge as a fellow of Trinity and Claverhouse

4

Professor of Ancient History at thirty-five.

Just after Munich, he had been approached by British Intelligence and had worked with Masterman at MI5, helping to destroy the German spy network in England.

Someone bright in personnel had picked up on the fact that he had been in Sicily in '32, studying the Greek ruins in the hills around Syracuse, and again in '34 on excavations along the volcanic eastern coast.

Colonel Bussaca, tough as a headmaster, had tested him on his command of the Sicilian dialects to see if he knew the Sicilian temper well enough to be able to deal face-to-face with Don Antonio Luca, *capo di capi,* who lived a deceptively simple life in a mountain village with his mistress and servants, and wouldn't lift a finger to help the Allies. Colonel Bussaca knew that Don Antonio liked to play bridge. Carter, a master at chess, knew how to lose gracefully at bridge. To help win the war he would have learned anything.

Three missions into Sicily by parachute earned him a medal, two oak-leaf clusters, weariness in his gray eyes, and permanent flecks of silver in his dark hair.

Carter flicked what remained of his

cigarette out into the garden.

"Careful, Harry," he said softly. "Next thing, you'll be starting to feel sorry for yourself."

There was a movement behind him and he glanced up as Captain Cusak appeared.

"Major Carter, General Eisenhower will see you now, sir."

The room was as ornate and Moorish in its furnishings as was the rest of the villa. The only signs that it was the nerve center of the headquarters of the Supreme Allied Commander for the North African Theater were to be found in the maps of the Mediterranean pinned to one wall and the three trestle tables covered with more maps, which had been placed by the terrace windows to serve as a desk.

Eisenhower was standing outside on the terrace as they went in, smoking a cigarette, wearing boots and riding breeches for he rode most afternoons. He turned and walked in briskly, his face illuminated by that famous and inimitable smile.

"Coffee, George," he said to Cusak. "Or maybe Major Carter would prefer tea?"

"No, coffee would be fine, sir."

Cusak went out and Eisenhower indicated

a chair and opened a file on his desk. "And just how does a man with your background get by as a Sicilian peasant?"

"Oh, you can thank the University Dramatic Society for that, General. There was a wild moment there when I was tempted to turn professional."

"You were that good."

"I wouldn't be here if I wasn't, sir," Carter said calmly.

"When S.O.E. sent you out to Cairo to take charge of the Italian section I don't think they envisaged your personal invasion of Sicily on . . ." here he glanced again at the file, ". . . three separate occasions?"

"I know, sir," Carter said. "But we didn't really have any choice. When it came to Sicily, there wasn't anyone else who knew the language or the people as well. I did a lot of work on archaeological digs there during the thirties."

"What exactly did you accomplish there?" asked Eisenhower.

"I wanted the Mafia to check on the harbors on the south coast, to make sure that if Germans mined the harbors the word would be passed along right away, including the location of the mined areas."

"Did they comply?"

"I delivered a certain consideration in both lire and large denomination U.S. treasury bills in accord with Mafia instructions."

Eisenhower nodded.

"And now you're going in again. Don't you think you're getting a little old for this sort of thing?"

Eisenhower pushed a document across the desk and Carter picked it up. It was a typical S.O.E. operation order in sparse, no-nonsense Civil Service English.

OPERATION INSTRUCTION NO. 592
For: Major Harry Carter.
Operation: Swordarm
Field Name: FORTUNATO
Name on Papers: Giovanni Ciccio
1. INFORMATION
We have discussed with you the possibility of your returning to Sicily to finalize the mission you were originally given when you left for that island in February of this year; namely, to coordinate the organization of Resistance groups in the general area of the Cammarata so that the maximum cooperation is available to Allied troops in the event of invasion.
2. METHOD

From Maison Blanche you will proceed to Sicily in a Halifax of 138 (Special Duties) Squadron and will land by parachute at a point 10 kilometres west of Bellona where you will be received by elements of the local Resistance movement. You have been given a cover story and papers in the name of Giovanni Ciccio which will enable you to live a normal life in the field.

3. INTERCOMMUNICATIONS

Your channel of communication with the Resistance movement in the Palermo area will be through the Contessa di Bellona who is at the present time in residence at her villa outside that town.

Your channel of communication with H.Q. will be by W/T radio transmission handled by Vito Barbera, coordinator, Bellona area.

4. WEAPONS

At your discretion, but only those you consider essential for hand-to-hand combat.

5. CONCLUSION

You are aware of the importance of this mission and nothing must take precedence over it. We anticipate completion in two weeks. Your return will be by submarine pickup. Details of this will be transmitted by radio in field code at the

appropriate time.
NOW DESTROY . . . NOW DESTROY
. . . NOW DESTROY

Carter took a cigarette lighter from his pocket, flicked it with his thumb, and touched the flame to the corner of the document. When it was well alight, he crossed to the empty fireplace and dropped it into the grate.

"Even you shouldn't have that, General."

The door opened and Cusak returned with coffee on a brass Arabic tray. "Thanks, George, I'll take care of it," Eisenhower said.

He poured the coffee himself and lit another cigarette. "I'd say it's a reasonable assumption that you know more about what's happening over there at the moment that anyone else in North Africa. So let's talk."

"What would you like to know, General?"

"I'd like you to tell me a bit more about the Mafia than I'm likely to know."

"You have the file on the Mafia connection, presumably?"

"Yes."

Carter lit a cigarette himself without thinking. "As you know, the Mafia began as a kind of secret society during a period of real oppression. In those days it was the only weapon the peasant had, his only means of justice."

"Go on."

"In understanding the landscape, sir, one has to see it as another world. Sterile, barren, where the struggle is not so much for a living as for survival. A world where the key word is *omerta,* which means manliness, honor, and never, never seek official help. If you have a problem, you go to the *capo.*"

"The boss."

"Boss, chief, put it how you like. Wherever you go in Sicily there will be a *capo mafia* who rules the roost."

"And still does."

"When Mussolini tried to crush the movement, it simply went under the surface. They can talk of Separatists, Communists, and other political factions as much as they like, but in Sicily, it's still the Mafia that has the real influence."

"You know this man Luca?" Eisenhower asked.

"Yes, sir."

"I mean you've actually met him face to face?"

"Yes, sir."

"He didn't take you for a Sicilian, did he?"

"No, sir," Carter said, smiling. "He's a very smart man."

Finally, as if coming to a decision, Eisenhower tapped the brown manila folder in front of him.

"Are you familiar with an individual mentioned here as Lucky Luciano?"

Carter nodded. "A New York Sicilian gangster and probably the most important *capo* in the American Mafia. He's serving a thirty-to-fifty-year sentence in Dannemora Penitentiary at the moment. I believe the charge was organized prostitution."

"Not now, he isn't," Eisenhower said. "According to the file, he's been moved to Great Meadow at Comstock. It seems that after the liner Normandie was burned out on the Hudson last year, Naval Intelligence became worried about increasing sabotage on the New York waterfront."

"I know, General, and when they approached the longshoreman's unions, they discovered that the man to see was Luciano, inside prison or out."

Eisenhower said, "Incredible. In the middle of the greatest war in history they have to go to a crook for help. As if that wasn't enough, I now find that our people have been putting agents into Sicily for some time now, usually Americans with an ethnic Sicilian background. Were you aware of this?"

"It's a specifically American project, General, but yes, I did know about it. The aim is, I believe, to insure Mafia cooperation in the event of an invasion."

"Aren't we supposed to be fighting the same war, for God's sake?" Eisenhower took another cigarette and struck a match so forcibly that it snapped. "They approached Luciano in the penitentiary again about giving his assistance. They seem to think he has some influence in Sicily also."

"Considerable, General. If he appeared in some of those mountain villages it would be like the Second Coming."

"Our Intelligence people certainly seem to think so. Apparently a yellow scarf with the initial L in black, which is Luciano's calling card, will be dropped extensively in appropriate areas at the right time."

"And they believe this will help?" Carter asked.

Eisenhower turned back to the map. "The theory is sound enough. The terrain Patton and his army have to pass through to reach Palermo is a soldier's nightmare. The area around the Cammarata particularly is a warren of ravines and mountains. It could take months to hack a way through it. On the other hand, if the Mafia used its power to promote an uprising of the people and to persuade Italian units to surrender, the Germans would have no other recourse but to get the hell out of it."

"Yes, General," Carter said.

"You don't sound too certain. Don't you think the Mafia can deliver?"

"Frankly, sir, not as the people in Washington who dreamed this thing up seem to expect. One major weakness: If you take the Mafia boss, the *capo,* in one particular district, you may find he doesn't have much influence elsewhere. Another thing, your Intelligence people have been recruiting American service personnel with Sicilian or Italian ethnic backgrounds."

"And what's wrong with that?" Eisenhower demanded.

"It's better than nothing, of course, but being Italian doesn't cut much ice in Sicily, and, as regards the language, there are at least five Sicilian dialects in Palermo alone."

"But surely the idea of using Luciano was to get over such difficulties by having someone whose name meant something to everyone."

"I don't happen to think it's enough."

"But Washington does?"

"So it would appear."

There was a brief silence, Eisenhower frowning down thoughtfully at the file, and then he looked up.

"All right, Major, you've had one briefing. Now I'm going to give you another. I want the facts on this Mafia thing and straight from the horse's mouth. When you return in two weeks or whatever I want you back here Priority One with a firsthand assessment of the situation in the field. You understand me, Major."

"Perfectly, General."

"Good. You'd better get moving, then."

Carter saluted. Eisenhower nodded and picked up his pen. As Carter reached the door and opened it, the General called softly, "One thing more, Major."

Carter turned to face him. "Yes, sir?"

"Leave the rough stuff to other people. I'd be considerably inconvenienced if you failed to keep our next appointment."

TWO

It started to rain as Carter went over the ridge, a heavy, drenching downpour, sheet lightning flickering beyond the mountain peaks. He leaned the cumbersome bicycle against a tree and took the field glasses from his pocket. When he focused them the houses of Bellona three miles away jumped into view. He followed the valley road to where it disappeared into pine trees, but there was no sign of life. Not even a shepherd.

He replaced the field glasses in his pack, moved back through the trees to the other side of the ridge, and looked down at the villa in the hollow below, quiet in the evening light, waiting for him.

He was tired and yet filled with a sudden fierce exhilaration, faced at last with the final end of things. He started down the slope through the pine trees, pushing the bicycle before him.

He entered the grounds by a gate in the rear wall and followed a path around to the front of the house. The garden was Moorish, lush, semitropical vegetation pressing in everywhere. Palms swayed gently above his head and, in the heavy downpour, water gurgled in the old conduits, splashing from numerous fountains.

He emerged into the courtyard at the front of the house, leaned the bicycle against the baroque fountain, and went up the steps to the front door. There was already a light in the hall and he pulled on the bell chain and waited. There was the sound of footsteps approaching and the door opened.

The man who stood there was perhaps forty, his heavy moustache and hair already grey. He wore a black bow tie and alpaca jacket and looked Carter over with total disapproval.

"What do you want?"

Carter removed his cloth cap, and when he spoke, his voice was rough and hoarse, pure Sicilian. "I have a message for the Contessa."

The manservant held out his hand.

"Give it to me."

Carter shook his head, assuming an expression of peasant cunning. "My orders were to deliver it personally. She's expecting me. Tell her Ciccio is here."

The manservant shrugged. "All right, come in. I'll see what she has to say."

Carter stepped inside and stood there, dripping rain on to the black and white ceramic tiles. The manservant frowned his displeasure, walked across the hall, and went through a green baize door into a large kitchen. He paused just inside the door, took a Walther automatic from his pocket, checked it quickly then opened a cupboard beside the old-fashioned iron stove and took out a military field telephone. He wound the handle and waited, whistling softly to himself, tapping the Walther against his thigh.

There was the murmur of a voice at the other end and he said in German, "Schäfer —at the villa. Carter's turned up at last. No problem. I'll hold him till you get here."

He replaced the telephone in the cupboard, turned, and, still whistling softly, moved back to the door.

18

Carter shivered, suddenly cold, aware for the first time that the rain had soaked through to his skin. *Almost over now. God, but he was tired.* In the gilt mirror on the other side of the hall he could see his reflection. A middle-aged Sicilian peasant, badly in need of a shave, hair too long, with sullen, brutalized features, patched tweed suit and leather leggings, a shotgun, the traditional *lupara* with sawed-off barrels, hanging from his left shoulder.

But not for much longer. Soon there would be Cairo, Shepherd's Hotel, hot baths, clean sheets, seven-course meals and ice-cold champagne. Dom Perignon '35. He still had, after all, an infallible source of supply.

The green baize door opened in the mirror behind him and the manservant came through. Carter turned. "The Contessa will see me?"

"She would if she could, only she isn't here. We took her away three days ago." His right hand came up holding the Walther and now he was speaking in English. "The shotgun, Major Carter. On the floor, very gently, then turn, hands against the wall."

Strange, but now that it had happened, this moment that he had always known would come one day, Carter was aware of a curious sensation of relief. He didn't even attempt to play Ciccio anymore, but put down the *lupara* as instructed and turned to face the wall.

"German?" he asked.

"I'm afraid so." A hand searched him expertly. "Schäfer. *Geheimefeldpolizei.* I was beginning to think you weren't coming." He stepped back and Carter turned to face him.

"The Contessa?"

"The Gestapo has her. They've been waiting for you in Bellona for three days now. I've just telephoned through from the kitchen. They'll be here in twenty minutes."

"I see," Carter said. "So what do we do now?"

"We wait." Schäfer motioned him through into the dining room.

Carter paused, looking down at the open fire, steam rising from his damp clothes. Behind him, Schäfer sat down at the end of the long dining table, took out a pack of cigarettes, lit one, then pushed the pack along the table. Carter took one gratefully and when he struck the match, his fingers trembled slightly.

Schäfer said, "There's brandy on the

sideboard. You look as if you could do with it."

Carter went around the table and helped himself. The brandy was the local variety, raw and pungent. It burned as it went down and he coughed, struggling for breath. He poured himself another and turned to Schäfer.

"What about you?"

"Why not?"

Carter found another glass and moved to the table. "Say when," he said, and started to pour.

Schäfer still covered him with the Walther. Raising the glass to his lips he said, "I'm sorry about this, Major. I don't like those Gestapo bastards any more than you do, but I've got a job to do."

"Haven't we all," Carter said.

He swung the decanter in an arc against the German's skull, at the same time grabbing for the wrist of the hand that held the Walther, desperately trying to deflect it.

He swung the decanter again so that it splintered into dozens of pieces, brandy spurting across Schäfer's head and face, mingling with the blood. Incredibly, Schäfer's left fist managed a punch of considerable force high on Carter's right cheek, splitting the flesh to the bone, before clutching him by the throat.

They fell across the table and rolled over the edge to the floor and Carter was aware of one blow after another to the body and the pistol exploding between them. Somehow, he found himself up on one knee, twisting the other's wrist up and around until the bone cracked and the Walther jumped into the air, landing in the hearth.

The German screamed in agony, his head going back and Carter punched him in the open throat with knuckles extended. Schäfer rolled over on to his face and lay still and Carter turned and ran into the hall. He grabbed for the shotgun, slinging it over his shoulder as he made for the front door.

There was a dreamlike quality to everything. It was as if he were moving in slow motion, no strength in him, so that even opening the front door was an effort. He leaned against the balustrade of the porch, aware now that the front of his jacket was soaked with blood, not Schäfer's but his own. When he slipped a hand inside his shirt he could feel the lips of the wound like raw meat where a bullet had ripped through his left side.

No time for that, not now, for he was

aware of the sound of vehicles approaching on the road, very fast. He went lurching down the steps, picked up the bicycle, and hurriedly retraced his steps through the garden to the rear gate.

He reached the shelter of the pine trees below the villa, turned in time to see a truck and two *Kubelwagens* appear on the main road above him. Carter didn't wait to see what would happen, simply pushed on through the trees until he came to the woodcutter's track that ran all the way down through the forest to Bellona. Just enough light to see by if he were lucky. He flung a leg over the broken leather saddle of the old bicycle and rode away.

There wasn't a great deal to remember of that ride. The trees crowding in on either side, deepening the evening gloom, the rush of the heavy rain. It was rather like being on the kind of monumental drunk where, afterwards, only occasional images surface.

He opened his eyes to find himself lying on his back, the rain falling on his upturned face, in a ditch on the edge of the village, the bicycle beside him.

The pain of the gunshot wound was intense now, worse than he would have believed possible. There was no sign of the shotgun and he forced himself to his feet and stumbled along the track through the swiftly falling darkness.

The smell of wood smoke hung on the damp air and a dog barked hollowly in the distance, but otherwise there was no sign of life except for the occasional light in a window. And yet there were people up there, watching from behind the shutters, waiting.

He made it across the main square, pausing at the fountain in the center to put his head under the jet of cold water that gushed from the mouth and nostrils of a bronze dryad, continued past the church, and turned into a narrow side street. There was an entrance to a courtyard a few houses along, barred by an oaken gate, a blue lamp above it. The sign painted on the wall in ornate black letters read *Vito Barbera — Mortician*.

A small judas gate stood next to the main door. Carter leaned against it and pulled the bell chain. There was silence for a while and he held on to the grille with one hand, staring up at the rain falling in a silver spray through the lamplight. A footstep sounded inside and the grille opened.

Barbera said, "What is it?"

"Me, Vito."

"Harry, is that you?" Barbera said, this time in the kind of English that came straight from the Bronx. "Thank God. I thought they must have gotten you."

He opened the judas gate and Carter stepped inside. "A damn near-run thing, Vito, just like Waterloo," he said and fainted.

Carter surfaced slowly and found himself looking up at a cracked plaster ceiling. It was very cold and there was a heavy, medicinal smell to everything that he soon recognized as formaldehyde. He was lying on one of the tables in the mortuary preparation room, his neck pillowed on a wooden block, his stomach and chest expertly bandaged.

He turned his head and found Barbera, wearing a long rubber apron, working on the corpse of an old man at the next table. Carter pushed himself up.

Barbera said cheerfully, "I wouldn't if I were you. He shot you twice. The one in the side went straight through, but the second is somewhere in the left lung. You'll need a surgeon who knows what he's doing."

"Thanks a million," Carter said. "That really does make me a feel a whole lot better."

On a trolley beside Barbera were the tools of the embalmer's trade laid out neatly on a white cloth: forceps, scalpels, surgical needles, artery tubes, and a glass jar containing a couple of gallons of embalming fluid.

There was a look of faint surprise on the corpse's face that many people show in death, jaw dropped, mouth gaping as if in astonishment that this could be happening. Barbera took a long curved needle and passed it from behind the lower lip, up through the nasal septum and down again so that when he tightened the thread and tied it off, the jaw was lifted.

"So you raise people from the dead, too?" Carter eased himself off the table. "I always knew you were a man of many parts."

Barbera smiled, a small, intense-looking man of fifty whose tangled iron-grey beard appeared strangely at odds with the Bronx accent.

"You fucking English, Harry! I mean, when you are going to learn? The days of Empire are over. What were you trying to do up there, win the war on your own?"

"Something like that."

The door opened and a young girl entered. Sixteen or seventeen, no more. Small, dark-haired with a ripe, full body that strained at the seams of the old cotton dress. She had a wide mouth, dark brown eyes in a face of considerable character and yet there was the impression of one who had seen too much of life at its worst too early.

She carried a tray containing an old brass coffee pot, brown sugar, and glasses. There was also a bottle of cognac—Courvoisier.

Barbera carried on working. "Rosa, this is Major Carter. My niece arrived from Palermo since you were last here."

"Rosa," Carter said.

She poured coffee and handed it to him without a word.

Barbera said, "Good girl. Now go back to the gate and watch the square. Anything — anything at all, you let me know."

She went out and Carter poured himself a brandy, sipping it slowly for the pain in his lung was so intense that he could hardly breathe. "I never knew you had a niece. How old is she?"

"Oh, a hundred and fifty, or sixteen.

Take your pick. Her father was my youngest brother. Killed in an auto accident in thirty-seven in Naples. I lost sight of his wife. She died of consumption in Palermo three years ago.''

''And Rosa?''

''I only heard about her two months ago through Mafia friends in Palermo. She's been a street whore since she was thirteen. I figured it was time she came home.''

''You still think of this place as home after Eastchester Avenue?''

''Oh, sure, no regrets. Something Rosa can't understand. New York is still the promised land to her whereas to me, it was somewhere to leave. My family ties are really here, in Sicily. We go back centuries, my friend.''

He was working cream into the old man's face now, touching the cheeks with rouge.

Carter said, ''What about the Contessa?''

''The Gestapo took her to Palermo.''

''Bad for you if they break her.''

''Not possible.'' Barbera shook his head. ''A friend passed her a cyanide capsule in the women's prison yesterday afternoon.''

Carter took a long, shuddering breath to steady his nerves. ''I was hoping she'd have news for me of Luca.''

Barbera paused and glanced at him in some surprise. "You waste your time. No one has news of Luca because that is the way he wants it."

"Mafia again?"

"Yes, my friend, Mafia again and you would do well to remember that. What are your plans?"

"I was supposed to go to Agrigento tonight. I'm due to put to sea with a tuna boat out of Porto Stefano at midnight."

"Submarine pickup?"

"That's it."

Barbera frowned thoughtfully. "I don't see how, Harry, not tonight. The roads will be crawling with Krauts. Maybe tomorrow." He gestured to the corpse. "I've got to take the old boy here down to Agrigento anyway."

Before Carter could reply, the door burst open and Rosa looked in. "They are here in the square. Many Germans."

Barbera moved to the window and parted the curtain slightly. Carter struggled up with difficulty and limped to join him. Several vehicles had pulled up in the square, *Kubelwagens* and troop carriers and two armored cars. Soldiers had gathered in a semicircle and were being addressed from the back of a field car by an officer.

Carter said, "SS paratroopers. Where in the hell did they come from?"

"The mainland last month. Specially selected by Kesselring to clear the mountains of partisans. The one doing the talking is their commanding officer, Major Koenig. He's good. They call him the Hunter in the Cammarata."

As they watched, the SS broke away to commence searching the village. Koenig sat down and his *Kubelwagen* started across the square, followed by another.

Barbera closed the curtain. "Looks as if he's coming this way." He turned to Carter. "Did you leave anybody dead up there at the villa, by any chance?"

"Probably." Carter caught him by the sleeve. "He'll take it out on the village if I don't turn up."

Barbera smiled sadly. "Not his style. Believe it or not very definitely a man of honor. Makes it difficult to stick a knife in his back. Now you stay here with Rosa and keep quiet."

He took the lamp and went out, leaving them in darkness.

They were already knocking at the outer

30

gate as he crossed the courtyard. He eased back the massive bolt and the gate swung open to reveal the first *Kubelwagen,* Koenig seated beside the driver. He got out and moved forward.

"Ah, there you are, Signor Barbera. I've brought some custom for you, I'm afraid," he said in fair Italian.

The two *Kubelwagens* drove into the courtyard. Barbera saw that there was a body strapped to a stretcher on one of them and covered with a blanket.

Two SS ran round to lift it down and Barbera said, "If you'd follow me, Major."

He crossed the courtyard and led the way in through a short passage. When he opened the door at the end, there was the taint of death in the air.

The room which he entered was quiet, a single oil lamp on a table in the center the only light. It was a waiting mortuary of a type common in Sicily. There were at least a dozen coffins, each one open and containing a corpse, fingers entwined in a pulley arrangement that stretched overhead to an old brass bell by the door.

Koenig entered behind him. His N.C.O.'s field cap was an affectation of some of the oldtimers, silver Death's Head badge glinting in the lamplight. The scarlet and black ribbon of the Knight's Cross made a brave show at his throat. He wore a leather greatcoat that had seen long service and paratroopers' jumpboots. He lit a cigarette, pausing just inside the door, and flicked a finger against the bell which echoed eerily.

"Has it ever rung?"

"Frequently," Barbera said. "Limbs behave strangely as they stiffen in death. If what the Major means is has anyone returned to life, that, too. A girl of twelve and, on another occasion, a man of forty. Both revived after death had been pronounced. That, after all, is the purpose of these places."

"You Sicilians seem to me to have an excessive preoccupation with death," Koenig said.

"Not to the extent that we are excited by the idea of being buried alive."

From the preparation room, peering through the crack in the door, Carter leaned against Rosa, fighting the pain, and watched them place the stretcher on a table and uncover Schäfer, the *Feldpolizei* sergeant. The face was streaked with blood, the eyes staring. Barbera closed them with a practiced movement.

"Sergeant Schäfer was a good man," Koenig said. "I need hardly point out that it would be most unfortunate for anyone found harboring the man who did this."

Barbera said, "What would you like me to do with him, Major?"

"Clean him up and deliver him to *Geheimefeldpolizei* headquarters in Agrigento."

Barbera covered Schäfer with the blanket again. "I had intended taking another corpse down to Agrigento tonight. See, in here."

He moved to the door of the preparation room, opened it, and led the way in, holding the lamp high so that Koenig could see the corpse of the old man. In the darkness of the rear cupboard, Carter slumped against Rosa and her arms tightened about him.

"I could take Sergeant Schäfer at the same time," Barbera said. "Of course, I would need a pass, Major. I presume your men will be active on all roads tonight."

He followed Koenig out and Carter waited there in the dark, the pain in his lung like a living thing. *God, he thought, perhaps I'm dying.* He clutched desperately at the girl as if she were life itself, conscious of the softness of her flesh, her breasts tight against him.

He groaned, struggling to control the pain, and she fastened her mouth over his as if to hold the sound in, her tongue working furiously. In spite of the agony, his flesh reacted to her practiced hands.

After a while she opened the door cautiously and led him out. Carter propped himself against one of the tables, aware of the sound of vehicles driving away down there in the courtyard.

"What were you trying to do, kill me or cure me?" he croaked.

She wiped sweat from his face with one of Barbera's towels. "We have a saying, Major. There is the big death and then there is the small death which may be repeated many times. Which would you prefer?"

He stared down into that old-young face, but before he could reply Barbera came back, holding a piece of paper.

"Signed by Major Koenig himself. Good for any roadblock between here and Agrigento. With luck, you should make that submarine after all."

"How?" Carter said.

"I wouldn't dream of having a hearse without a hidden compartment. Comes in handy. Of course, you'll be lying flat on your back with two corpses in coffins just inches above your nose, but I can guarantee you won't smell a thing." He grinned. "Stick with me, old buddy, and you'll live forever."

THREE

The JU52 which flew in from Rome with
Field Marshal Albert Kesselring landed at
the Luftwaffe base at Punta Raisi outside
Palermo just after nine in the morning. An
hour later, he was at German army headquarters in the old Benedictine monastery
near Monte Pellegrino, drinking coffee in
the office of Major General Karl Walther
who was temporarily in command.

"Beautiful," Kesselring said, indicating
the view. "Quite remarkable, and so is the
coffee."

"Yemeni mocha." Walther poured him
another cup. "We still manage some of the
finer things in life here."

"We had some difficulty driving through
the town. There seemed to be religious
processions everywhere."

"Some sort of holy week. They hold

them all the time. Everything grinds to a halt. They're a very religious people."

"So it would appear," Kesselring said. "When one of the processions passed us I noticed a rather unusual feature. The image of the Virgin they were carrying had a knife through its heart."

"Typically Sicilian," Walther replied. "The cult of death everywhere."

Kesselring put down his cup. "All right, what have I got?"

"There are eight this morning. All Iron Crosses. First Class, except for the two in whom the Field Marshal has a special interest."

"Let's take a look."

Walther opened the door and ushered him out onto a flagstone terrace, an ironwork grille between the pillars. Below in the courtyard eight men were drawn up.

"Koenig on the far end, Herr Field Marshal," Walther said. "The man next to him is *Sturmscharführer* Brandt."

"Who receives the Knight's Cross?"

"The third occasion that Koenig has put him forward."

"So," Kesselring nodded. "Then let's get on with it."

Major Max Koenig was twenty-six and looked ten years older. He had seen action in Poland, France, and Holland and had transferred to the newly formed 21st SS Paratroop Battalion in time for the drop over Maleme airfield in Crete in 1941 where he was seriously wounded. Then came the Winter War in Russia. Two years of it and it showed: in the gold wound badge that said he'd been a casualty on five separate occasions; in the general air of weariness, the empty look in the dark eyes.

Except for the silver Death's Head badge in his service cap and the SS runes and rank badges on his collar, he was all *Fallschirmjäger:* flying blouse, jump trousers tucked into paratroop boots. On his left sleeve was the *Kreta* cuff title, proud badge of those who had spearheaded the invasion of Crete. The gold and silver eagle of the paratroopers' qualification badge was pinned to his left breast beside the Iron Cross. The Knight's Cross with oak leaves hung at his throat.

Standing at ease at the end of the line waiting to receive the swords, he felt strangely indifferent and yet strove to find the right thing to say to Sergeant Major Brandt for whom this was a moment of supreme importance.

"So, Rudi," he whispered. "The great occasion at last."

"Thanks to you, Major," Brandt replied. He was an innkeeper's son from the Austrian Tyrol, a small, wiry man who could climb all day with no need of rest. He and Koenig had been together for more than two years now.

There was a clatter of boots on the stone stairs as Kesselring and General Walther appeared and someone called the parade to attention.

It was a pleasant enough affair, for Kesselring was in high good humor, full of his usual charm. He had a word for each man as he pinned on the ribbon. They responded well, as was only to be expected, for he was, after all, Commander in Chief South and arguably one of the half-dozen best generals on either side during the Second World War.

They had reached Brandt now and Kesselring did a marvelous thing, throwing all distinctions of rank to one side, clapping Brandt on the shoulders and shaking him warmly by the hand before hanging the coveted cross around his neck.

"My dear Brandt, a real pleasure, I

assure you as one soldier to another, and long overdue."

Brandt was overcome and Koenig was unable to keep a fleeting smile from his lips. A master stroke, but Kesselring knew how to handle men. Then the Field Marshal was standing in front of him, a slightly wry smile on his face as if he had noticed Koenig's reaction and was asking him to bear with him.

"What on earth can I say, Major? You are only the thirtieth recipient of the swords since the award was created. Normally, our Führer himself would wish to decorate you personally, but these are extraordinary times. I can only say how how delighted I am that the honor falls to me."

He held Koenig by the shoulders for a moment and then, as if in a sudden excess of emotion, embraced him.

Later, back in Walther's office having a cognac before lunch, Kesselring said, "A very impressive young man."

"He's certainly that," Walther agreed.

"Decent, honorable, chivalrous. A superb soldier. What every member of the Waffen SS would like to imagine himself to be. Let's have him in and get it over with."

Walther pressed a buzzer on his desk and an aide looked in.

"Major Koenig," Walther said.

The aide withdrew and Koenig entered. He paused at the desk, clicked his heels, and his hand went to the peak of his field cap in a military salute.

The Field Marshal said, "Pull up a chair, Major, and sit down."

Koenig did as he was told. Kesselring turned to the large-scale military map of Sicily on the wall. "I see you've applied for a transfer already."

"Yes, Herr Field Marshal."

"Well, it's denied."

"May I be permitted to ask why?"

"I could say because that silver plate they had to put in your skull after your last exploit in Russia makes you unsuitable for jumping out of airplanes anymore. But I don't need to. Your task here in Sicily is of vital importance."

General Walther said, "There is still too much partisan activity here in the central mountains, particularly in the region of the Cammarata. It would be fatal to our interests in the event of an invasion."

"I thought the Allies intend to try Sardinia first, General?" queried Koenig.

Walther and Kesselring glanced at each other and Kesselring laughed. "Go on, tell him. I don't see why not."

Walther said, "Actually, you're not far wrong, Major. The high command in Berlin, the Führer himself, feels that Sardinia will be the invasion point."

"A few weeks ago, the body of a British courier was washed up on a Spanish beach," Kesselring went on. "A Royal Marine major. He was carrying letters to General Alexander in Tunisia. There was another from Lord Louis Mountbatten to Sir Andrew Cunningham, Commander in Chief of the British Mediterranean Fleet. The gist of these letters indicates firmly that the target for the Allied invasion will be Sardinia and Greece. Any attack on Sicily will be diversionary."

There was a heavy silence. General Walther said, "We'd be interested in your opinion. Feel free to speak."

"What can I say, Herr General." Koenig shrugged. "Miracles do occur on occasions, even in this day and age. Presumably this British major's body being so conveniently washed up on a Spanish beach, where our agents could have a sight of the letters he was carrying, was one of them."

"But on the whole," Kesselring said, "You don't believe in miracles."

"Not since I stopped reading the fairy tales of the brothers Grimm, Herr Field Marshal."

"Good." Kesselring was all business now. "Give me your personal assessment of the situation here."

Koenig stood up and moved round to the map. "As regards partisan activity, two important groups. The Separatists, who want an independent Sicily, and the Communists. We all know what *they* want."

"They cut each other's throats as cheerfully as they do ours."

"General Walther was explaining to me about this Mafia movement," Kesselring said. "Are they a force to be reckoned with?"

"Yes, I think they have very real power under the surface of things and, again, they are peculiarly Sicilian. Mainland Italy and Mussolini mean nothing to them."

"And if an invasion comes, they will fight?"

"Oh, yes, I think so." Koenig nodded. "All of them. Our main worry would be the Italian army itself."

"You think so?" Kesselring asked.

Koenig took a deep breath and jumped in with both feet. "Frankly, Herr Field Marshal, I think the fact must be faced that the Italian people as a whole have lost any interest they ever had in the war and all enthusiasm for Mussolini."

There was a slight pause and then Kesselring smiled. "An accurate enough assessment. I wouldn't disagree with that. So, you think invasion will come to Sicily?"

Koenig ran a finger along the road south from Palermo to Agrigento. "Here is the most vital road in the whole of Sicily, passing through the Cammarata, one of the wildest and most primitive places in the island. There has been considerable partisan activity in that area recently. According to our informants, a number of American agents have been dropped by parachute during the past few weeks. So far, we haven't succeeded in catching any of them."

Kesselring picked up a folder from the desk. "And yet you almost had this man." He opened the file. "Major Harry Carter, in charge of the Italian desk at Special Operation Executive in Cairo. You had him, Koenig, and let him slip through

44

your fingers."

"With respect, Herr Field Marshal," Koenig corrected him firmly, "my task was to provide back-up forces on the ground. The affair was in the hands of the *Geheime-feldpolizei* and Gestapo. And I would remind you, sir, that, thanks to Russia, I have only thirty-five men remaining in what was once a battalion. Not a single officer is left on the strength except myself."

"Yes, well, the capture of Carter would have been an intelligence coup of the first order and Berlin, in the person of Reichsführer Himmler, is not pleased. To that end he has ordered the transfer of one of his most trusted intelligence officers from the Rome Office to work with you here."

"I see, Herr Field Marshal," Koenig said. "Gestapo?"

"Oh, no," Kesselring told him gravely. "Rather more important than that." He turned to Walther. "Show Major Meyer in."

The man who entered was broad and squat with a flat Slav fave and cold blue eyes. Koenig recognized the type at once, for the security service was full of them: ex-police officers, more used to the criminal underworld than anything else. He wore SS field uniform and his only decoration was the Order of Blood, a much coveted Nazi medal specially struck for those who had served prison sentences for political crimes in the old Weimar Republic. The most interesting fact about him was his cuff-title, which carried the legend RFSS picked out in silver thread. Reichsführer der SS, the symbol of Himmler's personal staff.

"Major Franz Meyer, Major Koenig." Walther made the introductions while Kesselring stood looking out of the window, smoking a cigarette.

Meyer took in everything about Koenig with the policeman's practised eye: The highly irregular SS uniform, the Knight's Cross with Oak Leaves and Swords.

"A pleasure, Major," he said.

Koenig turned to Kesselring. "There is a difficulty here, I think, Herr Field Marshal. Who is to be in charge? Meyer and I would appear to carry the same rank."

"No difficulty there, I hope?" Kesselring said, smoothly. "I see you as performing separate functions: you being responsible for the purely military side of the operation and Major Meyer for the, how shall I put it? The more political aspects."

"There will be no problem from my

point of view, I can assure the Herr Field Marshal of that," Meyer said.

"Excellent." Kesselring managed a wintry smile. "And now, if you would leave us, Meyer. There are still matters I wish to discuss with Major Koenig."

Meyer clicked his heels, delivered an impressive Heil Hitler and departed. When he'd gone, Kesselring said, "I know what you're going to say, Koenig, and you're quite right. It places you in a most difficult situation."

"Almost impossible, Herr Field Marshal. I will have no authority of rank, which means the wretched man can interfere as much as he likes."

He was angry and it showed. Kesselring said, "Rank has little to do with the matter. As a member of the Reichsführer's personal staff, he will always have considerable influence in certain situations, even were I myself concerned. However, I have done the best I can for you in the circumstances."

He nodded to Walther who handed Koenig a buff envelope. Koenig started to open it and Kesselring said, "No, keep it for later." He held out his hand in another of those unexpected gestures. "I wish you luck. You're going to need it."

"Herr Field Marshal-General." Koenig saluted, turned and went out.

Franz Meyer stood in the hall, pretending to read the noticeboard as he waited for Koenig.

His dislike for the Major had been immediate and it went beyond any personal jealousy of Koenig's military distinction. The truth was far deeper. Koenig was a gentleman, son of a Major General of the Luftwaffe. Meyer, on the other hand, was the third son of a Hamburg shoemaker who had served the last two years of the First World War in the trenches, who had starved like thousands of others in Germany during the twenties, thanks to the British and the French and the Jews until the Führer had come along, a man of the people, giving hope to the people. And Meyer had served him since those first days, one of the earliest party members in Hamburg. The Führer himself had pinned the Blood Order on him. The Koenigs of the world, who thought themselves so far above him, weren't even fit to polish his boots.

He turned as Koenig approached. "Ah, there you are, Major. I would very much appreciate an opportunity to discuss my

48

duties at the earliest possible moment. This Carter affair, for example.''

''Gestapo business, not mine,'' Koenig said, pulling on his gloves. ''I merely provided ground support.''

Meyer said, ''A valuable field officer murdered, Carter allowed to get clean away, yet you took no hostages in Bellona. Exacted no reprisals.''

''I'm a soldier, not a butcher,'' Koenig said. ''If the distinction doesn't appeal to you, take it up with the Field Marshal.''

''There are perhaps others I could take it up with,'' Meyer replied calmly. ''Reichsführer Himmler might well be interested in an officer of SS who expresses such sentiments.''

''Then you must discuss it with him,'' Koenig said, ''as I'm sure you will,'' and he went out of the entrance, down the steps and crossed to where Brandt waited for him behind the wheel of a *Kubelwagen*.

Koenig smoked a cigarette, furiously angry, as they drove down towards Palermo. Finally, he said, ''Pull over, Rudi. I must walk for a while.''

Brandt turned in at the entrance of the Pellegrino cemetery and Koenig got out and walked through the gates between even lines of Cyprus trees.

He stood looking up at a white marble tomb with a life-size statue of Santa Rosalia of Pellegrino on top. Brandt moved in behind him.

Koenig said, "The most vulgar thing I've ever seen in my life."

Brandt asked, "What happened back there?"

"Oh, nothing much. They've hung a Major called Meyer from Himmler's personal staff on my back, that's all. The Field Marshal was very sorry, but there wasn't much he could do about it."

He reached into his pocket for matches and the envelope Kesselring had given him fell out. Brandt picked it up as Koenig lit a cigarette.

"Major," he said, holding the envelope out.

"Kesselring's parting gift," Koenig told him. "Open it and let's see what it was he didn't have the courage to tell me personally."

He turned, looking out towards the sea, aware of Brandt ripping open the envelope and then the sergeant major's incredulous explosion of delight. Koenig swung around and Brandt held out the letter, smiling.

"It's your promotion, Lieutenant-Colonel."

Koenig stared at him for a long moment, then snatched the letter from him. The formality of the language meant nothing to him. The important thing was that Brandt was right. Kesselring had promoted him. When he looked at the envelope, he saw now that it was addressed to Obersturm-bannführer Max Koenig. What was it Kesselring had said? *I have done the best I can for you in the circumstances.*

He clapped Brandt on the shoulder. "A celebration, Rudi, is very definitely in order." As they started to walk back towards the *Kubelwagen* he laughed. "My God, but I'd like to see Meyer's face when he hears about this."

FOUR

It was four weeks later when the jeep carrying Carter deposited him at the ornate entrance of the villa at dar el Ouad. He went up the steps slowly, taking his time and passed into the cool darkness.

Cusak looked up from his desk and got to his feet instantly. "Major Carter. Good to see you, sir."

"I believe I'm expected."

"That's right, sir. I'll tell General Eisenhower you're here."

He moved away and Carter went out on the terrace. *Was it only six weeks since he'd stood here?* He had that pain in his chest again and in spite of that fact, or because of it, took the old silver case from his breast pocket, selected a cigarette and lit it, inhaling with great deliberation.

There was a quick step behind him and

as he turned, Cusak said, "The General will see you now, Major."

Standing in front of the desk, Carter was filled with a strange sense of déjà vu. Eisenhower, looking up at him, frowned. "You don't look too good, Major."

"I'll be all right, sir. I was just wondering whether it was then or now."

Eisenhower smiled. "Oh, yes, you've been here before, I can assure you. I get days like that myself. Sit down." He pulled a file forward and opened it. "I read your report with considerable interest."

Carter pulled forward a chair. "Thank you, sir." He hesitated. "Is the Sicilian invasion on, General?"

Eisenhower looked up and said calmly, "During the next few weeks the British under General Montgomery will invade at the Eastern end of the island, while General Patton and the Seventh Army will land in the South and strike for Palermo. Are you surprised?"

"Not really, sir, although there's been a strong opinion in Sicily for months now, which I might say the Germans seem to hold also, that Sardinia would be the target."

"Which is exactly what we want them to think. But let's get back to the original question I put to you when you were last here. According to your report, you seem certain that Washington is hoping for too much with the Mafia connection."

"I'm afraid so, General."

There was a brief silence, while Eisenhower stared gloomily down at the file. "All right, what's your solution?"

"Well, there is a man, General, named Luca. Don Antonio Luca. He's what's known in Sicily as *Capo di Tutti Capi*. Boss of all the bosses. The fascists imprisoned him in 1940. Sent him to prison on the mainland—Naples. He escaped later that year and returned to Sicily where he's been in hiding ever since. He's the one man they'll all listen to. I don't wish to blaspheme, but in Sicily he could pull a larger audience than the Pope."

"Then find him," Eisenhower said.

"He doesn't want to be found, sir."

"Could you find him?"

"I've tried. Total silence so far. I've got a better chance than your people though. He doesn't care for Americans. It seems he had a young brother called Cesare, who was a rum-runner on the Great Lakes during

54

Prohibition. One night in 1929 Cesare was ambushed by a rival gang outside Chicago and personally shot three men dead. He died himself in the electric chair the following year.''

Eisenhower stood up. ''That's all I needed.'' He paced up and down a couple of times, then turned to the map and stood looking up at it. ''Still, one thing's for sure. If George Patton and his boys have to fight their way through those mountains to Palermo, they'll die by the thousands. By the thousands.''

He repeated the phrase in a whisper as if to himself. Carter knew that in his mind's eye, Eisenhower was seeing again the American dead on the battlefield of Kaserine, that terrible debacle in which untried boys had found themselves faced with the cream of the Afrika Corps.

Carter cleared his throat. ''With respect, General, I do have a suggestion.''

Eisenhower turned, suddenly alert. ''And what might that be?''

''After all is said and done, Luciano still seems to me the key figure in the whole affair. His influence with the Sicilian Mafia is unquestioned. He might provide the right link with Luca. Enough to make Luca come out of hiding and declare himself for us. If he does that, General, then we have Mafia on our side one hundred and ten percent.''

Eisenhower stood there for a long moment, staring at him, then nodded slowly. ''Damn me, Major, but I have a sneaking suspicion you might be right.''

''Then you'll put Intelligence in Washington on to it right away, sir?'' Carter said. ''They could approach Luciano again during the next couple of days.''

''I'll think about it.'' Eisenhower glanced at his watch. ''And now you must excuse me. This is the time of day when the telephone lines start hotting up to Washington. I talk to the President most days. He likes to be kept informed.''

''I'll go then, sir.''

Carter got up, put on his cap and saluted. Eisenhower acknowledged the salute perfunctorily, already busy with papers again, and Carter walked to the door.

As he got it open, Eisenhower called, ''I'd like you back here at eleven.''

Carter turned in surprise. ''You mean eleven tonight, General?''

''That's it, Major,'' Eisenhower replied without looking up.

Carter closed the door, paused, then crossed the hall to the entrance and went down the steps to his jeep. He climbed in beside the driver and glanced at his watch. It was just after six. Almost five hours to kill.

"Where to now, sir?" asked the driver, a private first class who looked at most sixteen years of age.

"Do you know the RAF base at Maison Blanche?"

"Sure do, Major. About an hour and a half from here."

"Fine," Carter said. "Take me there."

The Douglas DC3, the famous Dakota, was probably the most successful general transport plane ever built, but the one which Wing Commander Harvey Grant was bringing back from Malta to his base at Maison Blanche just before dark had definitely seen better days.

Not that it was in any sense his regular place. The old Dakota did a milk run to Malta and back three times a week with medical supplies. The duty pilot had been taken ill that morning, and as there was no replacement readily available, Grant had seized the opportunity to vacate the

Squadron Commander's desk and do the flight himself. Which was very much contrary to regulations, for Grant had been forbidden any further operational flying by the Air Officer Commanding Middle East Theater himself only six weeks previously.

He sat at the controls now, alone and happy, whistling tunelessly between his teeth, the two supply sergeants forming his crew asleep in the rear.

Harvey Grant was twenty-six, a small man whose dark eyes seemed perpetually full of life. Son of a wheat farmer in Parker Iowa, the greatest influence on his life had been his father's younger brother, Templeton Grant, who had flown with the Royal Flying Corps in France.

At an early age, Grant learnt that you always watched the sun and never crossed the line alone under 10,000 feet. He soloed at sixteen, thanks to his uncle's tuition, then moved on to Harvard to study law, more to please his father than anything else. He was at the Sorbonne in Paris when war broke out, and promptly joined the RAF.

He was shot down twice piloting Hurricanes and had eleven German fighters to his credit before the Battle of Britain was over.

He'd then transferred to Bomber Command, completing a tour in Wellingtons, a second in Lancasters, by which time he was a Squadron Leader with a DSO and two DFC's to his name.

After that had come his posting to 138 (Special Duties) Squadron at Tempsford, the famous Moon Squadron that specialized in dropping agents into occupied Europe or picking them up again, as the occasion required.

Grant had flown over thirty such missions from Tempsford before being promoted and posted to Maison Blanche to handle the same kind of work, flying black-painted Halifaxes from the Algerian mainland to Sardinia, Sicily and Italy.

But all that was behind him. Now he was officially grounded. Too valuable to risk losing, that's what the A.O.C. had said, although in Grant's opinion it was simply another maneuver on the part of the American Army Air Corps to force him to transfer, a fate he was determined to avoid.

He was south-west of Pantellaria just before dusk, a quarter-moon touching the clouds with a pale luminosity, when a roaring filled the night. The Dakota bucked wildly so that it took everything Grant had to hold her as a dark shadow banked away to port.

He recognized it at once, a Junkers 88, one of those apparently clumsy, black, twin-engined planes festooned with strange radar aerials that had proved so devastating in their attacks on RAF bombers engaged on night raids over Europe. And he didn't have a thing to fight with except skill, for the Dakota carried no kind of armament.

The cabin door swung open behind him and the two supply sergeants peered in.

"Hang on!" Grant said. "I'm going to see if I can make him do something stupid."

He went down fast and was aware of the Junkers, turning and coming in fast, firing his cannon too soon, his speed so excessive that he had to bank to port to avoid collision.

Which was exactly what Grant was counting on. He kept on going down, was at six hundred feet when the Junkers came in on his tail. This time the Dakota staggered under the impact of cannon shell. The Junkers curved away to starboard again and appeared to take up station.

"Come on, you bastard! Come on!" Grant said softly.

Behind him one of the sergeants appeared, blood on his face where a splinter had caught him. "Johnson's bought it, sir."

"Okay," Grant said. "He's coming in again so get down on your face and hang on."

He was not more than five hundred feet above the waves as the Junkers came in for the kill, judging his speed perfectly now, sliding in on the Dakota's tail, opening up with more cannon shell. As the aircraft started to shudder under their impact, Grant dropped his flaps.

The Dakota seemed to stop in mid-air. The pilot of the Junkers banked steeply to starboard to avoid a collision and, with no space left to work in at such a speed, kept right on going, ploughing straight into the sea.

Grant walked towards the officers' mess at Maison Blanche, his flying boots drubbing on the tarmac, unaccountably depressed. He kept thinking of the way that Junkers had gone in, imagining the men inside. That was no good at all. He started up the steps to the mess and found Harry Carter standing at the top.

"Harry!" Grant said in delight. "I heard

61

you were in hospital in Cairo.''

''Not any more,'' Carter told him. ''I had business with the man himself at dar el Ouad and as I have an hour or two to spare, I thought I'd see how you were getting on.''

On the two occasions that Carter had dropped by parachute into Sicily, Grant had flown the plane, which was something of a bond.

''Feel like a drink?'' he asked.

''Not really. Let's take a walk.''

They moved towards the hangars. Carter said, ''I hear you got another one this evening.''

''In a matter of speaking.''

''And you're supposed to be grounded.''

''Damn nonsense. I had to see Air Marshal Sloane a few weeks ago on squadron business and he said I had a muscle twitching in my right cheek. Insisted I had a medical and the bastards stood me down.''

He was angry and it showed. Carter said, ''We can win the war without you, Harvey, but only just.'' He put a hand on the American's shoulder for a moment. ''What's wrong? What's really wrong?''

''I keep thinking about the men in that

Junkers this evening," Grant said. "I don't know how to explain this, Harry, but for the first time it was as if it was me. Does that make any kind of sense?"

"Perfectly," Carter told him. "It means that the doctor who stood you down knew what he was talking about."

Grant said, "And what about you? Are you going back over there again?"

"I shouldn't think it's likely."

"And a good thing, too." They were passing a hangar in which ground crew worked under floodlights repairing a badly damaged Halifax. Half the tail plane was missing and the rear gunner's compartment shattered. "Rear gunner and navigator both killed on a supply drop to Sicily two nights ago. The Luftwaffe really do have things their own way over there, Harry. We've lost four planes in ten days, all shot down, and in each case, the agents they were to drop were still inside. If you asked me to fly you in again, I'd give us no better than an even chance of reaching the target and dropping you."

"Oh, well," Carter said. "Someone else can worry about that one."

They had reached the end of the main hangar and he saw, to his surprise, a

Junkers 88 night fighter standing there in the gloom, RAF rondels painted on the fuselage and wings.

"What's this, for God's sake?"

"Forced down up the coast a few weeks ago after dropping a couple of Arab agents by parachute. See where they cut a special door in the fuselage. This is a Ju88S, one of their best night fighters, capable of around four hundred miles an hour. We've been doing evaluation flights."

"You have, you mean."

"Well, an hour here and there." Grant shrugged. "Who's to notice?" He clapped Carter on the shoulder. "So, what are you up to now? Something so secret the whole future of the war depends on it?"

Carter smiled. "There's no such animal, Harvey. Wars aren't won by men any more. They're run by large corporations, just like big business."

"Maybe you're right." Grant tossed his cigarette away. "You want to know something, Harry? I feel tired—I mean really tired. So I don't care any more."

"It's the war, Harvey. It's gone on too long."

"Good," Grant said. "I mean, that really does make me feel a whole lot better. Now let's get back to the mess and I'll buy you a drink.''

When the jeep dropped Carter in the courtyard outside the villa, there was a big Packard staff car outside. Carter went up the steps past the sentries and found Cusak still sitting at the desk.

"Doesn't anyone work around here except you?" Carter enquired.

Cusak smiled. "I must admit it feels that way some days. He won't be long, sir. He has General Patton with him."

Carter moved out on the terrace, wondering what it was Eisenhower wanted to see him about. A further discussion of the Sicilian situation perhaps, and yet, what more was there to say? It was all decided. Within the next few weeks, the big battalions would roll, the invasion would take place and, an unknown quantity of dead men later, Sicily would be in Allied hands. The Germans had lost the war, so much was obvious, so why didn't everyone simply get off at the next stop?

The door to Eisenhower's office opened and General George Patton walked across the hall. He wore field cap and heavy military greatcoat, his hands pushed deep into its pockets as if cold.

As Carter moved out of the shadows, Patton paused. "Are you Carter?"

"That's right, sir."

Patton stood there looking him over, a slight frown on his face. For a moment, it was as if he was about to speak; then he thought better of it, turned and walked out without another word.

The telephone buzzed, Cusak picked it up. "Yes, General?" He smiled briefly at Carter. "He'll see you now, Major."

The room was dark, the only light the table lamp on the desk where Eisenhower sat working on a file in a haze of cigarette smoke. He glanced up as Carter entered and put down his pen.

"You know, one thing they omitted to tell us when I was a cadet at West Point was the amount of paperwork that went into being Commander-in-Chief."

"If they did, maybe nobody would want the job, General."

"Exactly," Eisenhower grinned briefly and was then all business. "There's a Flying Fortress leaving Bone Airfield two hours from now, destination Prestwick in Scotland. From there, you'll fly straight on to Washington by the first available plane, Priority One. You should be there, with any luck, by early evening tomorrow. Captain Cusak will give you your documentation on the way out.''

''I'm afraid I don't understand, sir.''

''Of course you don't,'' Eisenhower replied. ''You don't know what the hell I'm talking about so I'll tell you. I liked what you said about the Sicilian situation. It made sense, particularly the bit about this man Antonio Luca and the effect he could have on the campaign if he were found and brought in on our side.''

''I see, sir.''

''I've spoken on the matter to the President during our phone call earlier this evening. He agrees that anything that can help save the lives of our boys is worth trying. To that end, I want you to proceed to this penitentiary at Great Meadow to discuss further with Luciano the whole question of Mafia involvement in the invasion.'' He passed a buff envelope across. ''There's your authority, in my name, to act in any way you see fit in this matter. It makes you answerable only to me and requires all personnel, military or civil, without distinction of rank, to assist you in any way you see fit. There will be a similar document waiting for you in Washington countersigned by the President.''

Carter stared down at the envelope, bewildered. ''To do what, General?''

''How in the hell do I know?'' Eisenhower said. ''Talk to the man. See what he has to say. Yank him right out of that damn prison if you have to. You've got the power. Now, are you going to use it or aren't you?''

Carter, filled with an excitement he had not known in years, slipped the envelope into one of his tunic pockets and buttoned it carefully.

''Oh, yes, sir.''

''Good.'' Eisenhower nodded. ''Another thing. I've arranged a promotion to full colonel for you. Only temporary, of course, but it should give you some extra muscle along the way.''

He turned before Carter could reply and switched on a lamp that illuminated the map of Sicily. He stood looking at it for a while and spoke without turning round. ''Are you surprised that I'm willing to have dealings with people like Luciano?''

''Frankly, sir, I think I've got well past

being surprised at anything."

"The Nazis have plundered and raped Europe, murdered millions of people. The stories that are beginning to emerge about their treatment of the Jews are past belief and I'm of German stock myself. Have you any idea how that feels?"

"I think so, sir," Carter said.

"Oh, no, you haven't," Eisenhower shook his head violently. "To beat these people, Major, finish them once and for all, root and branch, I'd shake hands with the Devil himself if it were necessary."

FIVE

On his twentieth lap of the exercise yard at Great Meadow, Luciano increased his speed, running fast and free, the best moment of the day when there was an infinite possibility to things. Then, as usual, the north wall got in the way and he had to slow down.

He walked back through a scattering of other prisoners, acknowledging a greeting here and there, to his usual spot in a corner by the landing where Franco waited with a towel.

"You're getting better each day, Mr. Luciano," Franco said.

He had the look of a professional wrestler and the build to go with it, a New York Sicilian who had killed many times on behalf of Mafia and was serving a double life sentence for murder.

Luciano caught the towel as Franco threw it. "You reach my age, you got to keep in shape. Did you get that book from the library?"

"I sure did, Mr. Luciano."

He passed it across, an English translation of *The City of God* by St. Augustine. Luciano sat on the step and examined it with a conscious pleasure.

He was forty-six, a dark, handsome, saturnine man of medium height. The lid drooped slightly over the left eye, relic of an old wound. In spite of the drab prison uniform he was a man to be looked at twice, and not just because of the authority and self-sufficiency that were plainly indicated in the face. There was also that perpetual slight smile of contempt directed at the world in general.

Franco said, "Excuse me, Mr. Luciano, but there's a kid here called Walton from D block. He needs a favor."

Luciano looked up. Walton was a tall, gangling young man of twenty-one or two with flat brown hair and arms that were too long for his shirt.

"What's he in for?" Luciano asked softly.

"One to three. Liquor store holdup.

No previous."

"Okay, let's see what he wants."

Franco nodded to the boy, gave Luciano a cigarette and lit it for him. "Okay, speak your piece."

Walton stood there, twisting his cap in his hand nervously. "Mr. Luciano, they say you can do anything."

"Except sprout wings and fly out of this place." Luciano smiled softly. "What's to do, boy?"

"It's like this, Mr. Luciano. I've only been here two months and my wife, Carrie, well, she's on her own now and she's only a kid. Eighteen is all."

"So?"

"There's a detective from the eighth precinct called O'Hara. He was one of the guys who pulled me in. He knows she's on her own and he's been pressuring her. You know what I mean?"

Luciano looked him over calmly for a long moment then nodded. "Okay. Detective O'Hara, eighth precinct. It's taken care of." He returned to his book.

The boy said, "Maybe I can do you a favor some time, Mr. Luciano."

Franco said, "That's what friends are for, kid. Now get out of here."

As the boy turned away, Luciano looked up. "Is it true that liquor store heist was your first job?"

Walton nodded. "That's right, Mr. Luciano."

"And one to three was the best your lawyer could do? He should have got you probation."

"I didn't really have no lawyer, not a proper one," Walton said. "Just a man the court appointed. He only spoke to me the once. Said the thing to do was plead guilty and throw myself on the court's mercy. I didn't see. . . ."

"All right!" Luciano put up a hand defensively. "I'll speak to my lawyer when he comes up Wednesday. Maybe he can do something."

The boy walked away and Franco said, "Keep that up and you'll have them standing in line at the bottom of the steps every morning."

One of the guards approached, an ageing Irishman named O'Toole, with the weary, bitter look of one who had long since faced up to defeat.

For Luciano, he managed a smile. "The Warden would like to see you in his office, Mr. Luciano."

73

"Now?" Luciano said.

"That's what he told me."

Luciano got up, still holding his book, and nodded to Franco. "See you later, Johnny."

They moved across the yard, O'Toole in the lead. He said, "They're waxing the entrance hall so we can't use the main door. We'll go through the showers and up the back stairs."

His forehead was damp with sweat and his hand shook a little as he unlocked the door to the shower block.

Luciano smiled easily, every sense sharpened. "Something bothering you, O'Toole?"

O'Toole gave him a sudden quick push inside and slammed the door and Franco, halfway across the yard, started to run, already too late as O'Toole turned, back to the door, the club ready in his hand.

Walton moved out of the first shower stall. He stood there, no expression on his face at all, no light in the dark eyes.

Luciano said easily, "I thought that story of yours was strictly from the corn belt. They send you up here specially?"

"That's right." Walton's hand came up

holding an ivory Madonna. When he pressed her feet, six inches of blue steel appeared, sharp as a razor on both edges. "Nothing personal, Mr. Luciano. With me, this is strictly business."

"Who sent you?"

"Fiorelli. He sent you his regards and gave me strict instructions to leave you with your prick in your mouth. He said being Sicilian, you'd know what that meant."

"Oh, I do," Luciano said and kicked his right foot, catching Walton just under the left kneecap.

Walton shouted in agony as bone splintered, and slashed out wildly. Luciano seized the right wrist with both hands, twisting it so cruelly that the knife dropped to the floor.

"You're going to cut someone up, kid, do it, don't talk about it."

He twisted round and up, locking the arm as in a vise. Walton screamed as muscle started to tear and Luciano ran him face first into the wall of the nearest stall. The boy slid down the wall, leaving a smear of blood on the tiles.

Luciano picked up the knife and closed the blade. The Madonna was about eight inches long and obviously extremely old, carved by some master of ivory and chased with silver. He slipped it into his belt against the small of his back and picked up his book.

Walton crouched at the base of the stall, moaning. Luciano turned on the shower and the boy clutched at the wall.

"So long, kid," Luciano said softly and he opened the door and went out.

O'Toole swung to face him, instant dismay on his face. Franco dodged past him. "You all right, Mr. Luciano?"

"Oh, sure," Luciano said, "But that Walton kid looks as if he's slipped in the shower in there. I'd say he needs a doctor bad."

Franco moved inside without a word and Luciano turned to O'Toole. "I'd better get moving or the Warden will wonder what's happened to me. You did say he wanted to see me, didn't you?"

O'Toole licked his dry lips. "Oh, sure, Mr. Luciano," he said feebly. "Right away."

Luciano smiled and moved off across the yard and Franco came out of the showers and leaned against the door, lighting a cigarette.

"Heh, O'Toole," he said softly, a terrible

smile on his face. "I don't know what they paid you, but I think maybe you just made the biggest mistake of your life."

Harry Carter, wearing a dark blue suit in place of his uniform, stood at the window of the Warden's office and looked down into the yard.

The Warden said, "He doesn't like to be called Lucky. He's supposed to have gotten the name because of an incident in 1929 when rival mobsters kidnapped him, took him to a deserted wood in Staten Island, hung him up by his thumbs, and tortured him. Left him for dead."

"I wonder how he paid them off?" Carter said.

"I can imagine." The Warden went round his desk and opened a file. "Charles Luciano, born Salvatore Lucania in the village of Lercara Friddi near Palermo, November 24, 1897. Arrived in New York in 1907 with his family, who, I might add, are all honest people. You know how the Mafia works, Colonel Carter?"

"Only the Sicilian variety."

"It's pretty much the same in New York. They start them young. First there are the boys, the *picciotti,* gaining advancement, what they call respect, by acting as executioners when required. Some of them graduate pretty quickly to the next rank, *sicario,* the professional assassin who's a specialist in that line of work."

"I know," Carter said. "In Sicily they prefer the *lupara,* the sawed-off shotgun, for that kind of thing. You have to get close, but then, that's really the point."

"They say Luciano's killed at least twenty men himself and that isn't counting those he's put a contract out on."

"Just how powerful a figure is he?" Carter asked. "I mean, he is in here, isn't he? You close a cell door on him every night."

"Inside or out, it doesn't really matter. He's still the single most important influence in the Mafia. Rose to power in the liquor business during Prohibition. What made him different from the others was his brain. He's a hugely intelligent man with a genius for organization. When Prohibition ended, he diversified into every possible racket that would make a dollar. Even invented a few. In 1936, Governor Dewey, who was then Special Prosecutor, brought him to trial for offenses concerned with organized prostitution and succeeded in obtaining a conviction."

"Strange," Carter said. "It's the one thing that doesn't seem to fit."

The Warden smiled. "That's what a lot of people say, but don't expect any comment from me. This is a State appointment. I know one thing. He can always be relied upon to do the unexpected thing. He was at Dannemora in 1941 just after Pearl Harbor. That was a bad time with Christmas coming up. People's minds were on other things, so there were no packages for the cons until Luciano put the word out. Christmas Day, three truckloads of gifts turned up from New York."

There was a knock on the door. He called, "Come in!" and Luciano entered.

He glanced at Carter casually then turned to the Warden. "You sent for me."

The Warden stood up. "This is Colonel Carter. He's from the Government and he has full authority to speak with you on a matter of national importance, so I'm going to leave you to it."

He went out and Carter took out his silver case. "Cigarette, Mr. Luciano?"

"Heh, you're English."

"So are the cigarettes."

Carter gave him a light and Luciano sat

down by the window. "So what the hell are you doing here?"

"I believe you've had some visitors in recent months," Carter said. "From Intelligence. To discuss the Sicilian invasion."

Luciano said, "Not again, for Christ's sake. Look, I gave them all the information I could. All the right names."

"I know," Carter said. "I hear they've going to drop flags with an L for Luciano on every village in the Cammarata. Was that your idea?"

Luciano moved to the window and looked down into the Yard. "You got an ace in your hand, you play it."

"I don't think that's going to be enough."

"You don't think!" Luciano laughed. "What the hell has it got to do with you, anyway?"

Carter replied in good Sicilian, "Sure, in the Cammarata they still talk about the great Luciano. Salvatore the savior to a whole generation of tough young men, Luciano, who went to America and took the power there, is an idol to follow. But turning out to fight Nazi tanks with shotguns just because someone drops his flag on their village . . . I don't think so."

Luciano frowned. "How come you speak such good Sicilian?"

"Before the war I was a university professor, ancient history, archaeology. That kind of thing. I used to spend a lot of time in Sicily excavating."

"Excavating?"

"Digging up old ruins."

"You mean you're only a part-time soldier? Just for the duration? A professor, eh? Now that I can respect." He passed across his copy of *The City of God*. "Have you ever read this?"

Carter examined it. "St. Augustine. Oh, yes. You read a lot, do you?"

Luciano nodded. "He knew what he was talking about. God and the Devil, they both exist, only these days God's outnumbered."

"I see," Carter said. "So you've settled for reigning in hell?"

"It's a point of view. Milton knew what he was talking about." Luciano smiled softly. "I've read him, too."

"You know, Mr. Luciano, you interest me—both of you."

"Both of me?"

"But of course. There's Luciano number one, a street-wise hoodlum, who leaves out verbs when he speaks and manages to sound

81

as if he's had the same script writer as James Cagney.''

''I'm complimented.'' Luciano was smiling. ''A great little guy.''

''And then there's Luciano number two, who reads Augustine and Milton, speaks discreetly, sounds remarkably upper-class. . . .''

''So a good actor changes his performance according to his audience.'' Luciano shrugged. ''I mean, who are *you* playing today, *Professore?*''

Carter smiled. ''Point taken. You're a remarkable man, Mr. Luciano.''

''And you, Professor, are a remarkable judge of character. Tell me, does Tom Dewey know you're here? When he was Special Prosecutor he pulled enough strings to get me put away. Look at him now. Governor of New York State. The White House next stop.''

''You think Dewey was unfair to you?''

''What's fair? What's unfair? There's only life. Some kid's born with twisted legs or half a brain. Is that fair?'' He got up and walked to the window. ''Look, Professor, I don't give a damn what you think, but this is the way it was. I was boss of the rackets. I had an interest in most things, but never girls. Tom Dewey tried every damn way he could to get me and failed. Finally, they brought me to trial with nine other guys and some of them were in the prostitution business. At the end of the day, the jury couldn't tell the difference between us. It's called guilt by association."

"A nice turn of phrase," Carter said.

Luciano turned to face him. "Sure, I did a lot, but I never ran girls. If I needed girls, I called Polly Adler. She kept the best house in New York."

Carter held out his silver case. "Have another cigarette."

"Okay." Luciano took one. "Now, what do you want with me?"

Carter sat down in the Warden's chair. "When the invasion starts, General Patton's Seventh Army is going to have the task of hacking its way through some of the worst mountains in Sicily to reach Palermo. If the Mafia can be persuaded to organize a popular uprising and make the Italian Army in the Cammarata surrender without firing a shot, then thousands of American lives could be saved. If not. . . ."

"Look, I've done everything they asked me to do," Luciano said.

"I know, but as I said, I don't think it's

enough. I was in Sicily myself only a matter of weeks ago and I can tell you this. There's only one man with the muscle to achieve what we're asking and that's Antonio Luca. And he isn't coming out of hiding for anyone."

Luciano had stopped smiling. "Don Antonio? You know him?"

"We've met. And you?"

"Sure I do." Luciano shook his head. "I still get the word in here. I know about him getting out of that prison in Naples and going back to Sicily. But you're wasting your time. Even if you could find him, he hates Americans. His brother went to the chair during Prohibition."

"I know about that. But what about his daughter?"

"Sophia. During the First World War, while she was supposed to be at school in Rome, she joined the Red Cross as a nurse. Met an Englishman called Vaughan, an infantry lieutenant serving on the Italian front, and married him. He was killed in the last month of the war and she went back home to live with her father in Palermo. Had a daughter called Maria the following year. She was the light of Don Antonio's life."

"What happened?" Carter said, although he had heard the story many times before.

"July 1936. The kid must have been about seventeen. Her mother borrowed her father's Ferrari one day so they could go shopping. When she put her finger on the starter, the car blew up. I guess whoever was responsible was after Don Antonio."

"So the mother was killed?"

"That's right. Maria was in the hospital for a while then one day she just walked out. I think maybe she'd had time to think, lying there on her back for so long."

"That if her grandfather hadn't been the kind of man he was, the whole thing would never have happened . . ." Carter said. "Did she ever turn up again?"

"She wrote to him once from London to say she was well, but never wanted to see him again. She had British nationality because of her old man. Don Antonio put people on to it, but they never managed to find her. After that, he grew more and more into himself."

"Would he see you?"

"See me?" Luciano frowned. "I don't get you."

"If you were in Sicily," Carter said. "If he knew you were there. If the word was out, would he see you?"

Luciano was genuinely astonished and it showed. "You're crazy."

"You're right," Carter said. "After all, look what you'd be giving up. Another twenty laps around the exercise yard tomorrow and the day after that. Thirty to fifty years, isn't that your sentence? I should say you'll be able to apply for parole around 1956 but I wouldn't count on it."

"Fuck you!" Luciano said. "I shouldn't even be in here in the first place."

"All right," Carter said. "So maybe this could be a way out."

"Go to hell!"

Carter sat there staring at him for a moment, then he got up and went out into the outer office where the Warden was sitting talking to a secretary.

Carter took a card from his wallet and passed it across. "Would you mind getting that number for me? It's priority one. The code word is Scorpion. That gets you through right away."

The Warden's eyes widened as he read the card and he whistled softly. "I certainly will."

Carter stood at the window, coughing over a cigarette. In spite of Luciano's attitude, every instinct cold him he was on the edge of something hugely important. When the Warden finally called him, he came to the phone at once.

"Is that you, Carter?" the voice at the other end of the line said. "How goes it?"

"Problems, Mr. President," Carter said and started to explain.

Luciano was standing at the window looking down into the exercise yard when the door opened and Carter and the Warden entered.

Luciano said, "Can I go now?"

The Warden moved round the desk and sat down. "I'm afraid not, Mr. Luciano. Colonel Carter's got a car waiting. You're being transferred to Washington under his care."

"Transferred?" Luciano cried. "To Washington? What for?"

"Let's just say for the good of your health," the Warden said. "They've got one of the best chest clinics in the country in Washington and we've been worried about that cough of yours for some time now."

Luciano turned to Carter. "You'll have to do better than this, Professor."

Carter smiled. "Oh, I intend to, Mr.

Luciano. You can count on it."

It was late evening as the Packard turned along Constitution Avenue and moved towards the White House. Carter and Luciano were seated together in the rear and Luciano wound down the window and looked out at the lights of Washington.

"I hear it's impossible to get a hotel bed in this town these days, is that true?"

"Not if you know the right people."

Luciano smiled.

The Packard turned in at the White House and delivered them to the West Basement entrance where Carter presented his pass to the Secret Service agents on duty.

Luciano wore a dark felt slouch hat and a trenchcoat over a grey tweed suit, clothes he had selected for himself from the prisoners' stock at Great Meadow. He stood there, a cigarette dangling from his mouth, amused by the proceedings.

"Hey, Professor, you sure we're not just waiting to see some half-assed paper-shuffler?"

An aide appeared, a young Marine Lieutenant in razor sharp uniform. "Colonel Carter? If you'd come this way the President will see you now."

When they entered the Oval Office, the room was in half darkness, the only light the table lamp on the massive desk, an array of service flags behind it. President Roosevelt was seated in his wheelchair at the desk working on some papers, the inevitable long cigarette holder jutting from his mouth.

He looked up at Carter and smiled. "Colonel Carter, how are you?"

"Fine, Mr. President."

The President nodded to the young Marine. "If I need you, I'll call."

The door closed quietly. There was silence for a moment while the President fitted a fresh cigarette into the holder. He lit it carefully, then finally acknowledged Luciano's existence.

"So you're Luciano?"

"That's what they tell me."

"I hear from Colonel Carter you've been giving him trouble."

"Now that, Mr. President, depends entirely on your point of view," Luciano said. "I'm sitting in my cell last year when your people come and ask to see me about doing something about saboteurs on the docks after they burned the *Normandie,* so

I arrange things with the unions. Then they come again the other month asking for help in Sicily. Again, I do what I can. And for what? I mean, what in hell is there in it for me except another thirty years in the pen? And then this guy turns up with some crazy idea I'm going to Sicily with him and put my head on the block, and you think *I'm* giving *him* trouble?''

The President leaned back and said softly, ''I'll tell you what I'm going to do, Luciano. I'm going to give you a chance to be an American again.''

''By going to Sicily with the Professor here?'' Luciano said. ''Why should I? What's in it for me?''

The President said, ''A bullet in the head if the Nazis catch you.''

''And if they don't? I mean, if his whole crazy idea works, what happens then?''

''Oh, I suppose you could take to those Sicilian mountains and be a fugitive for the rest of your life. On the other hand, you could go back to that cell of yours and take your chances. I'm sure a parole board would be suitably impressed.''

''You wouldn't care to guarantee that?''

Roosevelt fitted a fresh cigarette into his holder. ''Excuse me, but I've got pressing work to do. Thanks for coming to see me."

Luciano stood there staring at him, glanced at Carter, then spread his hand wide in a very Italian gesture, turned and walked out.

The President said, "Anything more I can do, Colonel?"

Carter took a folded piece of paper from his wallet and passed it across. "If you could ask Intelligence to trace that person for me, Mr. President, preferably before I leave, it would be helpful."

"I'll see to it," the President said.

"Mr. President."

Carter turned and followed Luciano, who was already on his way out. The Marine lieutenant said, "I'll only be a moment, Colonel," and went into the Oval Office.

Luciano was smiling again. Carter said, "Well?"

"Well, what?" Luciano said. "He didn't exactly leave me any choice, did he?" He grinned. "I'll say one thing for that old man. He's got balls."

"It's been said before."

"But he didn't promise me a thing."

"Not on paper. He couldn't do that. On the other hand, if you can't trust F.D.R., who can you trust?"

"All right. You've made your point. So what happens now?"

"We're flying out just after midnight. Scotland first stop. A place called Prestwick. Direct flight to Algeria from there."

"That gives us five hours to kill."

The Marine lieutenant returned and led the way back along the corridor to the West Basement entrance.

"I've got us a hotel room to keep us out of sight," Carter said.

Luciano gave that slight smile. "Professor, with your kind of contacts, I can believe it."

As the Flying Fortress gained height, climbing out over the Atlantic, the New England coastline falling away, Carter made himself as comfortable as possible in the sleeping bag the quartermaster had given him. Beside him, Luciano was having the same problem.

"One thing's for sure, they didn't intend these things to carry passengers."

Carter took an envelope from his pocket and passed it across. "Your name is now Frank Orsini. You're a field operative in the Office of Strategic Services with the rank of Captain. Everything you need to back that up is in the envelope."

"Christmas in June," Luciano said.

He took the Madonna from one of his pockets, jumped the blade and sliced open the envelope.

Carter said, "Where on earth did that come from?"

"With the clothes, from good old Great Meadow." Luciano smiled. "You can get most things in there, Professor. It was a parting gift from a friend."

A sergeant radio-operator appeared and crouched down beside Carter, holding a signal. "Colonel Carter, this came through for you just as we were leaving. Plain language. I hope it makes sense, sir."

Carter glanced at it and smiled. "Perfect sense, Sergeant."

The boy moved away and Luciano said, "You seem pleased."

"You could say that. An interesting fact about this war, Mr. Luciano, is that the British are actually more thoroughly documented than the Germans. Every man, woman, and child has to have a National Identity Card. Remember the piece of paper I gave the President? It was a request for our Intelligence people in London to see if they could run down Maria Vaughan. It didn't take them long."

He passed the signal across and Luciano's eyes widened. "Sister Maria Vaughan. Convent of the Little Sisters of Pity, Liverpool. Holy Mother of God."

"Careful," Carter told him as he took the signal back. "You almost crossed yourself."

"Little Sisters of Pity. That's a new one on me."

"It's a nursing order."

"Liverpool. Isn't that a port?"

"On the northwest coast of England. Lancashire."

"You intend to go see her?"

"Yes, I would say that's a distinct possibility."

"Everything's click-click with you," Luciano said. "I bet you're one hell of a chess player. But no emotion. You ever love anybody, Professor? I mean really love?"

Carter nodded. "Oh, yes, very definitely."

"When was this?"

"About a thousand years ago—when I was sixteen. Farmer's daughter in Norfolk where we used to go for family holidays. I can see her now, running over the sand dunes in a cotton frock."

"What happened?"

"She died during the influenza epidemic just after the war. Now me, I ran away from school and joined an infantry battalion just before my seventeenth birthday. I thought it was a romantic thing to do."

"That figures," Luciano said, but he was no longer smiling.

"We started the big push in 1918 with a battalion of 752 men. Within three months, we were down to seventy-three. I couldn't get killed and she had to die of bloody influenza."

Luciano said calmly, "So you never married?"

"Yes, my second cousin, Olive, in 1923."

"You loved her?"

"She was a childhood friend and she loved me."

"You got children?"

"No, she had the worst kind of miscarriage very early on."

"You going to see her when we get in?"

Carter shook his head. "Not possible. She died of cancer in thirty-eight."

Luciano nodded. "So, the war came just in time for you."

Carter gazed at him blankly. "You think so?"

"Don't you?" Luciano tipped the slouch hat over his eyes, folded his arms, and slept.

SIX

It was raining hard in Liverpool the following night when JU88 pathfinders made their first strike on the Liverpool Docks. At the General Infirmary, Sister Maria Vaughan had been due to go off duty at seven, but there was a severe shortage of experienced theater nurses and at the last moment, she had been asked to assist Professor Tankerley with a post mortem in the mortuary. It was not a duty she cared for, but it had to be done.

In the preparation room, she quickly pulled a fresh white gown over her habit and adjusted her cowl, checking herself in the mirror. She was twenty-three and slightly built with a grave, steady face. One of those plain faces that, for some reason, most people found themselves looking at twice. Only the eyes betrayed her, full of a kind of restless searching that showed that any visible repose had had to be fought for.

When she went into surgery, Tankerley was already there, a small intense man in a white gown that, from its condition, had already seen considerable service. There was no one else there except for the corpse under a sheet.

Tankerley pulled on rubber gloves impatiently. "Do get a move on, Sister. I've got a ward round in an hour."

He was three years past the retirement age, had only stayed on because of the war; a fine surgeon and convinced atheist who had little time for nuns at the best of times and certainly not in a hospital.

An assortment of surgical instruments was laid out on a trolley beside the operating table. Sister Maria pulled the sheet away and folded it neatly. The body was that of a middle-aged man who had obviously been in remarkably good condition, with powerful shoulders and strong muscular arms. The eyes were closed, the face peaceful.

"The general staff shortage being as bad as ever and no stenographer available, I'm going to have to do the report from memory later," Tankerley told her. "He was found on the pavement near a bus stop in Lime Street at five-thirty. Age around fifty, good physical condition, no evidence of external bruising, so obviously not the victim of an assault. What would your diagnosis be, Sister?"

"Coronary?" she said.

"Yes, I'd go along with that. Everything fits, including the age, so in the circumstances, we'll dispense with the whole works and go straight for the heart."

He held out his hand. She passed him a large scalpel and he opened the body from throat to belly with one practiced stroke. A living patient was different, but this was something she had always found difficult to take. She swallowed hard as Tankerley started to break the ribs with a pair of large cutters.

"Raw meat, Sister." He was, as usual, unable to resist taunting her. "That's all there is to a man at the end of the day. Where's your God now?"

She passed him a small scalpel. "A superior piece of engineering. Totally functional. There seems to be no task a human being is not capable of, wouldn't you agree?"

"Except learning how to live forever."

"No, but it is people at their most extraordinary I am interested in," she said. "Is this all that's left, a body on a mortuary slab? I don't think so. Christ, Professor, was once only a man dying on a cross. Two thousand years later he is a visible presence to millions."

He glanced up and half smiled in grudging admiration. "Oh, you have a way with the words, I'll say that for you."

And then, as the first stick of bombs fell across the docks, there was an explosion close at hand. The whole building shook, there was the crash of breaking glass. The lights dimmed for a moment and, somewhere, a woman screamed in fear.

"They certainly pick their time," Tankerley said. "On your way, Sister. They'll be needing you in Casualty. I'll finish up here on my own."

As she reached the door, another stick of bombs dropped across the docks. The steel instruments rattled on the tray as the building shook again. Tankerley reached for another scalpel and continued with his task while Sister Maria wrenched open the door and hurried out.

There was a tremendous hubbub in

Casualty, people running up and down the corridor and a smell of burning. The bombing had stopped and Maria could hear fire engines in the distance.

The hospital was working at full capacity now and she was on her own, patiently inserting twenty-five stitches into the left leg of a young seaman who had been brought in from the docks half an hour previously.

He watched her carefully, an unlit cigarette dangling from the corner of his mouth. "You're doing a good job there, Sister. How about giving me a little kiss for being a brave boy?"

"Not part of the service, I'm afraid."

"What a waste," he said. "I mean, a good-looking girl like you. It must be hell."

Behind her, Tankerley moved into the room. He produced a cigarette lighter and flicked it on. "Here, light your cigarette and shut up." He leaned down to examine the leg. "Very nice, Sister. You can go now. I'll finish here."

She moved out through the curtain and started awkwardly to unfasten the ties at the back of her gown. Tankerley appeared behind her. "Here, let me." He pulled the bows one by one and she was aware that he was angry. "Young swine," he muttered.

She turned, shaking her head. "He doesn't understand, that's all. So many people want everyone else to be as they are. And he's right. It can be hell. St. Chrysostom called celibacy the little crucifixion."

"And is it?" he asked.

"Not really, Professor. A very fair exchange in return for what is gained."

He scowled and gave her a push. "Go on, get out of here before you seduce me entirely. Go home." For once, she did as she was told, too tired, too spent to argue.

The Convent of the Little Sisters of Pity was behind high walls in Huby Road, a large redbrick building that had once been a college for the training of elementary school teachers. The teachers had long since moved out and the Little Sisters, with a considerable amount of faith and a large mortgage, had taken over. For twenty years this had been the base for all their work in the city.

The chapel was cold and smelled of damp, which was hardly surprising as no heating of any kind was possible because of fuel rationing. It was a place of shadows, candlelight and darkness alternating.

Maria Vaughan genuflected at the altar

102

rail and lit a candle to the Virgin. She knelt in prayer for a moment, then rose, picked up her mop and bucket, moved to the central aisle, and started to clean the floor. In spite of the tiredness she did not mind, for it was a simple enough task and gave her time to think.

High up in the gallery, Sister Katherine Markham, the Mother Superior of the convent, stood with Harry Carter and Luciano watching her.

"I thought you said she'd been working all day at the hospital?" Carter said.

"That's so. She's a theater sister there."

"Then why this?"

"However hard the day has gone, each member of the Order has an allotted task to perform each evening. However menial, Colonel, it is a symbol of the love that binds us all together. We'll go down now and I'll introduce you."

She started along the gallery to the stairs. Luciano grinned and said softly, "Ask a stupid question, Professor, and see what you get."

Maria looked up as they approached and paused in her work. "Sister?" she said.

Sister Katherine smiled. "You have

visitors, Maria. This is Colonel Carter and this is Mr. Orsini.''

Maria stood there, transfixed, staring at Luciano. He smiled easily and said in Sicilian, "Hello, pretty one. It's been a long time."

Sister Katherine gently took the mop from Maria. "I'll finish here. You can take these gentlemen to my office."

Maria looked again at Luciano, turned, and walked away. As Carter and Luciano started after her, Sister Katherine said, "We use the lodge as a guest house, Colonel. You're welcome to spend the night with us."

She dipped the mop in the bucket and started to work on the floor as they went out.

The office was small and cluttered, barely room for the desk and filing cabinets. Luciano leaned against the door, smoking, while Carter and Maria faced each other across the desk.

"So there you are," Carter said. "It's really very simple. All it requires is a yes or a no. Mr. Orsini and I. . . ."

"The subterfuge is not necessary, Colonel," she said calmly. "I am familiar with Mr. Luciano. He is a part of a past which I no longer wish to acknowledge. Which no longer forms a part of my life."

"Can you cut off a leg, an arm, and be the same person?" Luciano asked in Sicilian.

She answered in the same language. "Good husbandry, Mr. Luciano, to lop off the rotten branch to save the tree."

Carter said patiently, "Sister, to save thousands of lives it's necessary to persuade your grandfather to come over to our side publicly. You could just be the one to do it."

"You're wasting your time, Colonel. I have had no dealings with my grandfather for years. This entire affair is preposterous and has nothing to do with me. And now you must excuse me. I have work to do."

She brushed past Luciano and went out. Carter picked up the telephone and gave the long distance operator the number of S.O.E.'s headquarters in Baker Street in London.

Luciano said, "So, what happens now?"

"She'll go," Carter assured him.

"How can you be so sure?"

"Oh, the thought of all those dead men should do it. She's a *good* woman, after all. Can't you tell?''

The phone rang and he picked it up. ''Give me Control Two. Carter here. The code word is Scorpion.''

He reached for a cigarette and Luciano lit it for him as a voice echoed faintly in Carter's ear.

He said, ''Hello Jack, Harry here. Yes, all systems go. This is what I'm going to need. A safe house for a few days near Manchester. Is Bransby Abbey still on the list?''

Luciano said, ''Heh, wait a minute.''

Carter ignored him. ''Two heavies as part of the backup team. Good Italian essential plus all the usual skills, but I must have them within forty-eight hours. And signals to 138 Squadron at Maison Blanche and our friends in Bellona to make ready for a drop seven to ten days from now.''

He listened for a while then smiled. ''No, no problem.''

He replaced the receiver. Luciano said, ''Like I said, no emotion. Everything click-click-click. Only you're wrong about one thing, Professor.''

''Tell me,'' Harry Carter said.

''If Maria goes, it won't be because of the thought of all those lives she might save.''

"So what's your theory?"

"Simple. She's so eaten up with guilt that it's impossible for her to say no."

Sister Angela's one vice was cigarettes. Maria knew where they were kept. Behind the flour bin in the kitchen pantry. She lit one with trembling fingers and stood there in the dark, smoking furiously, like a defiant child.

The Sicilian half came to the surface rather easily on occasion, something to be fought against, but not now. The sight of Luciano's face, the old sardonic smile, had opened up wounds, and things walked out of dark corners to confront her again.

She could smell the burning, see again the blood on her mother's face as she crawled towards her. And afterwards, the pain. The long weeks in the hospital, the skin grafts for the burns, and her grandfather, sitting there day after day beside the bed, in spite of the fact that she would not speak to him.

The hate in her, the rage, was so strong now that, in a kind of panic, she dropped the cigarette in the sink, turned on the tap, and bathed her face with cold water.

After a while, she felt better. The past was over and done with. She had buried her dead and that included her grandfather. Sicily and all that it stood for was a matter of total indifference to her now. She had her work, her daily routine, the hospital. There was no place for anything else. Luciano and Carter would have to understand that. She smoothed her robe, took a deep breath and went out.

The Refuge, in what had been the old stables at the back of the convent, wasn't much of a place, but the stone walls had been neatly whitewashed, there was a coke fire in the stove, benches and blankets for those who waited in line there each night.

They were a strangely assorted group. Whole families, mother, father, children, who had been bombed out, servicemen on leave or between trains and needing a bed. And then there were flotsam and jetsam to be found in any great city, the unwashed, the destitute, the drunks who could no longer cope.

Maria and two other nuns stood together behind a trestle table doling out bread and hot broth to the slowly moving line of people.

Two young soldiers in khaki battledress were arguing at the end of the line. There was a sudden cry, a flurry of blows. Maria went round the table like a strong wind and flung herself between them. The one she was nearest to, a young, redheaded Scot, hit out wildly, still trying to reach his opponent, and struck her in the face.

Suddenly Luciano was there looking like the Devil himself. His right hand slapped across the boy's face very fast, his left seized him by the throat.

Maria had him by the arm now with both hands, exerting all her strength. "No, please. This isn't the way."

And Luciano was smiling now and released his grip so that the boy fell to his knees. "Okay, pretty one. Whatever you say," he said, in Sicilian.

There was a sudden buzz of conversation as the crowd came back to life. The soldier stood up and gingerly touched his throat.

"I'm sorry, miss," he said to Maria. "I don't know how it happened."

"I know," she said. "Get your soup and sit down," and she turned and went after Luciano.

"It's been a long time," he said. "The

summer of thirty-five. How old were you, sixteen?''

"And you," she said. "You don't change."

"So you've kept up with what happened to me?"

"Oh, yes, I know all about the great Lucky Luciano whose answer to everything is still violence. And where did it get you? Thirty years in prison."

"On a bum rap and I'm out now, aren't I?''

"You were my hero that summer when you visited my grandfather, you know that? Robin Hood and Richard the Lionheart rolled into one. When we walked in Palermo and people stopped to kiss your hand, I thought it was a mark of respect. But I was wrong. It was only that they were afraid."

"What about Don Antonio. You ever hear from him?"

"No."

It seemed colder than ever in the chapel and Luciano leaned against the end of a pew as he looked down at her. "You still love him, don't you, and that tears you apart because you should hate him."

"Very clever," she said.

"Listen, when I was in Sing-Sing, a

psychiatrist gave me all those fancy tests and told me I was below average intelligence. Wrote it on the report. Said I should learn a trade.''

She was unable to stop the slightest of smiles from touching her lips. "That's better," he said. "You laughed a lot that summer. That's what I remember best. Your smile.''

She shook her head. "Oh, Mr. Luciano, what's to become of you?''

"Look," he said. "I'm not making any excuses. I could say Eastchester Avenue was no place for any kid to grow up, but I won't. I made a choice. When people talk to me about the war, I say what war? I've been at war all my life, but I engage in a combat that's nothing to do with civilians.''

"Gangsters," she said. "Dope-peddlers, thieves, murderers.''

"I know," he said. "It sounds more like the Old Testament every minute.''

"You don't need to tell me," she said. "The world can't be innocent with Man in it.''

"And what the hell is that pearl of wisdom supposed to mean?" he demanded. "What do you want me to do, drain the cup? All right, I'll tell you how it is.''

He walked to the altar rail and turned. "We're fundamentally alone. Nothing lasts."

"God," she said. "There is always God."

"Well, if he exists, your God, I wish to hell he'd make up his mind. He's big on how and when. Not so hot on why."

"Have you learned nothing?" she said. "Has life taught you nothing?"

"Oh, yes," he said. "I've learned to kill with a smile. I'll probably die with one. But those soldiers who are going to die in the Cammarata, will they be smiling, do you think?"

She stood staring at him for a long moment, then turned and walked out.

Sister Katherine was at her desk in the office when there was a knock at the door. Maria entered. She stood there, hands folded, obviously deeply troubled.

"Sit down, my child," Sister Katherine told her.

Maria said, "Sister, has Colonel Carter told you why he has come here?"

"Yes," Sister Katherine said. "As much as he needed to."

Maria went round the desk and dropped

on her knees. "Sister, you know my story, you know why I came here."

"Of course," Katherine said. "You came seeking refuge. Instead you found God, is that not true?"

"Sister, my Bible tells me that we must love one another, but when I think of my grandfather, I know only hate." She gripped the older woman's hands tightly. "I am afraid of the violence I feel in myself. They would return me to everything I renounced, turned my back on. I will not do it," she added forcibly.

Sister Katherine smiled. "Such arrogance. You did not choose God, Maria. He chose you. For you, as his servant, there is no such thing as choice. You must do what is right. You may do no other."

Maria stayed there for a long moment, head bowed, then she looked up. "Which means I must go to Sicily."

Sister Katherine nodded. "Having no choice means there is no choice in the matter. A paradox, but true. What Colonel Carter has asked you to consider, this mission to Sicily, is one thing. The question of your hatred for your grandfather is another, hardly relevant to the greater issue. Is that not so?"

Maria took a deep, shuddering breath. "Help me, Sister."

Sister Katherine's hands tightened on hers, they bowed their heads together in prayer.

It was very quiet in the chapel when Carter and Luciano went in. The door banged, echoed in the silence. She was at the altar rail on her knees, and they paused halfway down the aisle and waited. She knew they were there, of course, the head coming up slowly. She stayed like that for a long moment, then got to her feet and turned. Her face was pale, but quite calm.

"Sister Katherine said you wanted to see me," Carter said. "You've made your choice, I presume?"

"Did I ever really have one, Colonel?"

Carter, suddenly desperately sorry, said, "Put like that, I don't suppose you did."

"When do we leave?"

"The morning would be fine." He hesitated and said, "Look, there's something we'd better get over with now. The only way we can get into Sicily at the moment is by parachute."

"That's all we need," Luciano said.

Carter ignored him. "I've known agents

going into the field for the first time drop cold, as we call it. In other words, their jump over the target is the first jump they've ever made. I'm not too keen on that. I'd like to think you had some idea of what you're doing."

"What would you suggest?"

"We'll be staying at a house in Cheshire for a while not far from Manchester. There's a parachute school there. Most S.O.E. agents pass through it. A six-hour course of instruction and one jump is usually enough."

"With any luck, I could break a leg," Luciano said.

Maria seemed totally indifferent. "Fine, Colonel, whatever you say." She looked around her as if taking everything in for the last time, then put a hand on the altar rail. "I've been happy here. Truly and deeply content for the only time in my life. Perhaps that was wrong."

Luciano said softly in Sicilian. "Now you go out into the world again. Maybe there are answers waiting."

"Yes, Mr. Luciano," she said. "That could be true." She smiled slightly. "I will hang on to that thought, believe me. Till the morning then, gentlemen."

She walked away along the aisle, the door closed behind her. Luciano said, "Well, Professor, you got what you wanted. Keep this up and maybe they'll give you a medal."

Carter shook his head. "I'm not sure at all that I've got what I wanted. Did you see her face, Mr. Luciano? She said yes—but I wouldn't be surprised if she reneged on that yes before we get to Sicily."

In the darkness of the chapel the flame of Luciano's cigarette flared briefly, illuminating his face. He was smiling. "That's why I'm here, Professor. With Luciano as her guardian, she'll get to Don Antonio's door."

"Safely?"

Luciano's smile vanished. "I think you'd better trust me, Colonel."

In Maison Blanche in Algeria just after dawn Harvey Grant walked across to the operations building. He was in a thoroughly bad temper. His mouth tasted like a sewer and his eyes were gritty from lack of sleep.

When he went into the Operations Room, he knew they were in trouble straight away, because it was deserted except for Joe Collinson, the squadron senior navigator who was night duty officer.

"Anything?" Grant asked him.

Collinson shook his head. "I'm sorry, sir, but I'm afraid they must have bought it. Way past their fuel time now."

"Four in a row," Grant said. "That's bad news, Joe."

Collinson turned to the map of Sicily on the wall behind him. "Jerry knows something's building up over Sicily, sir. Too much traffic over the past few weeks. Those Junkers 88s are out hunting every night and they're good, sir. Too damned good for a Halifax."

"You don't have to tell me," Grant said. "I've seen the faces in the mess. It's reaching the stage that when you brief a crew for a Sicilian drop, you might as well give them their death certificates while you're at it."

"So what do we do, sir?"

"What can we do except inform the A.O.C. of the situation. If they say go, we go, you know that."

He lit a cigarette and helped himself to coffee. Collinson said, "There's something for you, sir, just came in."

He pushed the envelope across the map table and Grant ripped it open. He stood there for a moment, reading Harry Carter's signal.

"Jesus," he whispered, and slumped down into a chair.

"Is anything wrong, sir?" Collinson asked, concerned.

"Oh, yes, I think you could say that," Grant told him heavily, and passed the signal across.

It was raining in Sicily that morning as the 21st Paratroop Battalion, or what was left of it, moved along a forest road towards the village of Vilalba. Max Koenig's 35 *Fallschirmjäger* fitted comfortably into three armored troop carriers. He himself was at the rear of the column in a field car with a driver and machine gunner. Rudi Brandt was riding point in another field car way out in front.

There was a ragged volley of rifle fire, flattened by the rain, and Koenig nodded to his driver who pulled out to overtake the column. Koenig signaled them to halt.

Brandt's field car had halted in pine trees on the ridge and the sergeant major stood beside it, a pair of Zeiss field glasses raised, examining Vilalba below. It was a miserable place, typical of the mountain villages.

A small church, a square, forty or fifty houses. There were two military trucks drawn up in the square and what seemed to be the entire population of the village watched as a firing squad went to work. There were already half a dozen bodies face down, or sprawled on their back in the unnatural postures of death. Another half dozen were being hustled forward to take their place against the church wall.

Koenig got out of his field car and Brandt handed him the glasses. *"Einsatzgruppen, Obersturmbannführer."*

Einsatzgruppen were units of the SS which had been formed by Himmler prior to the invasion of Russia. They were extermination squads, recruited from the jails of Germany, officered by the SD and Gestapo. Occasionally soldiers of the Waffen SS, convicted of some serious crime, were transferred to them as a punishment, and a number of Russian prisoners of war, mainly Ukrainians, were also employed by them.

Koenig handed Brandt his glasses back, his face grim. "All right, we'll go down. I'll lead."

As his field car led the convoy into the square, the small crowd was already beginning to disperse, herded away by half a dozen SS armed with rifles. Fifteen or twenty women were crowded into one of the trucks, some of them very young girls, most of them sobbing bitterly.

Koenig got out of his field car and walked forward to examine the dead. Three of them were teenage boys and there was another who could not have been more than ten years of age.

There was a cry behind him and someone called, "Signor Colonel, please!"

As Koenig turned, an old man ducked past the guards and ran before them. One of them raised his rifle and Koenig called, "Leave him."

The man was very old, with patched clothes and a heavy white moustache, and there were tears in his eyes.

"Please, Colonel, I am Angeli, the Mayor here, and you are a just man, everyone knows this."

"What happened here?"

"They came an hour ago saying that a German sentry was murdered in the next valley yesterday. That someone from here was responsible. They took every fifth man for the firing squad and every fifth woman. . . ." He appealed to Koenig passionately now, hands raised. "In the

120

name of God, Colonel. In the name of justice, tell your people not to do this thing.''

Koenig said calmly, ''These are not my people. You will not mention scum like that in the same breath as Waffen SS, you hear me?''

The old man was totally distraught now. He gestured towards the truck. ''Colonel, please, my granddaughter. The Russian, he took her inside.''

Before Koenig could reply, Brandt approached, his face grave. ''There is a difficulty here, I think, Colonel. These are Major Meyer's men.''

''Indeed,'' Koenig said. ''He's inside, presumably?''

''No, he's not here personally, Colonel.''

The *Fallschirmjäger* waited for orders by their vehicles, weapons ready. Koenig looked them over, then adjusted his gloves.

''Release the women, *Sturmscharführer*,'' he said clearly so that everyone could hear. ''If anyone tries to stop you, shoot them.''

Brandt responded instantly. *''Zu Befehl, Obersturmbannführer.''* He swung to face his men. ''All right, you heard the Colonel.''

There was a burst of laughter and singing from the inn as Koenig approached. He paused at the bottom of the steps, selected a cigarette from an old leather case, lit it, and passed inside.

There were half a dozen men drinking at the bar, rifles stacked. A burly *Untersturm-führer* was seated at one end of a long table by the fire. He was more Eastern than European with narrow eyes and high cheekbones. The girl on his knee was small and dark, no more than fifteen, her face swollen from weeping. There was a sudden silence as conversation died at the sight of Koenig standing there.

He said, "You are in charge here?"

The *Untersturmführer* pushed the girl away and stood up. "That's right. Suslov."

Koenig smiled down at the girl. "Go now, your grandfather is waiting for you outside."

She stared up at him for one brief moment then, as she turned to run, Suslov grabbed at her. Koenig stepped in his path and behind him the girl ran for the door.

Suslov said angrily, "Here, who in the hell might you be?"

"Your superior officer," Koenig said calmly. "And from now on, you will speak only when I invite you to speak. You will also stand at attention in my presence."

"*Sturmbannführer* Meyer is my commanding officer, not you."

Koenig raised his voice and called, "Sergeant Major!"

The rear door was kicked open and Brandt appeared, flanked by two paratroopers. All three of them carried machine pistols and looked perfectly willing to use them.

Koenig said softly, "In future, when I give you an order, you get those heels together and shout, *Zu Befehl, Obersturmbannführer.* Do you understand me?"

There was murder in Suslov's eyes, but he did as he was told and stood to attention. *"Jawohl, Obersturmbannführer."*

"Good. Now answer some questions. The executed—who were they?"

"Every fifth male."

"And the women?"

"For the army brothel in Palermo. Every fifth female." He hesitated. *"Sturmbannführer* Meyer's orders."

Koenig nodded. "You'll be interested to know that I've had them released. All that remains is for you and your men to remove yourselves. You have exactly two minutes in which to do that, otherwise I might be tempted to start operating in fifths myself."

Suslov, by that stage, knew better than to argue. He turned to his men, gave a sudden command in Russian and made for the door and they followed.

Koenig selected another cigarette and Brandt offered him a light "This could mean trouble, Colonel."

"Good," Koenig said, as engines roared into life outside.

He moved to the door and stood at the top of the steps as the trucks moved out of the village. At the same moment, a Mercedes staff car came over the ridge. The leading truck stopped and Koenig saw Suslov get out and lean down to the Mercedes window. After a while, the Russian got back into the truck, it moved off and the Mercedes came down towards the village.

Koenig stood watching the villagers moving the bodies of the dead. The Mercedes pulled up and Meyer got out.

"I was under the impression that I was in command here."

"Of this butcher's shop? You should be pleased."

An old woman and two girls came by, pulling a handcart behind them containing the body of the ten-year-old boy.

"One of our men was murdered last night. I had good reason to believe the culprits came from this village."

Koenig said, "Among the women selected on your orders, were twelve- and thirteen-year-old girls. I've had them all released, by the way. I presume Suslov told you."

"Naturally I shall make a full report of this entire affair to Reichsführer Himmler and also to Field Marshal Kesselring."

Koenig said, "You know what your problem is, Meyer? You believe yourself to be a soldier of the German Reich, a natural assumption in view of the uniform you wear, but you are mistaken. Now, would you like me to tell you what you are, in simple terms, so you fully understand?"

Meyer showed no emotion whatsoever, but stood there looking at him and Brandt came across and saluted. "Ready to leave, Colonel."

"Good," Koenig said. "We move out now."

He walked across to his field car and got in. He nodded to the driver and, as they drove away, the troop carriers formed up in the line to follow them. The convoy disappeared over the hill and the sounds of the engines faded into the distance.

Meyer, standing beside the Mercedes, became conscious of the silence. He was suddenly aware that everyone in the square had stopped what he was doing. The old men, the women, the children working on the bodies, all stood perfectly still, looking at him.

There was infinite menace there, and as someone bent down to pick up a stone, he realized that, except for the corporal driving the Mercedes, he was entirely alone.

Braun, his driver, jumped out of the Mercedes and opened the rear door. "Please, Major," he said urgently. "I think we should go now."

Meyer ignored him. He walked a few paces toward the villagers, hands behind his back, stopped and stood there, waiting. There was a long moment and then the youth who had picked up the stone dropped it. Meyer took out his case, selected a cigarette and lit it, taking his time, then he turned and went back to the car.

Braun was only eighteen and there was terror in his eyes now, his skin damp with sweat. Meyer took out his handkerchief, keeping his back to the villagers.

"Wipe your face. Did you know I used to be a police inspector in Hamburg?"

"No, *Sturmbannführer.*"

"Well, I did. St. Pauli was my beat. The red-light district. The worst bars in town. Pimps, cutthroats, murderers. I dealt with them all, and you know what I learned, boy? You never turn back and you never show fear."

"Yes, *Sturmbannführer.*"

"Remember that. Now let's get out of here."

He settled back against the seat as they drove away and considered the problem of Koenig with no particular rancor. There was no need, for Koenig was so vulnerable, both in his actions and the things he said, that it was really only a matter of time before he did something totally unforgiveable. And when he did. . . .

SEVEN

The old Dakota lifted off the main run-way at Ringway and climbed quickly to two thousand feet. Carter slid back the door and saw Manchester in the distance, shrouded in rain.

Besides the RAF sergeant-instructor, there were only the three of them, Carter, Luciano, and Maria, all wearing British paratroopers' camouflaged smocks and helmets and X-type parachutes.

Maria seemed smaller than ever under all the equipment. As he clipped her static line to the anchor line, Carter felt that she was totally vulnerable, a child playing at some grown-up game that was beyond her.

"If possible on the real target, we'll jump from four hundred feet," he told her, "because that way you'll hit the ground in twenty seconds, which has its points; but today, we'll do it from a thousand. All right?"

She nodded. "Fine."

The Dakota was banking back towards the airport now. Carter said to Luciano, "You first, Maria second, and I'll bring up the rear."

Luciano grinned as he moved towards the door. "I hope you're getting a picture of this for my parole board."

The sergeant-instructor moved into position as the red light blinked above the door. Luciano turned and called. "With my luck, I'll probably break that leg. Then what happens?"

The green light flared and the Sergeant yelled, "Go!" and slapped him on the back.

Luciano went headfirst into space and Maria, terrified, heart pounding, throat dry, went after him without hesitation. Carter clipped on to the anchor line and followed.

There wasn't much time to think. Luciano was aware of himself turning over a couple of times, the sudden slap of the parachute opening, a jerk, and then he was swinging beneath a khaki umbrella.

The airport was laid out like a child's plaything beneath him, the hangars, the aircraft standing outside in neat rows, and there were faces, lots of them, turned up to watch. He looked up and saw Maria above and to one side, Carter perhaps sixty or seventy yards further away. Then suddenly, the airport was much larger and he seemed to be going in very fast.

He hit the tarmac hard, rolled, and miraculously found himself on his feet, the parachute itself giving him no problem because of the almost total lack of wind. As he turned and unclipped the harness, he saw that Maria was down forty or fifty yards away.

Carter was just hitting the ground on the far side of her. He rolled expertly, for this was his fifteenth drop, and came to his feet. As he disengaged from his harness, he saw Luciano running towards Maria, who was still on the ground, crouched over her chute.

Carter hurried towards them anxiously, but before he reached them, Luciano had turned and was coming to meet him, a smile on his face.

"Is she all right?" Carter called.

"Oh, sure." Luciano fished out a crumpled pack of cigarettes and lit one.

"What's wrong then?"

"Nothing. Two Hail Marys and three Our Fathers for a safe deliverance or something like that." He offered Carter a cigarette. "That was great. We must do it again sometime."

"You will, Mr. Luciano," Carter said. "Soon."

Bransby Abbey was close to Alderley Edge, one of the most beautiful parts of Cheshire and about ten miles from Ringway Airport. Parts of it dated from the fourteenth century, but it had been heavily restored in the 1850s. It was constructed in mellow grey stone surrounded by a high wall. Bransby was one of a number of safe houses operated by the S.O.E.; a place where agents could be prepared for specific missions or receive last minute training.

On the afternoon of the following day, Luciano and Carter went for a run through the grounds. There was a trail through the woods, an assault course with commando nets, ropes stretched between trees, and similar hazards. Luciano was enjoying himself in spite of the rain. He wore a commando stocking cap and army fatigues and was soon soaked with rain and mud.

He crawled through a line of barbed wire,

aware that he had lost Carter somewhere back there in the woods. As he got up, a voice called, "Heh, you down there."

Luciano glanced up and saw a United States Army officer standing on the hill, wearing a field cap, captain's bars on his military trenchcoat.

"I want a word with you."

It wasn't so much a request as an order and delivered in fine Bostonian tones of the kind you usually got in New England and nowhere else in America. Luciano didn't like that kind of voice, never had, so he didn't bother to reply.

"I'm talking to you, soldier."

"Great," Luciano said. "I'm very happy for you."

Then a hand had him by the shoulder and a voice that was straight out of New York said, "When the Captain speaks, you answer, you bum, hear me?"

Luciano glanced over his shoulder and found himself in the grip of an army sergeant who was considerably larger than he was, with a raw, bony face swollen by the scar tissue of a professional prizefighter.

"Heh, you got real medals," Luciano said. He dipped one shoulder in under the big man's arm and twisted and the sergeant went headfirst down into the hollow.

Luciano looked up at the officer. "He made a mistake. Don't let him make another."

He was tall, with very fair hair and a handsome, arrogant face. Something moved in the blue eyes, and then the sergeant was up out of the hollow, arms reaching to destroy. When he was about six feet away, Luciano's hand came out of his hip pocket holding the ivory Madonna. There was a nasty click and the blade jumped into view. The sergeant stopped dead, then crouched to move close.

He frowned suddenly and stood very still, his jaw slack with amazement. "Heh, I know you."

The captain called, "Detweiler, stay where you are! That's an order."

And then Carter joined in, appearing from the trees on the run. "What's going on here?"

"Colonel Carter?"

"That's right."

The captain saluted and produced a buff envelope from inside his trenchcoat. "Jack Savage, captain, Ranger Division, and this is Sergeant Detweiler. My orders were to report to you here as soon as possible."

He glanced at Luciano. "I'm sorry for any apparent misunderstanding, but this soldier. . . ."

"Captain Orsini, O.S.S.," Carter said.

As Luciano started to grin, Detweiler said angrily, "Orsini, my ass, sir. I was raised in New York, lived most of my life on Eastchester Avenue, and I've seen this guy a hundred times or more. He's a gangster named Lucky Luciano."

Jack Savage was twenty-four, the younger son of a career diplomat who had spent his time in places like Paris and Rome. As a result, the boy had been raised to be fluent in both languages. The Savage family was one of the wealthiest in Boston, with huge interests in oil and steel, none of which interested Savage in the slightest.

The fact was that, from an early age, he had shown a quite extraordinary talent for drawing. Out of deference to his parents, he had gone to Yale to study economics, but enough was enough, and after taking his first degree he had moved on to London to study painting at the Slade.

He was in Paris living in the artists' colony in Montmartre when the Germans took the city and had stayed for another six months before moving on to Madrid. He had finally returned home to join the army just before America entered the war.

The Americans had no equivalent to the British S.O.E. until June 1942, when Wild Bill Donovan, who had firsthand knowledge of British methods, set up the Office of Strategic Services, the O.S.S. Jack Savage, by then a very bored Intelligence lieutenant at the Pentagon, had been one of the first recruits.

He made a brave show standing in front of Carter's desk in the library at the Abbey, a tall, handsome young man in olive drab battledress, his pants tucked into jump boots. On his right sleeve he carried a double set of parachutist's wings, a rare distinction for that handful of members of the American Special Forces who had completed jump training with the British.

Detweiler was still letting his views be known forcibly. "Orsini nothing, Captain. That guy is Luciano!"

Harry Carter held up the orders Savage had given him. "You have read these, Captain. You do appreciate that they place you and the sergeant entirely under my command?"

"Of course, sir."

"Good, I thought there might be some misunderstanding." He turned on Detweiler coldly. "Which means that in future, when I want your opinion, I ask for it."

Detweiler was badly shocked and it showed. He turned in a kind of appeal to Savage, "For Christ's sake, Captain . . ."

Carter cut in fast. "Get your feet together and stay that way until I tell you different. Come on, man! Move!"

Detweiler, red in the face, did as he was told.

Carter took the envelope from the inside pocket of his battle dress tunic, extracted the letter of authorization General Eisenhower had given him in Algeria and the similar one he had obtained from President Roosevelt.

"Read those."

Savage did as he was told and looked up in astonishment. "Good God!" he whispered.

"Exactly," Carter said. "I'm not going to mince matters. I don't like your sergeant's attitude. If there was time to dump him, I would, but there isn't."

"Colonel, Detweiler's a good soldier. We've been through a lot together. I know."

"Good. Then show him those letters and see if you can talk some sense into him. I'll be back in five minutes to explain exactly what's going on here."

Luciano was sitting against one of the stone lions on the terrace. He had changed into black sweater and pants, but still needed a shave.

He looked up at Carter, shaking his head. "Where in hell do you find them?"

"His uncle's a three star general."

"And I used to know Al Capone very well indeed. What the hell does that have to do with the price of tomatoes? Listen, Professor, I know the type. Boston, the kind of people who fell over each other in their scramble to be first off the Mayflower. Who needs him?"

"We do."

"Would you mind telling me why?"

"Because, strictly speaking, the whole thing is an American operation, so it seemed like a good idea to the powers that be to have people like Savage and Detweiler along."

"Oh, I see. You mean I didn't count?"

"Something like that."

Carter smiled, aware that there was no

strain with Luciano at all. That for some reason it was like old friends talking. No need to pretend or pull punches.

"Great," Luciano said. "That really makes me feel wanted."

"He's a good man. Two DSCs, a Silver Star. Even the French have decorated him. When he operated in France as an O.S.S. agent, the Gestapo had him and he got away. Since then he's raided across the Channel into France with the Special Forces on a number of occasions."

"France isn't Sicily. What's he doing here?"

"His father was a diplomat at the American Embassy in Rome before the war for four years. Savage went to school there. Speaks good Italian."

Luciano said. "Rome Italian. Professor, there are villages in the Cammarata where that will sound like Greek. Anyway, what's Detweiler's story?"

"He was born and raised in New York, but his mother is Italian. I've already given them a brief rundown on the whole affair. I've arranged to meet in the library for a full briefing. Do you know where Sister Maria is?"

There was a rumble of thunder overhead

as if rain threatened again. Luciano said, "I think she went for a walk in the grounds. I'll find her."

"Good. The library in half an hour then," Carter said and went inside.

Maria sat on a stone bench by the fountain in the rose garden. She wore slacks, an olive green army sweater that was at least two sizes too large for her, and a scarf twisted around her head like a turban.

It was very calm, peaceful, the only sounds rooks calling to each other in the beech trees at the end of the rose garden. The fact that she was here and in the open, instead of inside the house, was in itself significant.

She was trying to come to terms with freedom for the first time in years. It was nothing as simple as being away from the convent on her own. That happened every day of her life because of her hospital work. This was different. Now she was once again responsible for herself in a way that she had not been since her entry into the Order. She had not only pledged herself to God, but to a community and a way of life which had sustained her totally during that dark night of the soul she had gone through for so long. Now, she was responsible once again for her own destiny.

As thunder rumbled again, she glanced towards the sky and turned to move towards the house. Luciano came into the walled garden through the arched entrance carrying a spare trenchcoat.

"Now you see why they baptized me Salvatore," he said cheerfully.

"Thank you, Mr. Luciano."

"Carter wants us in the library in twenty minutes, just to tie up all the loose ends. The rest of the team has turned up. A Captain Savage and a Sergeant Detweiler."

"We'd better get moving then."

"No hurry." He lit a cigarette and carried on in Sicilian. "Poor Maria, I worry you, don't I? Disturb the calm order of your life. The serpent in Eden."

"Is that how you see yourself? As some romantic outsider?"

As they went out through the arch the rain increased in force and he pulled her under the pergola to avoid the worst of it.

"And you?" he said. "How do you see me? No, don't answer that." He put a finger to his lips. "Because whatever you think I am, that's what I'm not."

"True for all of us."

"Tell me something," he asked her. "The religious thing. How did that happen?"

"Oh, when I first reached London I had very little money. I worked in a shop for a while and then I became ill—very ill. For a while, I was in a charity ward in a hospital where some of the nurses were Sisters of Pity."

"So you decided that was for you? A blinding flash, God sending someone down off the mountain to tell you, or what?"

She remembered so clearly that final day during Special Mass on her knees, asking Mother Superior for permission to make her perpetual profession in the Society of the Little Sisters of Pity, resolving to undertake a life of perfect chastity, obedience, poverty, and service. It still made her uneasy to discuss it and yet it could not be avoided.

"No, I think it's obvious enough now why I joined the Order. I sought a refuge. I should add that I found God, Mr. Luciano, but only in His own good time."

"And Carter turns up like something out of a bad movie, saying I've come to take you away from all that."

"I suppose you're right," she smiled.

"With the Devil trailing behind?"

141

"Is that supposed to be you? If so, where are the horns?"

"Oh, I don't know. We all end up the same way," he said, suddenly somber. "The one absolute certainty, death." He took her arm before she could reply "Come on, let's get out of here."

Carter was waiting in the library with Savage and Detweiler when they went in. "Ah, there you are," he said, and started to make the introductions. "Sister Maria Vaughan, Captain Savage."

She put up a hand. "Plain Maria will be better in the circumstances."

She took Savage's hand briefly and sat down, pulling off her turban as she did so, revealing dark hair cropped very closely to her skull, giving her a boyish look.

"Christ Almighty!" Detweiler said in a whisper.

Carter said, "Mr. Luciano, you've already met." Savage nodded, Detweiler glared, and Luciano, indifferent to both of them, lounged in the window seat.

Carter said, "May I make one thing clear? I've been concerned with this kind of intelligence operation for some time now and, as far as most of them go, the truth is that, succeed or fail, it isn't going to make a scrap of difference to the war as a whole."

Savage frowned, as he was bound to do at a suggestion which so put down his own war career. "Don't you think that's going a little far, Colonel?"

"No, I don't, but one thing is for sure. It isn't true of this present venture. If we can get into Sicily in one piece, if Mr. Luciano and Maria between them make the contact we hope for, then thousands of lives will be saved. If we fail, Patton's army will sustain thousands of needless casualties. It's as simple as that."

There was silence. It was Savage who finally said, "When do we go, sir?"

"Tomorrow night from RAF Hovington in a Lancaster bomber, straight across France and the Mediterranean to Algiers."

"And then?"

"Sicily any time within four or five days after that, depending on the best conditions for the drop. One more thing, Captain Savage. You and Detweiler will be operating in civilian clothes. You understand what that means if you fall into enemy hands?"

"They've been shooting Ranger and Commando prisoners in uniform under the terms of Hitler's *Kommandobefehl* for two years now, sir. I can't see that it makes much difference.''

"As long as you understand that. Now gather round the map, all of you, and I'll go over the whole thing in detail.''

In Bellona, at the same moment, Vito Barbera was climbing a short wooden ladder to the coffin room above the mortuary. He opened the cupboard at the far end and felt for a hidden catch inside. The entire back, shelves and all, swung open to reveal a cubbyhole containing a radio receiver and transmitter. He switched on the light, sat down, put on the earphones, then waited patiently for the allotted hour as he did three times a week.

He straightened, suddenly excited as he started to receive a signal. He reached for a pencil and made notes. Behind him, the secret door opened and Rosa entered with coffee on a tray.

He motioned her to silence and continued to write. After awhile, he took off the headphones and sat there, reading what he had written, a look of astonishment on his face.

"Is it something important?'' she asked.

"Carter is returning.''

"On his own?" she said.

He shook his head. "No, Rosa, not on his own."

Looking for Carter after supper, Luciano was directed to the firing range in the basement, where he discovered Carter and Savage on the firing line. Detweiler was helping the armorer, an Ordnance Corps major named Smith, to load.

As Luciano stood watching, Carter took careful aim with both hands and squeezed one off, chipping the right arm of one of the replicas of a charging German at the other end.

"Very good, sir," Savage told him.

"Not if you consider that I was aiming for the heart," Carter said. He fired another five rounds and hit the target twice more, once in the neck and again in the arm. "Oh, well, I never was much good with handguns."

"It's a knack, sir, like anything else," Savage said cheerfully and fired, like Carter, double-handed, but much more rapidly, hitting the general area of the chest in a solid group.

Detweiler said, "I don't recall anyone being much better at it than you, Captain."

Carter turned to Luciano, "What about you?"

Luciano hefted one of the Brownings in his hand and shook his head. "The trouble with automatics is they can jam." He turned to the armorer. "What else you got?"

"Webley .38, sir?" Smith suggested.

"Too clumsy."

"The only other revolver I have here at the moment is a Smith and Wesson .32 with a three-inch barrel."

Luciano tried it in his right hand, then the left. "That's more like it. You got a silencer for this?"

"Sure—over here."

Smith got one from the cupboard and screwed it into place. As he handed the weapon to Luciano, Detweiler said, "A popgun. You'd need to get damn close to do any good with that. But then, that's your style, isn't it?"

Luciano turned and fired twice very fast, right arm extended, both rounds hitting the heart.

There was a respectful silence. Savage said, "I'd say the second round was rather superfluous, Mr. Luciano."

"I like to cover my bets," Luciano told

him, "And a wounded man can always shoot back."

Savage said to Detweiler, "I think we could do with a couple of fresh targets down there."

As Detweiler obediently moved down the range, Luciano laid down the Smith and Wesson, following normal safety precautions. Detweiler replaced two of the targets and turned.

Luciano called, "Heh, Detweiler! Like you said, I always do my best work in close." He picked up the Smith and Wesson, fired twice without apparently taking aim, and shot out the eyes of the target next to Detweiler.

Detweiler cried out in alarm and ducked and Luciano started to laugh, was still laughing as he walked out.

"They say he's killed at least twenty men personally," Carter observed.

"Well all I can say, Colonel, is I'm damn glad he's on our side," Savage told him.

Maria awakened early on the following morning from a deep sleep. Pale sunshine filtered in through the curtains. She lay there for a few moments, remembering that this was the last day. Tonight, she would be on a plane for Algeria, set on a course from which there would be no turning back.

It was not that she was afraid anymore. It was simply that nothing fitted. It was as if this were all a dream. A few days before, her world had consisted of the convent and the hospital, a daily round that filled her time and life, work for the mind and for the body. Nothing that ever needed to be questioned. But now?

She got up and stood beside the bed for a moment. She had slept in the nude, something she had not done for years, always wearing the nun's linen shift of modesty.

"A crack in the fabric already, Maria," she said softly, and pulled on a terrycloth robe.

Her room was on the ground floor and she opened the French window, looked out into the garden, and moved on to the terrace. It was incredibly beautiful in the early morning sun, the trees touched with a kind of nimbus, the rooks cawing lazily to each other.

And yet she felt detached, not part of any of this at all, not really aware. It was as if she were looking at things under water in slow motion. She went down the steps without thinking about it, barefooted in the damp grass.

Luciano had also awakened early. He was sitting at the window of his bedroom in pajamas, smoking the first cigarette of the day as she crossed the lawn and entered the wood. He stood up, frowning slightly, watching her go, then tossed his cigarette out of the window, turned and started to dress quickly.

She advanced through the wood, still caught in that dream-like state, and the sound of the rooks seemed to fade and there was the most profound silence she had ever known. She came out on to a long jetty beside an ornamental lake and stood there looking across the water.

Suddenly, a voice said quite distinctly: *Having nothing, yet possessing everything.*

It was her voice which had spoken, she broke through to reality again, aware of the rooks in the beech trees above her head, the smell of the damp grass, the golden glory of the morning.

"So this is what it's like!" she thought. "Total certainty."

She had never felt so much at one with

everything, so much a part of the whole. It seemed the most natural thing in the world to slip out of her robe and wade into the cold water of the lake. She turned on her back and floated there in the lily pads, face up to the sun, eyes closed.

Luciano, walking along the path through the wood, paused, aware of Detweiler crouched behind a tree where the path dipped down towards the lake. He went forward quietly, until he was close enough to see the object of the sergeant's attention, Maria Vaughan floating in the water lilies below.

"Heh, Detweiler!" Luciano whispered softly, and when the Sergeant turned, lifted a knee into his face, sending him over on to his back.

Detweiler rolled over once, then was on his feet and moving in fast. Luciano's hand came up clutching the ivory Madonna, there was a click and the point of the needle drew blood under Detweiler's chin.

Luciano said, "Now hear this and hear good because I only say it once. If I catch you anywhere near her again, they'll find you in a ditch with a very personal part of your anatomy stuffed into your mouth.

An old Sicilian custom.''

Detweiler glared, an expression that was a compound of fear and hatred on his face. "Damn you to hell, you guinea bastard!" he said hoarsely, took a step back, turned and walked away.

Luciano folded the knife and replaced it in his hip pocket. "Heh, pretty one!" he called in Sicilian. "You decent?"

"Mr. Luciano," she called back. "Please stay where you are."

He took his time lighting a cigarette and finally went down the path to find her on the jetty, tying her robe.

"You're crazy," he said. "You know that?"

Her smile was enchanting. "I've never felt so hungry."

"Then we'll get back and have some breakfast."

She shook her head. "Not possible just yet. There's a little Catholic church in the village. I'm going to early morning Mass. What about you?"

"Do I look as if I would?"

"It's possible for anyone to end up on his knees, even Lucky Luciano."

He laughed, "Okay, I'll tell you what I'll do. I'll walk you down to the church, wait for you outside. How about that?"

"It's a start."

They went up the path together. A small wind blowing across the lake brought with it the dark wet smell of rotting leaves. She paused, smiling.

"Isn't it wonderful? Doesn't a day like this make you feel good to be alive?"

She ran up the path, lifting the skirts of her robe, and Luciano watched her go, cold in spite of the sun, as if someone somewhere had stepped on his grave. Reverting to his Sicilian childhood, he instinctively formed two fingers and a thumb into the ancient sign to ward off the Evil One and went after her.

EIGHT

The Avro Lancaster was the most successful Allied bomber of the Second World War. Its exploits included the sinking of the German pocket battleship, *Tirpitz*. Only three weeks previously, Lancasters of 617 Squadron had carried out one of the most daring raids of the war, breaching the Ruhr dams and flooding the most important industrial area in Germany.

It was shortly after nine o'clock that evening when Lancaster *S-Sugar* lifted off the main runway at RAF Hovington and joined on the tail end of a stream of heavy bombers from stations all over the Midlands and east England.

By the time they converged over the North Sea, they comprised a force of over six hundred in a tail back a hundred miles long. The target was the Genoa docks, all the way across France and the Alps except for *S-Sugar,* which, at an appropriate point, would leave the mainstream and change course for North Africa.

It was bitterly cold in the cramped interior, and the noise from the four great piston engines was almost intolerable. Carter's party had been issued with heavy flying suits and sleeping bags, and they huddled together in the body of the plane.

Luciano looked up at the gunner in the mid-upper turret above his head, then glanced across at Maria, who was sitting opposite him, apparently asleep. Her eyes flickered open and he leaned across.

"You okay?"

"Fine," she smiled.

Which was a lie, of course, for she was afraid again. Not only of the danger that lay ahead, but desperately afraid of the prospect of meeting her grandfather. At the thought of what that might unleash inside her, her stomach cramped in panic.

Luciano leaned back and burrowed into the sleeping bag, aware of the vibrations of the fuselage, the roar of the engine, the fierce cold. *What in the name of God am I doing here?* he asked himself, and closed his eyes and tried to sleep.

From further along the plane, Detweiler watched him, eyes filled with hate.

The Franciscan monastery of the Crown of Thorns lay five miles outside Bellona. Centuries earlier it had been a Saracen castle sited on a ridge a thousand feet above the valley with views across the surrounding countryside for twenty miles in every direction. And a castle was what it still most resembled, with smooth stone walls more than a hundred feet high.

It took Vito Barbera an hour and a half to get there by mule from Bellona, following the dirt road which zigzagged up the side of the mountain. The defensive ditch from the old days was still there at the base of the walls, choked with weeds and rubbish now. He crossed the wooden bridge that gave access to the only entrance and reined in at the oaken gates.

There was a bellchain to one side and he leaned over and pulled it, staying in the saddle. The sound was remote, unreal in the heat of the afternoon, and he waited, tired, gazing out across the valley.

After a while, a small shutter opened and a young bearded monk peered out. He said nothing, simply closed the shutter. A moment later, the great gates cracked open and Barbera rode inside.

Padre Giovanni, the prior of the monastery, was a tall, frail old man of seventy, full-bearded as indeed were all the Franciscans at Crown of Thorns, although in his case it was almost pure white except for the nicotine staining around his mouth.

He wore a brown beretta on his head, a plain brown habit with knotted cord at his waist from which hung a large crucifix. His face was full of strength, firm, aesthetic, and yet shrewd good humor was never far from his eyes.

The red-pantiled roofs of the monastery extended like a series of giant uneven steps to the highest point on the ramparts where he kept his pigeons, the great love of his life. He was working on them now when young Brother Lucio brought Vito Barbera to him.

"Ah, Vito," the old prior said. "How good to see you."

Barbera pulled off his cap and kissed the extended hand; not for religious reasons only for Padre Giovanni's connections with the Mafia were a matter of public knowl-edge. Mori, Mussolini's notorious Chief of Police, had expended considerable time in attempting to prove the fact. He had even succeeded in bringing Giovanni to court, a trial that had descended to low farce and had ended with the jury finding Padre Giovanni and other members of his order not guilty of even feeding pigeons in the park.

He helped himself to a cigarette from the tin on the parapet. "How are things in the village?"

"Bad," Barbera told him. "The man from the Gestapo, Meyer, and those Russians of his. . . ." He shook his head.

"And the other, this Colonel Koenig?"

"A good man in the wrong uniform." Barbera shrugged. "A holy fool, Padre. He thinks you can still fight wars according to rules, like a game of cards."

"So." The old man nodded. "What can I do for you?"

"I have a message for Don Antonio."

The old man smiled, "My dear Vito, who knows where Don Antonio is?"

Barbera moved to the pigeon loft and scratched the wire, cooing at the birds inside. "I'm sure he has a friend or two in here who could find him, and not too far away."

Padre Giovanni sat down in the old wicker chair by the low parapet. "Vito, if you have heard from your friends in Algeria again, if this is to do with the Mafia and the American invasion, I tell you now you are wasting your time. Don Antonio's dislike of the Germans is followed closely by his hatred of all things American. No, in this case he stays in the mountains. He does not wish to be involved."

"But it's all different now, Padre," Barbera told him. "Don Antonio's granddaughter is coming, Maria."

The old man looked up, astonishment on his face. "You mean to the Cammarata? But how can this be?"

"I've had word on the radio. Carter returns, very soon now."

Padre Giovanni stubbed out his cigarette angrily. "The fool. I told him when he was last here that enough was enough. He seeks death, that one. But tell me more about the girl? Carter brings her with him, does he? They hope she will influence Don Antonio in a way no one else has been able to." He shrugged. "I'm not too sure that they are right."

Barbera said, "There's more, Padre, a great deal more. Luciano comes with them."

The old man stared at him. "Lucania?" he whispered, using Luciano's Sicilian name. "Salvatore Lucania comes here? But he is in prison." Then comprehension dawned. "Ah, I see now—the whole strategy. Luciano and the old Don's granddaughter. Harry Carter must think the game is his."

"And you, Padre? What is your opinion?"

"How could that be of the slightest importance? I will see that one of my little friends here," he touched the pigeon loft, "takes news of this to Don Antonio. He will act as he sees fit. When do they come?"

"Within the next few days. I'll be getting a further radio communication."

"When you have the exact date, let me know. Have you spoken of this to the district committee."

"No," Barbera said.

District committees had been set up during the previous summer to coordinate the activities of the various groups which made up the Resistance movement.

Padre Giovanni put a hand on Barbera's shoulder. "And now, my friend, you will join me at the table. Something to sustain you on the journey back to Bellona."

Harry Carter was waiting on the terrace of the villa at dar el Ouad when Eisenhower rode into the courtyard. The General dismounted, gave his reins to a groom, and went up the steps to the entrance, acknowledging the salute of the sentries. As he moved into the hall, Cusak stood up at this desk.

"Colonel Carter's waiting, General."

Eisenhower turned as Carter came in from the terrace. He looked at him fixedly for a moment, then said, "Come in, Colonel," and led the way into his office.

He dropped his riding crop on the table. "I've read your report, Colonel. You've been busy."

"A fair description, General."

"Where are you staying?"

"A small villa near the airfield at Maison Blanche, sir."

"Comfortable?"

"Adequate, sir."

"Luciano and this man Luca's granddaughter. That's like aces back to back. Sit down."

Carter did as he was told. "The invasion's still on, sir?"

"Oh, yes. Of course, they know about our preparations, we know that. They're expecting us any day now. Our deception plan is that any attack on Sicily will be only a feint; the real targets are Sardinia and Greece."

Carter said, "When, sir?"

"Privileged information, Colonel, for your ears only. You don't tell the rest of your party except in circumstances of some extraordinary nature."

"Very well, sir."

"The ninth." Eisenhower flipped the date pages of the desk calendar and smiled. "It says here: 'A good day to sit back and take stock of your life.' "

Carter was astonished. "But that gives us only four days."

"I know, but the weather boys have guaranteed us storms on that day. The Italians won't be expecting any attack in that kind of weather."

"Then if we go, it would have to be tomorrow night at the latest and that would give us only three days to work in."

"How much time do you need?" Eisenhower asked. "One meeting with this man Luca is all it takes. If he decides to join us, the rest is simply his people spreading the word, isn't that so?"

"In theory, sir."

"Well, theory is all we've got." Eisenhower stood up, went to the map and jabbed his finger at the Cammarata. "Here, overlooking the two main roads we'll be using to reach Palermo. Mainly Italian troops with artillery of every description, including 88s, and you know what they do to our tanks. They've even got a few Tigers up there as well. If they decide to fight, they could hold us for weeks. If they surrender, then the few German units in the area will have to get out fast, leaving the road to Palermo clear for George Patton."

"Yes, sir, I'm well aware of the situation."

"What you don't know is that since we last talked, information's reached us from Rome that the whole house of cards is ready to fall. Mussolini's on the verge of being kicked out. One more push is all it takes and Marshal Badoglio takes over and that means a negotiated peace with Italy."

Carter said, "There is another aspect to consider. I called in at Maison Blanche before coming here to make arrangements for the drop with Wing Commander Grant. He tells me the A.O.C. has suspended any further operations. It seems we lost the last four Halifaxes we sent to Sicily."

"Yes, I know about that," Eisenhower said calmly. "But the written authority you hold allows you to countermand that order."

"The point is that, in Grant's opinion, the odds are heavily against one of their Halifaxes being able to reach the target."

"You mean he says it's impossible?"

Carter remembered Grant's exact words and rephrased them. "Let's just say that he didn't rate our chances very highly."

Eisenhower said, "Are you saying it's not on?"

"No, sir, I'm simply being realistic."

Eisenhower stood up and walked to the window. He spoke, gazing out into the garden at the same time. "You know something I've discovered about command, Colonel? That even Napoleon was only as good as his worst soldier. No matter how well you plan, the success of an entire battle can come down to half a dozen brave men denying a bridge to the enemy. My personal theory is that every battle is like that. Somewhere in the middle of all the action, although we may never know it, a single incident can be the balance point that decides which way victory will go."

"Yes, I think I'd go along with that, General," Carter said.

Eisenhower turned. "Whatever happens, we go into Sicily. We take our chances. We may win with heavy casualties, but for all I know this man Luca could be the kind of balance point I'm talking about. The difference between winning and losing."

"So we go, sir?"

This time the smile was touched with sadness. "Difficult decisions have always been the privilege of rank, Colonel. I say you go and take your chances." He held out his hand. "I can only wish you luck."

Harvey Grant, seated at his office desk at Maison Blanche, finished reading the two letters of authorization from General Eisenhower and President Roosevelt. He passed them back to Carter.

"This madness. As good a way of committing suicide as I can imagine. Like I told you, I can't even offer you a fifty-fifty chance. Another thing, we've not been grounded just because of losses. I know the invasion's coming any day now. They'll tell you that in every bazaar in Algiers plus the fact that it's just a part of a mammoth deception to fool the enemy. For Sicily, read Sardinia. What the eye doesn't see."

"I can't comment on that," Carter started to say, and Grant suddenly slammed a hand against the windowsill.

"Christ, Harry, I think I've got it. What the eye doesn't see. Correction, what the eye expects to see, it ignores."

"I don't follow you."

"You will. Come on, I'll show you."

They went down the steps and walked towards the hangars. "How many did you say there'll be?"

"Five. Four men and a woman."

"A woman?" Grant said. "My God. Still, I think it should do."

"What exactly."

"This."

Grant waved a hand and led the way into the end hangar where the black-painted Ju88S night fighter crouched in the gloom.

"You really think it would work?" Carter said.

"We'll need a quick paint job. Replace those RAF rondels with Luftwaffe markings again. The point is, this baby has an engine boosting system that takes it up to around four hundred. That means we can hit your drop zone in just under an hour from here.

In and out, Harry and to anyone around, we're just another night fighter."

Carter nodded slowly. "You could be right."

Grant said impatiently. "The Krauts used the thing for the same purpose themselves, so it has the right modification, that special door they've fitted for a fast exit. More than coincidence, Harry. The Gods are smiling."

"All right," Carter said. "Let's say it works, but how about coming back? This thing will have every RAF fighter in the area on its back the moment it crosses the coast."

"No problem," Grant said. "Naturally, I'll have to tell the A.O.C., Air Marshal Sloane, that I'm going, but there won't be any problem there, not when he sees your authorization. He'll arrange the right kind of reception for me when I get back."

Carter said, "You're grounded, Harvey, remember?"

"Not on this one, old son." Grant patted the side of the Junkers. "I'm not saying I'm the only pilot in the squadron who can fly this plane, but I'm the only one who can give this operation half a chance. I'll take Joe Collinson with me, the squadron's senior navigator. He's flown as many hours as I have in her so he's familiar with the equipment.''

Carter, no choice in the matter now, nodded. ''All right, Harvey.''

''When do we go?''

''Tomorrow night, if that suits you.''

''The same drop zone as you used last time? Outside Bellona?''

''Yes.''

''If you come with me now to the met. office we'll check on the weather, but all things being equal, I'd say you could send a message to your people in Bellona telling them to expect you around eleven.''

''Fine by me.''

''Good, then let's get moving. There's work to be done.''

In Palermo, at his temporary headquarters in the Grand Hotel, General Alfred Guzzoni, commanding the Italian Sixth Army, was holding a staff conference. It was attended mainly by Italian officers although there were a handful of Germans present, among them Meyer and Koenig.

Guzzoni, a first-rate soldier and veteran of numerous campaigns, had spent an hour explaining the strategic situation in the Mediterranean.

"So, gentlemen," he ended. "They come soon, we know that. A feint at some point on the Sicilian coast and the main attack probably Sardinia. One thing seems certain. We can expect no activity for at least a week. The meteorological report indicates some very stormy weather. Any questions?"

There were a few, and, after a while, Meyer raised his hand. "General, I'd like to discuss the question of partisan activity in the mountains."

Guzzoni said, "In what respect, Major?"

"A question of cooperation, General," Meyer said. "I expect none from these damn peasants in the mountains, but when I experience what I can only describe as a total lack of assistance from units of the Italian Army. . . ."

There was an angry murmur from the Italian officers present, and it was Koenig who defused the situation by standing up and saying, "You must excuse Major Meyer, General. He is perhaps not familiar with the fact that Italian dead lie as far east as the outskirts of Moscow and in considerable numbers in Stalingrad. I have been lucky enough to have Italian soldiers on my flank on more than one occasion and have been grateful for it.''

A number of Italian officers around him broke into spontaneous applause. Meyer glanced at him calmly, picked up his brief-case, and walked out.

Guzzoni walked through the crowd and held out his hand. ''You've made an enemy there, I think.''

''Then I'll just have to live with it, sir.'' Guzzoni put a hand around his shoulder. ''I had the pleasure of meeting your father in Berlin when I attended the OKW conference last month. Come and have lunch with me and I'll tell you how he was.''

The villa Carter's party was using was five miles along the coast from Maison Blanche. It wasn't much of a place, being run down and badly in need of a coat of whitewash, but the area behind it was astonishingly beautiful. Sand dunes separated the over-grown garden from the sea. Beyond them, a white beach ran as far as the eye could see into distance.

Carter had assembled the whole party in the living room of the villa for a general briefing. There was a map of Sicily on the wall and several large envelopes were on the table.

Most of what he said was simply a reworking of what had already been discussed before. When he was finished, he said, "Any questions?"

Detweiler asked, "When is the invasion to take place, Colonel?"

"No need for you to know that yet," Carter said. "I believe it's a sound principle to keep knowledge of dates, facts, identities of sympathizers to a minimum when going into the field. The less you know, the less you can disclose under pressure. False papers have, of course, been prepared for each of you."

Savage said, "But if anything goes wrong with the landing? If one of us becomes separated from the others, where do we make for?"

"Here, at the head of the valley. The Franciscan monastery of the Crown of Thorns. That will be our general headquarters. Any further questions?"

There was silence.

Maria was sitting in a hollow in the dunes when Luciano found her. He flung himself down beside her and lit a cigarette.

"Carter's back. He wants to see us all together in thirty minutes."

"Is it on?" she said.

"Apparently."

She turned away, gazing out to sea, hugging her knees and he said, "What are you trying to see—Sicily?"

"It's been a long time."

"And your grandfather. That's been a long time, too."

"Yes," she said. "Maybe too long for both of us. Have you considered that?"

"I have, but I don't think the Professor has."

She shook her head. "The omnipotent Luciano. Is nothing impossible to you?"

"Some things. Even the Devil has his off days." He held out a hand and pulled her to her feet. "Come on, time to eat."

They walked away side by side and disappeared over the sand dunes. There was a stirring in a patch of long grass near by and Detweiler stood up. He brushed sand from his fatigues for a moment, a strange, dazed look in his eyes, and then went after them.

NINE

In the living room of his house at the back of the mortuary, Vito Barbera presided over a meeting of the district committee. There was Pietro Mori, the schoolmaster, a thin, intense man of forty-six with steel-rimmed glasses, who had fought with the International Brigade in Spain. So had Ettore Russo, the one thing they had in common, for the fact that Russo had inherited his father's sheep farm made him suspect in the minds of many of the comrades.

The Christian Democrats were represented by Father Collura, the parish priest for the Bellona district, and the Separatists by Verga, the innkeeper. And although it was not stated, had never needed to be, Vito Barbera stood there for the Honored Society—for the Mafia.

When he finished talking, there was a

172

long pause. It was Mori who spoke first. "So, what do you want us to do? Genuflect because this Mafia cutthroat comes amongst us?"

"Salvatore comes as a savior," Ettore Russo mocked. "Who from?"

"The Germans," Barbera suggested.

"Yes, but not from Mafia." It was Verga, the innkeeper speaking now. "We of the Separatist movement want a Sicily that is genuinely free, not just separated from Italy, but with the same old Mafia gang running things as before."

Father Collura said mildly, "Shouldn't our primary task be to aid the American invasion as much as possible? The question of who is going to run the country can come afterwards. A matter of free democratic election."

"Marvelous," Mori said. "Free democratic election with a Mafia hand on every throat."

Barbera said, "Whatever else may be said, the Mafia has always stood outside politics. I think no one here can deny that."

"And behind whoever was in power," Russo replied.

Barbera sighed. "I may take it, then, that

no one is in favor of any concerted action at the moment?''

''When the Americans come, we will rise in the mountains,'' Mori said. ''But as for Luciano. To hell with him.''

''And Don Antonio Luca's grand-daughter? To hell with her also?''

There was silence at the mention of that name. Mori glanced at Russo and forced a smile. ''Now look, Vito, old friend, we certainly meant no offense to Don Antonio.''

''No, that's what I thought.'' Barbera looked at his watch and stood up. ''My friends will be here in approximately three hours, so you must excuse me. I know, of course, that this information is safe with you. If anything did go wrong, one would so obviously know where to start looking.'' He shrugged, smiling. ''But what am I saying.''

They moved out into the darkness of the side street and went their separate ways, except for Mori and Russo who walked together for a while.

Mori said, ''I know we don't always see eye to eye, but in this present affair I sense a considerable agreement. If Luciano adds his strength to Luca's our movement may

174

have to contend with a two-headed giant.''

"If you mean something should be done quickly about Luciano, then I'm with you," Russo told him.

Mori put an arm around his shoulders. "Come back to my house for supper. We can talk things over in peace there and I have an excellent bottle of Chianti.''

At Maison Blanche, a heavy, damp fog rolling in off the Mediterranean reduced visibility to no more than two hundred yards. The Junkers, once more with Luftwaffe markings, squatted on the runway, had been there for something like half an hour. Carter and the rest of his party were crowded together into the narrow fuselage, their bodies swollen with parachutes and equipment.

Flight Lieutenant Collinson, the navigator, was already on board, familiarizing his eyes with the Lichtenstein radar set that, in effect, enabled the Junkers to see in the dark.

Harvey Grant stood outside the crew room with Air Marshal Sloane who had come down to see them off personally.

"It's not good, Harvey," he said. "About as bad as I've seen. If you go, you might not be able to land, even if you get back."

A young pilot officer appeared and handed Grant a weather report. "Rain and thunderstorms predicted," Grant said cheerfully. "That's good enough for me, sir. See you in a couple of hours. This soup will all be washed away by then."

He turned and walked towards the Junkers, pulling on his flying helmet. Sloane watched him go up the ladder and pull it up behind him. A moment later, the engines, which had already been warmed up, rumbled into life.

As Grant boosted power, the Junkers moved forward with increasing speed, following the line of flares. The fog swallowed it from sight, and Sloane and the others standing outside the crew room, waited, holding their breaths.

Not that there was any need, for at precisely the right moment, Grant hauled back the column, and the Junkers lifted, climbing up out of the fog into clear air. Grant put pressure on the right rudder and turned out to sea.

After a while he spoke to Carter over the intercom which had been specially set up. "How are things back there?"

"Fine," Carter said.

"Good. Estimated time of arrival in the target area, fifty minutes. The weather isn't too good there. Raining, but visibility should be okay. Thunderstorms forecast so it may get bumpy."

He settled the Junkers at a thousand feet exactly and sat back, barely touching the controls, thoroughly enjoying himself as they skimmed the surface of the fog.

Twenty minutes from target and sixty miles southwest of Cape Granitola in Sicily, Collinson, leaning over the Lichtenstein set, gave a sudden cry.

"I've got something, sir, probably a night fighter."

Grant said over the intercom, "Red alert, Harry, we've got company."

In their cramped quarters in the body of the Junkers, Carter, Luciano and the others couldn't see a thing. Carter said, "Are you sure?"

"Now I am," Grant told him as a Junkers, twin to his own, burst out of the fog to starboard and took up station. Grant raised a hand and could see the pilot of the other plane return the gesture. It stayed with them for a while, then peeled off to starboard and vanished into the night.

"Worked perfectly," Grant said cheerfully over the intercom to Carter. "He just took off. We've got exactly fifteen minutes so better make sure you're ready."

In a meadow at the head of the valley beyond the Contessa di Bellona's villa, Vito Barbera and Rosa waited. It was raining steadily and they sheltered under the trees at the edge of the meadow. Rosa wore a tweed cap and an old belted raincoat.

"Are you all right?" Barbera asked. "This stinking weather is something I hadn't counted on."

"Why don't you worry about something important like those Communist bastards Mori and Russo? They could bring the Germans down on us any time they liked."

"No," he said. "I don't think so. Mori is no fool. He wouldn't put his head on the block so stupidly."

She grabbed his arm. "Listen, they come."

In the distance, there was the rumble of engines. He said, "You know what to do."

She ran across to the far side of the field and Barbera tossed a match to the gasoline-soaked bonfire they had prepared an hour earlier. It roared into life, and on the other side of the meadow flame blossomed also as Rosa performed her part.

Barbera looked up into the night and waited.

The Junkers was down to a thousand feet when Harvey Grant saw the two fires marking the north and south edges of the meadow.

"Did you see that, Joe?" he said to Collinson.

"Got it, sir."

Grant banked to starboard, lifting over a ridge, turned and started his run.

"You've got two minutes, Harry," he called over the intercom.

Carter said, "Fine, Harvey, all we need."

He nodded to the rest of the group and they all stood, crouching awkwardly in the confined space and clipped their static lines which opened the parachute automatically when they jumped to the anchor cable. Carter moved down the line, checking each of them personally, first Maria, then Savage followed by Luciano, Detweiler bringing up the rear.

He went back to the head of the line,

179

clipped his own static line in place, then slid back the exit door. Rain and cold air rushed in, and a moment later the green light flashed above his head.

Carter, already aware of the fire blossoming in the night below, jumped without hesitation. Maria froze for the briefest of moments only and Savage shoved her out bodily and went after her.

What happened next was not by any design. It was a kind of reflex gesture, a reflection of the hate Detweiler had come to bear Luciano. He pulled the razor-sharp gravity knife from its scabbard on his right knee. Luciano, poised in the entrance clutching his supply bag, was aware of the knife slicing through the static line above his head before the sergeant shoved him out into space.

Collinson, looking back through the open door of the cockpit, saw nothing of this action; in the half-light, he knew only that Detweiler was still with them, for the sergeant had paused in the doorway, frozen, his mind numb, stunned by the enormity of what he had done.

Grant, already way beyond the target, was pulling back the column to take the Junkers over the ridge ahead and Collinson clapped him on the shoulder.

"We've still got company."

And then, as the line of the ridge lifted to meet them, Grant boosted power and banked to port and Detweiler lost his balance and pitched headfirst into darkness.

At four hundred feet, it takes twenty seconds to hit the ground. Luciano falling, already past the half-way mark, remembered Carter's words in the Dakota at Ringway. He turned over once, twice, then released the supply bag he had been clutching and his fingers tore at the cover of the emergency chute, strapped across his belly, found the handle of the ripcord and pulled.

There was a sudden jerk, the crack of the chute catching air no more than a hundred feet to go and then he was swinging beneath that dark khaki umbrella, the supply bag below on the end of a line clipped to his waist.

And he was right on target, dropping fast towards the fire at the north end of the meadow, aware of Carter and Maria already down. He glanced up, but there was no sign of Detweiler's parachute. He drifted in over Savage as the Captain hit the grass and then the fire seemed to be rushing towards him

181

and he was aware of someone standing there looking up at him, a boy in an old raincoat and cloth cap.

The supply bag hit the ground with a solid thump, warning him to get ready. He followed it a split second later, rolling into wet grass, the breath going out of him. Then the boy in the raincoat and tweed cap was moving in to help, clutching the billowing waves of silk, and Luciano saw that it was a young girl.

He stood up, unlocking the quick release on his harness and she paused, examining him in the firelight.

"You are Luciano?"

"That's right. And you?"

"Rosa Barbera—Vito's niece."

She started to bundle up the parachute and Harry Carter arrived on the run, Savage not far behind.

"Where's Detweiler? Vito says you were the last to jump, then the plane passed over into the next valley."

Luciano divested himself of the main chute, the one that hadn't opened, and held up the static line, the clean knife-cut evident to all. "I knew the bastard didn't like me. I just didn't realize how much."

Detweiler, drifting down into the next valley, landed in a pine-wood, his parachute snagging in branches, leaving him suspended ten feet above the ground. He snapped the release buckle, fell to the turf, and lay there for a moment.

What in the hell was he going to do now? He hadn't intended it, not any of it. It had been a moment of pure madness which had left him on the wrong side of the mountain and miles off target, alone and totally vulnerable.

One thing was certain. He had to get moving fast and try to reach Bellona on his own. He unzipped the flying suit in which he had jumped. Underneath he wore a patched tweed suit and shirt without collar. There was a cap in one pocket. He pulled it on, crouched down and opened the supply bag. He took out a Colt .45 automatic pistol and a carbine, slipped the Colt in one pocket and slung the carbine over his shoulder.

He threw the supply bag into the bushes and pulled on the parachute to bring it down. It refused to budge so he abandoned it and started to work his way cautiously down through the wood. It had stopped raining for the moment and a pale moon showed through a gap in the clouds. In its light, he saw a dirt road on the far side of a low stone wall and scrambled over. He could smell woodsmoke, saw a farmhouse down below, a light in the window.

He paused, slipping a hand inside his jacket to make sure the wallet was there containing the false papers Carter had given him at Maison Blanche. Reassured, he carried on down the track and turned in at the farmyard, leaving the M1 still slung from his shoulder, but with a hand in his pocket on the butt of the Colt.

A dog barked excitedly inside the house as he walked through the mud of the farmyard to the door. He knocked. There was a certain amount of movement inside and then the top half of the door opened.

Smoke drifted out into the cold air and in the dim light of an oil lamp, Detweiler was aware of a man standing there, holding a shotgun. He was perhaps sixty, with hollow cheeks and unshaven face and wore incredibly patched clothes. A small, ragged boy of about twelve stood beside him. Beyond them by the open fire, an old woman, face as wizened as an Egyptian mummy's, lay back in a wooden rocking chair, swaddled in blankets.

"What do you want?" the man asked hoarsely.

"I'm a shepherd," Detweiler said. "I was walking over the top of the next valley and lost my way, then it got dark. Can you put me up for the night?"

The man nodded, "Sure, why not. You can sleep in the barn. Giorgio here can put you on your way in the morning." He patted the boy on the head, who drew a sleeve across his nose, but said nothing.

The man eyed Detweiler speculatively. "Tell me the truth now. Aren't you with the boys in the mountains?"

Detweiler was uncertain what to say, but decided to take a chance. "Perhaps."

"I knew it." The old man smiled suddenly, revealing blackened teeth. "You've come to the right place, son, believe me. We're all patriots here," and he opened the lower half of the door and drew Detweiler in.

The atmosphere inside the Junkers was of tremendous excitement as they roared through the night to the Sicilian coast line. Collinson said over the intercom, "Cape Granitola coming up fast. We did it, sir. We did it! A perfect drop."

"Except for that stupid sod cocking things up at the end," Grant replied. "God knows where he's ended up. We were miles off target by the time he jumped. What in the hell was he playing at?"

And then Collinson, staring into the Lichtenstein set said, "We've got company. Big trouble."

A Junkers emerged from the cloud to starboard. A second later another took up station to port.

Collinson said, "Better check your tail. There's another bastard there. Now what?"

"I suspect the clever thing to do would be to switch to their air-to-air frequency," Grant said and did just that.

There was a little static and a voice said in fair English, "Big black bird, we've been lonely without you. Last seen over Algeria a month ago. You've taken your time coming home. Now let's all go down nice and friendly, land at Otranto base and sort things out."

"Go fuck yourself!" Grant said and dropped his flaps as on that memorable occasion in the Dakota on his way back from Malta.

The pilot of the Junkers on his tail shoved his column forward desperately and went into a steep dive, passing underneath, and Grant went after him, switching to his G2 system to boost power, holding his fire like all great pilots until he was close. His thumb pressed on the button, cannon shell and tracer ripped into the other plane, tearing great chunks out of the fuselage. There was a sudden tongue of flame in the night that mushroomed into a fireball as the Junkers disintegrated.

In the same moment, Grant's own aircraft staggered under the impact of cannon shell as one of the other planes came in on his tail. He went into a corkscrew instantly, the reflex of several years of combat flying coming to his aid, and a moment later was engulfed in cloud.

"Everything okay?" he called.

"We're in a mess back here," Collinson told him. "Hole in the fuselage you could drive a Morris Ten through."

They lurched again under the impact of more cannon shell and Grant said, "I'm going to go right down to sea level. Hang on, Joe, and we'll see if these bastards know how to fly."

He emerged from broken cloud at a thousand feet and kept on going, levelling out at the last possible moment. It was probably the most hazardous piece of flying he had ever attempted, for the only light was the moon occasionally shining through a gap in the cloud and the wind was such that the sea was already lifting into forty foot swells.

The two Junkers hung on grimly, even at that suicidal level, firing whenever they could get on his tail. Again and again, Grant's aircraft shuddered under the impact of cannon shell.

Half an hour at four hundred miles an hour. Engines overheating and the nitrous oxide tanks which fueled his booster system almost empty. They couldn't take much more of this, he knew that, and then as the aircraft bucked again, this time under a burst of machine gun fire, his windscreen shattered and he received a violent blow in the left arm, another in the right leg.

His fingers came up covered in blood and the port engine started to smoke. He feathered it at once and switched to the extinguishers. The Junkers started to slow, the needle falling rapidly.

And then that voice spoke again over the radio, "Good luck whoever you are. You've earned it."

Collinson cried, "They're going, Skip.

They've turned back. Why?"

"We're a hundred and fifty miles from the coast, the limit of their radius for a sea chase. See if you can find a field dressing in the box. I think I've got a bullet in the leg."

Collinson found the first-aid box and scrambled across. "You all right, sir?"

Grant said. "How could I be anything else. A bullet in the arm, another in the leg, the port engine burned out? Who could ask for anything more." He grinned through the pain. "Now cross your fingers, say a prayer, and let's see if I can still fly this thing."

TEN

Vito opened the door of the boiler in the basement at the Contessa di Bellona's villa. He had lit the fire earlier and it glowed red hot. He turned to Luciano and Carter.

"Okay, everything inside."

They tossed in the jump suits, the bundled parachutes, the equipment bags and Barbera closed the door. "Harry, it's good to see you."

"And you, Vito. When do we see Luca?"

"I don't know, Harry, don't even know where he is. Padre Giovanni is my only contact with him."

"Who's he?" Luciano demanded.

"Prior of the Franciscans at Crown of Thorns."

"The Mafia connection?"

"Oh, sure," Barbera said. "We got God on our side, too."

"Actually, that's more accurate than you know, Vito," Carter told him. "Do you know where we found Luca's granddaughter?"

"Not until you tell me."

"A convent in Liverpool in England. Little Sisters of Pity."

Barbera's mouth gaped in surprise. "You're kidding?"

Luciano said, "The old man should be pleased. Isn't it everyone's ambition to have a priest in the family? Maria's just the female equivalent."

They went upstairs and Barbera led the way through the back passageway to the enormous kitchen at the rear of the house. There was a fire on the wide hearth, which Savage was replenishing with logs.

Maria stood at the table slicing bread and salami. She wore a headscarf, a woollen jacket and a black cotton dress and looked perfectly at home in her surroundings. Rosa had taken off her raincoat and cap and crouched at the fire, stirring soup in a pot.

Savage got to his feet as the other three men entered. Like them, he wore a cloth cap; patched, shabby clothes; and leather leggings, the typical attire of the mountain shepherd or hunter.

Luciano shook his head. "It's no good, kid. Even in that outfit you still look like a whisky ad."

Savage found it difficult to raise a smile, for the knowledge of what Detweiler had done weighed heavily on him.

He said to Carter, "Look Colonel, about Detweiler. . . ."

"Nothing to be said," Carter told them. "Not until we hear the full facts."

"When I get back to my place in Bellona, I'll radio Maison Blanche," Barbera said. "They'll know if he returned with the plane." He put an arm around Luciano's shoulder. "And now, Don Salvatore. A drink to celebrate your safe delivery."

Double doors stood open to the terrace overlooking the rear garden. Savage moved out and Carter went after him.

"It wasn't your fault."

Savage shook his head. "Not good enough, sir. Poor judgment on my part. I thought I knew him."

Carter gave him a cigarette and Savage turned and looked across the kitchen at Rosa crouched by the fire.

"The girl—how old is she?"

"Rosa? Sixteen or seventeen. She's Barbera's niece."

"Rather young to be involved in this sort of game."

"On the contrary, she manages very well, and that's hardly surprising. She was left to fend for herself at the age of thirteen. When Vito found her, she'd been on the streets in Palermo for three years."

Savage, a product of the most conventional of upbringings, was shocked. "You mean she was a prostitute?"

"So it would appear."

Savage went and sat by the fire, watching her. She was aware of his presence, but scratched her backside, totally unconcerned. When she reached up for a ladle he saw that her dress was split under the arm so that a tuft of dark hair poked through.

"You hungry?" she said without looking at him.

"I could eat a horse."

"Heh, I like the way you speak." She turned. "Rome Italian, like a real gentleman."

"I lived in Rome for a few years before the war."

"But you're American? Truly American?" She spooned soup into a bowl and handed it to him.

"I think you could say that."

"From New York?"

"Boston."

She wrinkled her nose in disappointment. "That's a pity. New York's the place. Statue of Liberty, the Empire State building. Uncle Vito's told me all about it. I'm going to live there one day."

"Truly?"

"Maybe after the war."

The soup was excellent, but very hot and he burned his mouth a little.

"Good?" she said.

"Very good."

"Have some more."

She emptied the ladle again into his plate, then went to the table to serve the others. She walked with a kind of total movement of the body that he found disturbing. The black cotton dress was a size too small and molded her buttocks as she leaned across the table. He was aware of Luciano watching him sardonically and hurriedly returned to his soup. The other three men sat down and Maria brought coffee from the stove.

Barbera said, "Let's get down to business. You'll be safe here for a day or two until I get word from Padre Giovanni at Crown of Thorns. As I said before, any news from Don Antonio will come through him."

"Time is of the essence, Vito," Carter said. "How long will we have to wait?"

"I don't know, Harry, it all depends on Luca. I'll keep in close touch, I promise, and I'll leave Rosa to look after you."

"A couple of days," Carter said. "That's all we've got."

Maria bowed her head and murmured a grace before eating. When she looked up, Barbera said awkwardly, "Sister, Harry has been telling me about your situation. I'm sorry, I didn't know."

"It doesn't signify, Mr. Barbera."

Rosa said, "Is what he said true? Are you a nun?"

"Yes, Rosa," Maria told her. "A nurse in a hospital."

"Oh, that kind of nun. Like the General Infirmary in Palermo. I was in there once. The nurses were all nuns."

"You were in the hospital?"

"Sure, when I lost my baby," she said and continued round the table, serving the soup.

At Maison Blanche, the fog had lifted and it had stopped raining. Air Marshal Sloane was sitting at the desk in the Crew Room, working his way through some of the papers he had brought in his briefcase. Paperwork of the most stupefying kind, the sort one put to the bottom of the pile, hoping it would go away.

The door opened and the duty officer looked in. "He made it, sir. Coming in now."

Sloane went out of the Crew Room on the run, crossed to the control tower, and mounted the stairs. He snapped his fingers and one of the sergeants passed him a pair of Zeiss night glasses. In the pale moonlight, he could see the Junkers about two miles away.

Harvey Grant's voice sounded over the radio, totally washed out. "No time for procedure. I'm bringing one very tired baby straight home to bed."

Sloane lowered the glasses. "Not good. Full emergency."

The Junkers came in over the sea at five hundred feet. The wind whistled through the shattered screen. Collinson's face was blue with cold as he crouched behind Grant, hands on his shoulders as if to support him.

Grant sat there, hands frozen to the control column, a slight fixed smile on his face. According to the gauge, their fuel had run out fifteen minutes earlier.

As the airfield came into view, the runway clearly marked by twin lines of glittering flares, the starboard engine spluttered and started to die, the prop feathering.

"That's it," Grant said. "Hang on and pray, Joe."

He brushed across the line of palms at the north end of the runway, aware of the trail of vehicles moving from the control buildings on his right. The Junkers almost stalled. He gave a final burst of power to straighten her and, miraculously, the engine roared into life briefly.

And then the worst landing of his career, bouncing back up again twice, before they slowed to a halt, sand spraying in a great cloud as the tail spun round and they turned full circle. But they were down.

That engine had very definitely stopped now. Grant was aware of the screech of brakes as the emergency people arrived and of Collinson shaking his shoulder anxiously. There were voices, lots of them, a confused shouting, and then he opened his eyes again and found Sloane leaning over him.

Grant smiled. "Don't scold me, sir, not this time. Just for once, I'm rather proud of myself.''

Luciano moved out on the terrace, followed by Barbera. He could hear water gurgling in the conduits, splashing from numerous fountains. In the old days it was said that whoever held the meager water supplies of the island held Sicily, and the Mafia had done just that.

In the light from the rear windows, he was aware of the lush, semi-tropical vegetation pressing in on the house. Although he couldn't see it, he could smell an orange grove, almond trees. Palms swayed in a slight breeze and rain dripped from the eaves of the verandah.

He took a deep breath. ''I'd forgotten how it could be.''

''The real Sicily?'' Barbera said.

''That depends on your point of view.''

Below the verandah and five yards on the other side of the path, leaves trembled and a gun barrel poked through. Luciano sent Barbera sprawling with a stiff left arm and reached under his jacket for the revolver he carried in his belt against the small of his back. In the same fluid motion, he drew and fired twice. A machine pistol jumped into the air, there was a choking cough and a man fell out of the bushes and rolled on his back.

Luciano crouched. ''There will be another,'' Barbera whispered.

Savage came out through the open door in a hurry holding an M1. A shotgun blasted from the bushes over to the right, too far away to do any damage.

Luciano took a running jump into the greenery, landed badly, rolled over, and came up about six feet away from the other gunman. He was clutching a sawed-off shotgun in both hands.

Luciano fired, catching him in the left arm. The man screamed, dropping the *lupara,* and Savage, firing the M1 on automatic, emptied the magazines into the man, driving him back into the bushes.

Luciano said, ''The idea was to keep him alive so he could tell us what this is all about.''

Savage stared at him, a dazed look in his eyes, and Barbera and Carter hurried past him to Luciano who was looking down at the body of a boy of about seventeen.

Barbera picked up the shotgun. The *lupara,* traditional weapon used in a Mafia ritual killing. He turned to Luciano. ''It was you they were after."

"Me?" Luciano was astounded. "Mafia? It doesn't make sense."

"Not Mafia. See, over here." He crossed to the other gunman who lay on his face. Barbera turned him over with his foot.

Carter said. "I know him. That's Ettore Russo."

"Who is he?" Luciano demanded.

"A Communist," Barbera said, "and no friend to the Mafia. A member of the district committee which coordinates the work of the various factions that go to make up the resistance movement. I met them earlier tonight to discuss your arrival and what we hoped to achieve. He was less than pleased."

"So decided to knock me off?"

"Not really," Barbera said. "I think he was used by someone much cleverer than himself. Look at it this way. If he and his boy kill you, it looks as if it's done by the Mafia. You're out of the way and everyone's confused."

"And with this result?" Carter said.

"Lucky Luciano and his friends have butchered one of the most important Communists in the district, which won't go down well with his friends, so we'd better bury these two as soon as possible.''

Maria moved past them, dropped to her knees beside Russo, and started to pray. Barbera looked down at her, embarrassed. Luciano inclined his head and they all moved back up on the verandah.

''You think you know who's behind this?''

''Sure I do. Don't worry. He'll be taken care of,'' said Barbera.

''So what happens now?'' Luciano asked.

Barbera turned to Carter. ''I think you and I had better go down to Bellona and see what the situation is.''

''While the rest of us stay here?''

''No.'' Barbera shook his head. ''I can't be sure someone else won't try the same thing, not until I've fixed that bastard, Mori. I think maybe Rosa better take you up to the Franciscans. Padre Giovanni will look after you. No one will dare touch you up there.'' He turned to Carter. ''Okay, Harry?''

Carter looked at the others, then nodded. ''It doesn't seem as if we've got much choice.''

''Good,'' Barbera said. ''Then let's dispose of those bodies and get moving.''

Luciano sat at the table reloading the revolver. It was the short-barrelled Smith and Wesson .32 he had used at the firing range at the Abbey.

Carter moved up behind him. "Where did you get that?"

"Did a deal with that armorer." Luciano took the silencer from his pocket. "He was very accommodating." He slipped the Smith and Wesson back in its place in his waistband at the small of his back.

Savage slid his arms through the straps of his rucksack and picked up his carbine. Rosa came in from the bedroom, once more dressed in her old raincoat and cloth cap. Maria wore a waterproof poncho and was tying a scarf around her head.

Barbera said, "Good, we go now. You'll be at the monastery in three hours. No problems. We'll see you up there some time tomorrow."

He turned out the light and they all moved out on the verandah. He and Carter stood there and waited until the others had disappeared into the darkness, Rosa leading the way. When they were out of sight, Barbera turned to Carter.

"Okay, Harry, now for Mori," he said and went down the steps.

ELEVEN

Pietro Mori had sent his wife to bed early and waited for Russo's return, sitting in the old easy chair by the fire with a bottle of brandy. Not that he was particularly worried. Russo, after all, was taking the risks and it couldn't go wrong, whatever happened. That was the essential cleverness of the whole scheme.

He dozed off and was awakened by a tapping at the window. He got up and opened the casement an inch or two.

"Who is it?"

"It's me, Vito," Barbera said. "I must speak with you."

"Just a minute. I'll open the door," Mori said.

He pulled back the bolt and Barbera slipped inside.

"What is it?" Mori demanded.

"I've just come from Russo, you bastard," Barbera told him. "He says he's waiting for you in hell."

His left hand went around Mori's neck, pulling him close and he kissed him full on the lips, the Mafia kiss of death. At the same time he drove the needle point of the stiletto he held in his other hand up under the ribs, probing for the heart.

Pietro Mori groaned once and died and Barbera eased him back into the chair and left him there by the fire, head back, eyes staring into eternity.

At that same moment, the others were moving down a sloping meadow in the side of the valley toward trees below, Rosa leading the way. Luciano, like Savage, carried a rucksack on his back and an M1 slung over one shoulder.

It was raining again. As they reached the trees he said to Maria, "You okay?"

"Fine."

Rosa motioned them to halt and they crouched down. Luciano could just make out a low wall and a road on the other side, more trees beyond.

"We cross over here," the girl said, "then climb the mountain on the far side.

The monastery is on the ridge at the other end of the valley from here, beyond Bellona.''

''Okay,'' Luciano said. ''Let's get moving.''

Rosa scrambled over the wall, followed by Savage who turned to assist Maria. They started across the road when suddenly a spotlight was turned on and vehicle head-lamps.

A voice called harshly in bad Italian, ''Stay where you are.''

Rosa was already running, scrambling over the other wall, dropping out of sight followed by Savage. Luciano pulled his Smith and Wesson, fired twice in the direction of the lights, shattering one of them, then followed Maria who was running for the wall.

As he went over after her, a burst of machine gun fire chipped the stonework. He grabbed her hand and they ran together, through the darkness, toward the trees.

Even when they were into their shelter, a machine gun chattered again, slicing branches above their heads. They could hear voices calling as their pursuers came over the wall and started to follow, firing their weapons blindly.

Luciano ducked as a bullet plucked at his cap and pulled Maria down. He could hear Rosa and Savage still moving on ahead somewhere; then the voices of the soldiers seemed very close and he dragged Maria to her feet.

"This way!" he said and ran to one side, moving fast through a plantation of young pine trees, an arm raised to protect his face.

After a while, the sounds of the pursuers faded and he paused.

Maria said, "What about Rosa and Captain Savage?"

"They'll have to make out the best way they can."

"And what about us?"

"We climb. She said the monastery was on the ridge at the far end of the valley, didn't she?"

He took her hand. As they waded across a small stream and up the other side, it started to rain heavily.

Detweiler had dined well on boiled mutton and goats' cheese, washed down with a bottle of red wine and the wine particularly helped him to see things in a much more hopeful light. Now, he was desperately tired. The old man gave him a couple of blankets and took him out to the barn. Detweiler lay down, rifle close at hand, and was almost instantly asleep.

Five minutes later, as he lay snoring gently, the barn door creaked open and the old man appeared with the boy. He held up a lantern, peering down at Detweiler, then withdrew, closing the door behind him.

He gave the boy a push. "Go now. You know what to do."

The boy turned and walked across the farmyard and out of the gate. When he reached the track, he started to run. The old man watched him go for a while, then turned and went back to the house.

In the second cubbyhole on the other side of the coffin room above the mortuary, Vito Barbera sat at the radio. Carter walked up and down impatiently, smoking a cigarette.

Finally Barbera took off the headphones and turned. "He got back in one piece."

"And Detweiler?"

"You aren't going to like this. Apparently he did jump, but far too late. Probably came down in the next valley."

Carter exploded. "That's all we need.

Detweiler wandering around the countryside totally at sea. The man must have blown his top. I mean, what if he's picked up?''

"It'll be all right, Harry, you'll see," Barbera said. "I'll put the word out. We'll pull him in soon enough." He grinned and put a hand on Carter's shoulder. "I've told you before, all you have to do is live right."

The previous year, operating as an OSS courier in occupied France, Jack Savage had called at a cafe in Tours, a staging post on the route to Spain. He had promptly been arrested and hauled off to SD headquarters where he had been interrogated with considerable brutality for three days before being put on a train for Paris under guard, his final destination, Gestapo Headquarters on the rue des Saussaies. He had killed a guard stupid enough to turn his back on him and managed to jump from the train just outside Orleans, the start of five active days that had ended with him crossing the Pyrenees into Spain on foot.

It was a strange sensation to be hunted again, nothing quite like it, and he was conscious of the familiar nervous excitement, sharpening all the senses, as he paused on the rim of a small plateau and looked back.

There was nothing to be seen, but he could hear the soldiers calling to each other, faint and far away now.

Rosa said, "They can't catch us, not in these hills."

"What about Maria?" he asked. "And Luciano?"

"There's nothing we can do," she said flatly. "They must take their chances. Now we must go."

The rain had slackened again, but a strong wind began to lift through the pine trees and the clouds above them were storm-tossed, the moon showing through occasionally.

Instead of working her way across the steep hillside, she went straight up. The slope lifted until it was almost perpendicular, with rough tussocks of grass sticking out of the bare rock. They came to the foot of an apron of loose stones and shale and she started to climb and Savage went after her.

Once he heaved strongly on a boulder and it tore itself free and bounced and crashed its way down the mountainside. The sound of it echoed away into the night.

She looked down at him. "All right?"

"Sure. Just keep going."

A moment later, the ground sloped away and he found himself standing on the edge of a broad plateau. He turned to peer down into the darkness of the valley, but could see nothing, was aware only of space and the increasingly strong wind cold on his face.

Rosa moved beside him. He said, "Now what?"

She pointed across the plateau and in the dim light he saw that a great rock wall faced them. He said softly, "Are you sure it can be done?"

"Oh, yes. You will see."

She led the way across the plateau, picking her way between boulders. When they reached the base of the rock, Savage saw that it wasn't perpendicular at all, but lifted back in great slabs, most of which were split and fissured.

She said, "Boys herd goats up here."

Savage ran a hand over his mouth, his throat dry, fear churning his guts. His one secret was a fear of heights. He was a brave man who had placed himself in maximum danger on several occasions, had killed men in hand-to-hand combat, and yet he had never jumped from a plane with his eyes open, had gone through a private hell abseiling down the rock faces on the Commando course at Ashnacarry in Scotland.

Rosa started to climb. He swallowed hard and forced himself to follow her. The wind cut through his old tweed jacket. Lightning flickered on the mountain tops and it started to rain again.

At least when he looked down he could see nothing. He paused, breathed deeply to steady himself, eyes closed. When he opened them, the girl was crouched beside him.

"Are you all right?"

He nodded. "Fine."

But she knew, he could sense it, reaching out to touch his face briefly with the fingers of one hand. She turned, starting to climb again, and Savage took another deep, shuddering breath and went after her.

Suslov, the Ukrainian *Einsatzgruppen* lieutenant, crossed the farmyard cautiously followed by a corporal and two men carrying machine pistols. The old man and Giorgio, the boy who had brought the message, waited at the barn door.

The old man opened the door. From inside came the sound of Detweiler's heavy breathing. Suslov nodded to the corporal who moved in with the two SS.

There was a sudden muffled cry, the sound of blows, and they reappeared dragging Detweiler between them. They dropped him in the mud and he lay there groaning.

Suslov knelt down and searched him, finding the Colt automatic and the false identity papers Carter had given Detweiler at Maison Blanche. He examined them briefly, then took a silver whistle from his pocket and blew a single long blast. There was the sound of engines starting up and a few moments later, five *Kubelwagens* drove into the farmyard. The first two had drivers only, but the other three had heavy machine guns and carried three-man crews.

The corporal came out of the barn with Detweiler's rucksack and the rifle. Suslov examined it with interest, then stirred Detweiler with his toe.

"American M1, brand-new." He held up the Colt. "American handgun. You must have some interesting friends. Major Meyer's going to enjoy meeting you." He nodded to the corporal. "Get him in the car."

"*Zu Befehl, Untersturmbannführer,*" the corporal replied, for it was a strict regulation of Meyer's that all members of his *Einsatzgruppe* spoke German, however badly.

They handcuffed Detweiler's wrists behind his back and bundled him into the rear of one of the front *Kubelwagens*. The corporal and two guards got in with him. Suslov moved over to the three rear vehicles and addressed the crews.

"From the looks of things, we've got ourselves a nice one here. A partisan armed with brand-new American weapons. That means they've had a supply drop in this district recently. Patrol the villages on the heights. Anyone the slightest bit suspicious, haul them in."

He stood back and they drove away in echelon. As he returned to the front car, the old man pulled off his cap and patted the boy on the head.

"We did well, Lieutenant, Giorgio and me, eh?"

Suslov lit a cigarette and looked him over contemptuously. "You really are a disgusting old bastard, aren't you, but then I suppose every dog must have its bone."

He took a roll of banknotes from his pocket and threw them in the mud at the old man's feet, then got into the *Kubelwagen* and nodded to the driver who drove away at once.

The old man picked up the money and stood there, an arm around Giorgio's shoulders, listening until their sound had faded into the distance. Then he patted the boy on the head and they turned and went inside.

Savage was soaked to the skin and bitterly cold as he hauled himself up over the last slab. Rosa reached out and took his hand.

"Over here," she said. "Not far."

He followed her, head down in the howling gale which at that height threatened to blow them off their feet. They scrambled over rough grass and he was aware of another rock face looming out of the night. Then the wind seemed to drop away.

"Head down," the girl said. He put out a hand in pitch darkness and felt rough stone.

A match flared and he saw Rosa standing a few feet away. She held the match above her head and looked around her, searching. They were in a low roofed cave with every evidence of habitation. There was wood laid ready to burn on a crude stone hearth, a wooden table, sheepskins, blankets, and an assortment of cooking pots. The match went out and she struck another and lit an old oil lamp that stood on the table.

"What is this place?" Savage asked.

"The shepherds use it during the lambing season. They stay up here for weeks."

He put down his M1 and took off his rucksack. He was shaking with cold and folded his arms as if to hold himself together. She turned and put a hand to his cheek and there was the concern on her face that a mother might show for a child.

"Too cold, Savage. This is not your country, not your way." She picked up one of the blankets and unfolded it. "Undress and dry yourself with this. I'll light a fire."

She crouched at the hearth, striking another match, and the dry twigs flared. She took off her raincoat and knelt there, putting logs on the fire. The rain had soaked through to the cotton dress so that it molded her like a second skin.

Savage struggled to get his wet jacket off. "What about you?"

"I'm used to it." She filled a pan with water from a rivulet that trickled down one of the stone walls and set it on the fire.

"I thought you came from Palermo?"

She paused, turning from the fire. "Who told you that?"

"Colonel Carter. He said. . . ." Savage hesitated. "He said your Uncle Vito brought you last year from Palermo to live with him."

There was a calculating look in her eyes as if she were trying to assess how much he knew about her. Savage was confused and embarrassed. She was instantly aware of it, smiled slightly and turned back to feed more logs on the fire.

"I've lived in Bellona with Uncle Vito for nine months now."

He peeled off his shirt with difficulty. "You like it better?"

"Than Palermo? Oh, sure. I help Vito with the funeral business. And when he needs a runner, I handle that too."

"A runner?"

She picked up the blanket and started to dry his back and shoulders vigorously. "Runners carry messages between the various Resistance groups. They usually use boys, but Vito prefers me."

"Why?"

"I'm smarter, for one thing. Anyway, it's my choice. I like the mountains. I like the air up here and I like being alone." She started to unbuckle his belt. "Better get your pants off."

Her breasts were strong and firm, thrusting against the damp linen of her dress, perfectly outlined, and he could see her nipples. He panicked slightly, acutely embarrassed like some gangling boy.

His hands went to the belt, pushing her away. "That's okay, I'll do it."

She smiled, went across to a rock shelf and rummaged among various utensils and other items there. She held up a can. "Coffee. Old, but it will do."

She crouched down at the fire again, spooning coffee into the pan of simmering water. Savage, divested of his boots, managed the wet trousers with difficulty and quickly wrapped the blanket around him.

Rosa piled a sheepskin beside the fire. "You come over here and get warm," she ordered.

He hesitated, then did as he was told. She covered him with a blanket, piled another couple of sheepskins on top. They were old, certainly dirty and very possibly flea-ridden, but Savage suddenly realized that he didn't give a damn. They were soft and warm and smelled of wood smoke.

She took a cigarette from an old tobacco tin, lit it with a splinter from the fire and passed it to him without a word. He held it with shaking fingers, grateful for the comfort from the cheap, strong tobacco as he inhaled deeply.

For some reason, he remembered the dinner party his mother had given for him during his last leave in Boston. Dinner jackets, handsome men in uniform, pretty women, the Savage silver gleaming in the candlelight, discreet servants. And there was Joanna, of course, Joanna Van der Boegart who had been somewhere around since his earliest memories. Joanna whom he would marry one day, much to everyone's satisfaction.

He remembered her that last time in his arms on the terrace, up from Vassar for the weekend specially for the party. Cool, elegant, her lips firm and full, but never opening for him, not even on an occasion with the possibility of such finality to it.

Not like this—not anything like this. He watched Rosa, leaning over the fire pouring coffee carefully into an old tin cup. The damp cotton dress was so tight that he could see the shape of her pants underneath.

There was an immediate sexual stirring of a kind he had not known for some considerable time and he moved uncomfortably. Whatever a soldier monk might be, Jack Savage was a strong contender for the title. He had been celibate for over a year now. The kind of life he had led, the lengthy periods of training interspersed with brief forays into Europe, left little time for any kind of relationship with a woman. He had long since decided to cut that side of things out of his life altogether, at least for the duration.

In any case, he had never thought of himself as being any great shakes with women. The kind of upper-class girl he had been raised with, girls like Joanna, used their virginity as a bargaining factor. Episodes with the other type of girl at college had been unsatisfactory to say the least.

Even Montmartre had failed to work its magic on him during his painting days. There were plenty of girls interested in the handsome American painter with money, but whatever it took to keep them happy, he didn't have. He had long since come to that regrettable conclusion.

Rosa passed him coffee in the old tin mug, hot and black, and Savage swallowed it greedily, burning his mouth, his hand shaking. She stood looking down at him, a hand on her hips, the steam rising from her damp dress. God, but he was cold, shaking so badly that coffee slipped down his chin and she took the cup from him.

"I think you have a fever," she said. "And for that, you must sweat."

She piled more sheepskins on him, then started to unbutton the dress. As she peeled it down, firm breasts gleamed in the firelight. He closed his eyes, aware of her pants sliding down, the dark hair between her thighs, and then she was coming in under the sheepskin beside him.

There was an incredible unreality to it all, like one of those fantasies born in the mind when half asleep.

Her lips nibbled at his ear and then her tongue was probing his mouth. Her hand slid down the blanket across the flat muscular belly and touched him.

She laughed and breathed in his ear. "You take me to New York, eh? You take me to New York, Savage, and I make you a little bit crazy."

And then she moved, rolling on top of him, spreading her thighs, guiding him into her.

Later, lying there, half asleep, still in a fever, his arm around her, he was aware of her whispering.

"Savage, are you awake?"

He made no reply but lay there, thinking about what had happened. He had never known anything like it or like her. The warmth, the primitiveness, the total lack of shame.

Her head went down and he was aware of her tongue tracing a course across his belly. Then she had him in her mouth. He groaned and started to move.

She pulled away and looked up at him. "So, you are awake?"

"Yes," he said, pushing her over on her back. "I'm awake, damn you!"

She laughed and kissed him as he thrust into her, still half in a delirium, mounting to a climax that seemed to be without end. One thing he was aware of: the way her body moved, the sudden gasp, the hands tightening into his flesh, her smothered cries.

Then afterwards, he stayed on top of her and finally drifted into sleep as she gently stroked his face.

TWELVE

Luciano and Maria followed the same rough track for almost two hours. For most of the time its path lay through pine forest and they avoided the worst of the weather. When it emerged from the trees to climb a steep and rocky hillside, the wind drove rain into their faces so that they could only walk head down and she had to hold on to him for support.

They stopped in the shelter of an outcrop of rock and Luciano shouted, "This is no good."

She put a hand to his face. "Just a moment. I think I smell wood smoke."

She was right. He moved out of the shelter into the full force of the wind, aware instantly of the strong, pungent aroma, and they struggled on.

They came over a rise and saw a light in

a hollow among the trees. Dogs started to bark and they came to a fence, and beyond, on the other side of a mud yard, was a cottage. Luciano unslung his M1 and cocked it and they went across the yard. The top half of the door opened, light flooding through, and a man appeared holding a shotgun.

"Who goes?" he called.

"Travelers, caught by the night," Luciano replied. "We need shelter."

"None for you here. We have trouble enough."

He was perhaps thirty, a typical mountain man with a heavy black moustache and long unkempt hair under the cap.

He started to close the door and Luciano said, "I got a woman with me. What kind of man are you, anyway?"

He took a step toward the door and the man raised the shotgun to his shoulder. "I said no. Another step and I blow your head off."

"And answer to the Mafia," Luciano said. "To Luca himself."

The man froze, lowered the shotgun slowly. "What has Don Antonio to do with this?"

Luciano pulled Maria forward. "His

granddaughter. We're on our way to the Franciscans at Crown of Thorns.''

The shotgun came all the way down. The man hesitated; then a woman cried out in agony inside and he turned quickly.

Luciano and Maria paused at the door. The scene inside was incredibly primitive: bare stone walls, mud floor, an open fire on the hearth with the most rudimentary of chimneys so that the room was half filled with smoke. There were two goats tethered beside a couple of young children wrapped in a blanket, who watched what was happening at the other end of the room with great round eyes.

A young woman lay on a crude wooden bed, her face running with sweat and racked with agony. An old crone sat on a stool beside the fire stirring something in an iron pot. She had a face like wrinkled leather and wore a black scarf around her head, black dress, and broken boots.

The young woman moaned again, her knees sprawling apart under the blanket, her belly swollen. Maria unlatched the lower half of the door and went in. Luciano followed her.

She leaned over the girl, placing a hand on her brow, and the young man said,

"She's been in childbirth since yesterday. That's why I sent for the *strega.*"

Stregas were witches more than anything else. There was usually one in most villages, who sold potions and spells that were really only herbal medicine. In the back country, they were the peasant's substitute for doctors.

Maria started to pull back the blanket to examine the girl, and the old woman reacted angrily, turning on the stool.

"Infamita!"

The man got hold of Maria by the wrist and twisted it. "What are you doing? You think I want my wife shamed before strangers?"

Luciano took a handful of hair, dragged back his head, and rammed the muzzle of the M1 up under his chin.

"What's your name?"

The man gasped in pain. "Solazzo."

"Well, listen to me. God has smiled on you tonight because the good sister here is a nurse. A real nurse from a real hospital, so stand back and leave her to it or she'll have two patients."

The old woman at the fire started to protest. Solazzo silenced her with his hand, gazed at Luciano searchingly, then turned to Maria.

"This is true, what he says?"

"Yes," she said.

He took off his cap, wiped his face with the back of one hand. Maria turned back to the girl on the bed who was crying now, moving her head from side to side. Maria pulled down the blanket and raised the stained shift, exposing the swollen belly.

"How long did you say she has been in labor?"

"Since yesterday afternoon."

She leaned over the girl, examining her quickly, and finally turned, her face grave. "Mr. Solazzo, we have a serious problem here. The reason for your wife's long labor is plain. A child is normally delivered head first. This one is the wrong way round."

"God in heaven!" Solazzo said wildly and crossed himself.

"Isn't that what they call a breech?" Luciano asked.

"That's right."

The woman cried out sharply, pushing her body up from the bed and Solazzo said, "Help her, Sister, for the love of God."

She raised a hand to still him. "Exactly," she said. "For His sake and for hers. Now you will bring me hot water and cloths.

Tear up a sheet, a shirt, anything. And as clean as possible.''

Solazzo hurried to the fire. Luciano said, ''You've got to be joking. Clean? In a hovel like this?''

''We will do the best we can, all of us,'' she said. ''Including you, Mr. Luciano. Now listen to me closely and I will tell you what I want you to do.''

Maria leaned over the young woman. ''Elena, isn't that it? I want you to trust me. Do you trust me?''

Elena Solazzo nodded wearily and Maria wiped sweat from her face. ''When I tell you to push, use all your strength. You understand?''

Luciano was at the other end of the bed with a bowl of hot water and torn strips of linen ready. Solazzo and the old woman stood by the fire. One of the children at the other end of the room started to cry and Solazzo whispered to the old woman who went to comfort them.

Maria went to work, probing gently inside Elena for the first problem was to deliver the legs. She had wanted to turn the baby around but it was too late. She felt for the back of the baby's knee and prodded. The leg flexed instantly and so did the other when she repeated the trick.

"And now, Elena, push," she said. "Push hard!"

She held out her hands and Luciano wiped them clean and dried them. She grasped the baby firmly by the legs and pulled down until the shoulders were clear, but the arms were still inside, extended.

As Luciano watched she probed again gently, twisting to the left, hooking a finger into the left elbow and delivering the arm. A moment later, the other arm was also free.

Elena was gasping for breath like an animal, staring up at the ceiling, face contorted with pain.

"How's it going?" Luciano asked softly.

"Fine so far, but this is the most dangerous part, delivery of the head. If it's not done just right. . . ."

She paused and he completed the sentence for her. "She could have an imbecile on her hands."

Maria took a deep breath, trying to remember every aspect of her training. The essential thing was to bring the head out slowly and steadily. She put her right arm underneath the infant and got a finger into its mouth, which meant she was now supporting it.

Her other hand was on the neck, fingers spread and she started to pull. It was amazing how much strength it took; then suddenly it was clear and safe in her hands.

The baby was not breathing, was a deep shade of purple all over. She cleansed the nostrils and the mouth of mucus with strips of linen and placed a hand over the chest.

"Is it okay?" Luciano demanded.

"Oh, yes, a strong heartbeat."

She blew into the tiny mouth, very, very gently. Quite suddenly the chest heaved and the baby started to cry. Solazzo cried out as if responding to it.

Maria tied the cord, then cut that last essential link between mother and child. "A daughter, Mr. Solazzo, in case you hadn't noticed."

Elena was crying now, tears mingling with the sweat, and as Maria wrapped the child in strips of linen, Solazzo leaned over.

"What a little beauty. We name her after you, Sister." He laughed out loud, tension pouring out of him.

Even the old woman was smiling and she came forward, the two children shuffling beside her, wrapped in their blanket, and the goats bleating in the shadows.

Maria washed blood from her hands in the basin. Luciano said, "You did all right."

"Why thank you, Mr. Luciano." She smiled back at him. "Could I have more hot water?"

She turned and started to clean Elena's belly and thighs. Luciano went to the door and emptied the bowl into the yard. He lit a cigarette and leaned on the door, staring out into the rain. He hadn't felt so alive in years.

Solazzo appeared beside him with a bottle. "A drink, Signor?"

Luciano took a pull. It was cheap Sicilian brandy and it burned all the way down. He choked and handed the bottle back.

Solazzo took a swig himself. "What you said earlier about the good sister is true, Signor? She is Don Antonio's grand-daughter?"

"You are of the Society?" Luciano asked.

"Since I was seventeen years. And you also Signor." He shrugged. "I do not need to ask. May I have the pleasure of your name?"

"Luciano."

Solazzo's mouth gaped in astonishment. "You—you are Luciano, Signor?"

"That's right."

Solazzo grabbed for his right hand and kissed it. "Don Salvatore—the Savior. God sent you to us out of the storm tonight."

"Very possibly," Luciano said and glanced up. Maria was smiling sadly at him from across the room.

Fifteen miles north in a small lost valley high in the Cammarata, Don Antonio Luca, the most powerful man in Sicily, ate his evening meal alone, the windows to the terrace of the old rambling farmhouse open to the night. The long living room, though primitive in some respects with whitewashed walls and a stone floor, was comfortable enough with a log fire burning in the open hearth in one corner.

He sat at one end of a long dark oak table and ate sparingly of the dishes which were laid before him. *Narbe di San Paolo,* ravioli filled with sugar and ricotta cheese and fried, and *cannoli,* that most famous of all Sicilian sweets. He reached for the wine bottle and, finding it empty, rang a hand bell.

The woman who entered was no more than thirty, a shapely, fleshy peasant with wide hips that stretched the conventional black cotton dress to its extremity. Her hair was night-black and fastened into a tight bun at the nape of her neck. Her skin was olive, the lines just beginning to show, and she had kind eyes.

"Another bottle, Katerina," he said.

She went out without a word. He lit a cigar, then got up to stir the fire. He was sixty-five, the hair and carefully trimmed beard iron grey, a tall man still, the shoulders only slightly stooped with age.

The face was the most remarkable feature. Ruthlessness, pride, arrogance, but also a blazing intelligence. He wore the rough clothes of a mountain farmer, corduroy trousers, waistcoat, red flannel shirt, and yet there was a curious impression of elegance to him still, a suggestion of the aristocrat in gamekeeper's clothing that was strange in a man who had started life as a sharecropper's son.

Katerina came back with a fresh bottle of wine. "Mario's here."

"Good. Send him in and bring coffee."

He stirred the logs with a foot and turned as the door opened again.

The man who entered was in his mid-fifties and had the face of a confident gladiator who had survived the arena. A small, greying man with an engaging presence, he could still smile as he killed, and he had killed many times on the orders of his *capo*. Mario Sciara was Antonio Luca's strong right arm.

Luca said, "Well?"

The door opened again and Katerina came in with the coffee.

Sciara said, "They are here, Don Antonio."

"Luciano?"

"Yes."

"And my granddaughter? Where are they now?"

"I don't know exactly. They were at the villa of the Contessa di Bellona but there was trouble."

"What kind of trouble?"

Katerina paused in the act of pouring coffee, waiting. Sciara said, "You know how much the Communists have worried about increasing Mafia involvement in the Resistance movement. When they heard Luciano was coming, they didn't like it. They tried to give him the business."

"Who was it?"

"That sheepfarmer from Bellona, Russo, and some boy or other. Luciano took care of it, as I understand it. They're both dead."

"So, his hand hasn't lost its cunning. And my granddaughter? She was there?"

"Yes, *Capo.*"

Luca's eyes flared and when he picked the bottle of Marsala up from the table, his hand shook. *"Infamita.* To do such a thing. Luciano can take his chances, but to place my granddaughter's life in jeopardy." He emptied the glass in one quick swallow. "There were others involved?"

"Mori, the schoolmaster."

"That bastard. Another Red. He pays, Mario, in full."

"Already taken care of, *Capo.* Vito Barbera has seen to it on your behalf."

"Good." Luca nodded. "One can always rely on Vito. Now, to the other business. Is the Englishman, Carter, with them?"

"Yes, *Capo.*"

"Excellent—I like Carter." He turned to Katerina. "When he comes we can play bridge again with a dummy hand, but better than nothing."

"You will see them?"

"Of course. They can come here. Make

the necessary arrangements with Padre Giovanni. Now, have your coffee and tell me how the war goes."

Later, standing in the darkness of his bedroom with the window open to the terrace, Luca watched lightning flicker over the mountain. Katerina moved in from the other room and stood beside him. She wore a robe of heavy silk, and when his arm went around her his hand cupped her left breast, his fingers stroking the nipple erect.

"You are unhappy, Antonio?"

"Can you always be so certain?"

"Of course. It is Maria, I think. You do not wish her to come? Why not? She is of your own flesh. Your own surviving blood kin. It is not natural."

He shook his head. "How can I explain to you? As a child, I adored her and she loved me totally. She never knew her father, God rest him. I was the only man in her life. Then that day, that terrible day when she and her mother got in the car. . . ." His voice faded. She rested a hand on his shoulder.

"She turned from me, with words of hatred on her lips." He shook his head. "No, my love, when she comes now, it is as if we turn over an old stone and expose the corruption that lies underneath."

"No, Antonio. She comes with love I am sure."

He laughed harshly. "Is Antonio Luca a fool? Is this how he has survived all these years? She comes because I have refused to help the Americans in this coming invasion. She comes because they hope she will be able to change my mind. If it were not for that, she would not have come at all."

There was a terrible desolation in his voice and she turned into him, holding him tight. "Come to bed, Antonio."

"Soon, *cara,* very soon." He kissed her hair and pushed her gently away.

When he moved out on the terrace he could smell the mimosa, heavy and clinging on the damp air. The whole electric world waited for a sign. It came. The heavens opened and it started to rain.

THIRTEEN

Koenig was standing at the window of his office at the police barracks in Agrigento shortly after dawn, when Suslov and his Ukrainians drove into the courtyard below. As Koenig watched, the door opened behind him and Rudi Brandt came in with a cup of coffee.

Koenig nodded down into the courtyard as Detweiler was dragged from the *Kubelwagen*. He fell to his knees and one of the Ukrainians kicked him. Then two of them ran across the yard towards the entrance of the old police captain's house which Meyer was using as his headquarters.

"More work for the undertaker," Koenig said.

"So it would appear, Colonel."

"Find out who he is and report back to me."

Brandt went out at once and Koenig opened the window. The storm of the previous night seemed to have blown itself out, but rain drifted against the window in a fine spray. He felt old beyond his years, unaccountably depressed, as he sipped his coffee and watched Rudi Brandt cross the courtyard below.

Detweiler, his wits sharpened considerably by fear, stood in front of Meyer's desk and waited. The Major ignored him, watching while Suslov took various items from the rucksack: ammunition clips, several grenades, chocolate K-rations. He laid them down beside the M1 and the Colt automatic.

"So?" Meyer said.

"The weapons would appear to be brand-new, Major."

Meyer picked up Detweiler's false papers. "Who have we here?" He spoke without looking up. "Mario Brazzi, born Palermo, 1917. It says here you are a shepherd by profession?"

"Yes, sir," Detweiler said, keeping his head down.

"Employed by whom?"

Detweiler stayed with the story Carter

238

had outlined for him at Maison Blanche. "Times are hard. I move from place to place. A few days here, a few days there."

"Discharged from the Fifteenth Infantry Brigade in February as a result of a chest wound received in North Africa."

"That's right, sir."

Meyer nodded and Suslov put down the M1, reached across and tore open his shirt. The great raised scar of a gunshot wound was clearly visible on the left side of Detweiler's chest, souvenir of the ill-fated Dieppe landings.

Meyer sat back. "We would appear to have a paradox. Mario Brazzi, wounded veteran and honest shepherd, found wandering the hills with brand-new American weapons, American chocolate, and K-rations." He turned to Suslov. "What would that suggest to you, *Obersturmführer?*"

"A supply drop to partisans in the area, probably very recent, Major, judging by the M1 and the other items."

Detweiler pulled out all the stops to stay in character. "I'm an honest man, I swear it. I stayed the night in a shepherd's hut on the other side of Viterba, high in the mountains. I found all this stuff hidden under the straw.''

Meyer grimaced and Suslov picked up the M1 and drove the butt into the pit of Detweiler's stomach with all his strength. Detweiler lay on his face, retching.

Meyer said. ''Let's try again.''

They hauled him to his feet, and at that moment the door opened and Koenig entered. He wore a camouflaged jump jacket over his uniform, his old N.C.O.'s field cap slanted over one eye.

''Ah, there you are, Meyer,'' he said. ''I'm just off.'' He paused, suitably surprised. ''What's all this?''

Meyer had long since learned to control his anger in Koenig's presence.

He jumped to his feet. ''A partisan, or so we think, Colonel. Suslov picked him up in the mountains with various items of American equipment. It would appear some sort of drop's taken place in that area recently.''

Koenig picked up the Colt, hefted it and put it back on the desk. ''And what does he have to say?''

''That he found all this hidden under the straw in a shepherd's hut.''

Koenig looked Detweiler over, and the Sergeant, supported by the two Ukrainians, kept his head down, trying to catch his breath.

Koenig said, "It's possible, I suppose."

Meyer was astonished. "Colonel?"

"Put him in a cell, give him something to eat and twenty-four hours to think about his situation. I'm going up to command headquarters in Palermo, but I'll be back sometime tomorrow. I'll see him then."

Meyer smiled slightly. "As you say, Colonel."

Koenig walked to the door and opened it. He turned, "And I'd like to find him still in one piece. Do impress that on your men. They have a tendency to get a trifle overenthusiastic on these occasions and that would not please me at all."

"Certainly, Colonel, that goes without saying."

The door closed and Suslov said, "This is crazy, Major. Just let me have my way with this bastard."

Meyer shook his head. "When the right moment comes I intend to have Koenig's head, believe me, but I'm not going to jeopardize the situation by a conflict over something like this. It isn't important enough."

"So what do we do with this one?"

As Detweiler couldn't speak German he had been unable to follow what was going on. He waited fearfully, trying to play the cringing peasant, with only the expression on Meyer's face giving him a clue as to what was going on.

Meyer said thoughtfully, "Twenty-four hours to think things over, the Colonel said. Very well, let's give him just that. Take him down to twenty-two."

"*Zu Befehl, Sturmbannführer.*" Suslov nodded to his men and they dragged Detweiler out.

They descended stone steps, Suslov leading the way followed by the two Ukrainians holding Detweiler between them.

Detweiler's mind worked furiously, assessing the possibilities. He'd been prepared for this sort of situation in training, of course. Solitary confinement, that's what they usually started with, and in total darkness. He remembered what the psychiatrist lecturing to them had said. Sensory deprivation leading to total alienation of the individual. Okay, but all he had to do was hang on because he knew something these bastards didn't. That the invasion was due any day now.

They paused outside a cell door and Suslov unlocked it. The stench was appalling. When Detweiler was pushed forward he saw, as the light flooded in, that there were twelve or more filthy and ragged creatures huddled together on the floor in that confined space.

Suslov nodded and the two Ukrainians started to rip off Detweiler's clothes. When he was naked, they handcuffed his hands behind him. Detweiler had never felt so vulnerable in his life as Meyer came down the stairs and walked along the passage. He looked Detweiler over calmly, then moved into the entrance of the cell.

"Now listen to me," he said in his bad Italian. "This man doesn't lie down, doesn't sit, gets no rest whatsoever. And he isn't to sleep when standing. You take turns to make sure my orders are carried out, if you fail me, no water, no food for one week. Just each other."

He nodded to Suslov who shoved Detweiler down into the cell and slammed the door. Detweiler fell over a prostrate body, aware of the stench of the place, and kicked out frantically.

There were hands everywhere, crawling all over him, pulling him to his feet. Someone said hoarsely, "I don't know who you are, friend, and we couldn't care less. It's dog eat dog in here. That means we do what that Gestapo bastard wants and you do what we want."

Detweiler stood there in the darkness, suddenly terribly afraid. "Listen to me, for God's sake," he began.

The same hoarse voice said, "God has nothing to do with it, so be a good boy and do exactly as you're told."

In late spring and early summer, when the first real heat begins, violent thunderstorms are common in the Sicilian high country. It started to rain again as Savage and Rosa followed a track along a ridge between two mountain peaks.

He said, "Does it always rain this much in Sicily?"

She laughed. "No, this is not usual."

Not that Savage minded. Some people were rainwalkers by nature. It gave them a lift just to be out in the stuff. The rain-storm which broke over the Cammarata that morning worked its usual magic on him. The earth came alive and there was a freshness to everything.

She took his arm. "One thing I don't

understand. Last night when you were making love to me.''

"Which time was that.'' He tried to keep his face straight. "The third or fourth?''

"No, early this morning, when you woke from sleep. You kept apologizing for being no good. You said you were much better at shooting people.''

"I don't remember,'' he lied.

"But you are a wonderful lover. You made me happy many times.''

He was thoroughly embarrassed. "You shouldn't talk like that.''

"Like what?'' she demanded. "What did I say that was so terrible?''

"Let it go,'' he said. "Just let it go.''

She pulled him round and looked up at his face, grave beneath the peak of the old tweed cap. "I don't know what they've been telling you all these years, but you are not the man they think you are.'' She reached up and touched his face gently. "Or the man they have told you to be.''

He put an arm around her and pulled her close. "How come all this wisdom in one so young?''

"Because I was a whore,'' she said harshly. "In Palermo. But you knew this about me, I think?''

He was filled with a sense of overwhelming affection, and he leaned down and kissed her gently.

"Come on," he said. "We'd better make tracks for the monastery and find out what's happened to the others."

Luciano and Maria walked quietly together through the morning rain. She said, "I wish I hadn't had to leave that child."

"You've provided one miracle to start with," he said. "It'll survive. Bound to after such a start. Anyway, I thought you were in the faith business?"

"And you are not?"

"I deal in facts."

"You don't hate the Germans?"

"Do you?"

"I hate some of the things they've done."

"Life's a whole lot simpler than that for me."

"You reject any kind of personal commitment."

Luciano shrugged. "I know what I am. That tells me who I am. I like you, so I'm on your side."

"And the Germans?"

"I haven't even seen one yet."

"It's a game to you, all of it, isn't it, Mr.

Luciano, just like the Mafia?" She shook her head. "With your rules like some game for schoolboys. Your *omerta*. Manliness, honor, solve your own problems, and kill your enemy face-to-face."

"Everyone plays games," he said. "It helps you get by in life, haven't you noticed that? Flickering candles, mediaeval robes, plainsong, a man dressed in a woman's robe to wash your spirit clean at frequent intervals? Now what in the hell am I supposed to make of that?"

Before she could reply they emerged from the trees and saw a small village in the valley below.

"The place Solazzo mentioned," she said. "Viterba."

Luciano nodded. "Okay, let's go down and take a look. See if I can find this guy, Verga, that Solazzo spoke of."

It was a poor sort of place. Several streets slanted down to a square, mainly open sewers if the stench was anything to go by. Thin children played listlessly in the dirt, stopping to gaze apathetically as Luciano and Maria went by. There was a wine shop, an awning stretched over a few tables outside, rain pouring over the edge.

Luciano said to Maria, "Wait here, I'll

see if he's inside."

She sat at one of the tables and he went in. It was very dark, a few tables only and a cracked marble bar with bottles behind. There were no customers, only a short, thickset man in open-necked shirt and soiled white apron, who leaned on the bar reading a magazine.

He looked up warily. "Yes?"

"Mario Solazzo sent me."

"So?"

"I'm trying to get to the Franciscans at Crown of Thorns. He said you'd put us on the way."

"Us?"

"I have a woman with me." There was a long pause and Luciano said patiently, "You are Verga, aren't you? I was told you were of the Society."

Verga stared at him blankly and his hand was under the bar now. "So?"

Luciano said, "I'm going to take something out of my right hand pocket so don't shoot me. It isn't a gun."

He produced a yellow silk handkerchief and unfolded it. Verga looked down at the black L and his eyes widened. His hand emerged, holding a Beretta automatic of the type issued to Italian officers, and he placed it carefully on the bar.

"L for Luciano." He looked up slowly. Luciano stood there, head back, a hand on his right hip. Verga whispered, "You've come, just like they said you would."

He went round the bar and raised Luciano's hand to his lips, and at the same moment Maria cried out in pain. Luciano turned and ran for the door.

She was pressed back against one of the tables. The two men crowding her were typical of the young men of the region: Shabby clothes, broken boots, features brutalized and coarse from a life of toil.

One of them had his arms around her, hands moving over her buttocks, cruel smile on his face. He whispered some obscenity in her ear and she slapped his face. To a Sicilian, a woman is there to be used, to do as she is told. To be publicly humiliated by one is unthinkable. The young man raised his hand to strike.

Luciano grabbed him by the wrist and spun him around. They stared at each other, face to face. Already, the other man's expression was changing, first to dismay, then fear. It was not that he recognized Luciano, but what he saw clearly in that implacable face was the self-sufficiency, the quiet arrogance, the power of the *mafioso*.

Luciano slapped him. The man didn't say a word; simply stood there. His friend touched his arm and they walked backwards, faces blank, turned and hurried away.

Verga said, "Don Salvatore, what can I say? And you, Signorina."

"This good lady is one of the Sisters of Pity," Luciano informed him. "There are reasons for her being dressed like this. She is also Don Antonio Luca's granddaughter."

Verga turned in astonishment to look at her, then caught her hand and kissed it before she could prevent him. "Please come in. Eat with me and then I'll see you on the road to the monastery."

Savage and Rosa went over a rise and paused. There was a village about half a mile to the right and below them, in the side of the valley.

"What's that place?" he demanded.

"Viterba, but we keep going this way, where the track climbs up beyond the church to the ridge. The monastery is five miles on the other side."

As they started down the track he said,

"A strange place to have a church, out here on its own."

"Not really. The villages in the high country are not large enough to have their own church and priest. People walk from many places to this one. It is served by the Franciscans."

As they approached, Savage was aware of the sound of an engine close at hand and turned to see a *Kubelwagen* emerge from the trees in the valley below. It carried three men, one of them sitting behind a heavy machine gun.

He raised his field glasses and examined them quickly. "Germans."

"No," she said. "Ukrainians—members of the SS Special Group run by a man called Meyer. He's a Gestapo major operating out of Agrigento."

She grabbed his arm and hurried him along. "Heh," he said, "What is this?"

"The church—we'll hide in the church."

She was right, of course. They really had no other choice, for the track carried on for hundreds of yards across bare mountainside. Before they could get anywhere, they were certain to be spotted.

There was a donkey tethered outside. They moved past it and Rosa opened the door and led the way in. It was very quiet, only the candles, incense heavy on the damp morning air. Down by the altar, the Virgin seemed to float out of darkness, a slight fixed smile on her face.

Three people waited by a confessional box, a boy, an old man, and an even older woman who wore the usual black headscarf with a decaying sheepskin coat against the cold. She looked at Rosa and Savage curiously.

Savage peered through the partially open door as the *Kubelwagen* braked to a halt. The Ukrainians got out and stood beside the fieldcar lighting cigarettes and talking, then all three of them started up the path to the church.

They were casual enough, obviously expecting no trouble. The corporal who led the way carried a sidearm at his belt and the other two had Schmeissers. Savage unslung his M1, evaluating his chances of taking all three before they knew what was happening.

Rosa said softly, "You might get the corporal, but not the other two."

"So what do we do?"

"Give me that." She pulled the M1 from his hands. "And now the pack." He did as he was told and she quickly stowed them away behind the confessional box. The two old people and the boy watched impassively.

"We're here to see the priest to discuss our marriage plans." She pulled him over to a pew in the shadows behind the others. "No trouble, I can handle it."

"Like you have before?"

"Sure," she said. "They're men, aren't they? German, Russian—what's the difference?"

"I'm the difference, damn you! I'm the difference!"

He took off his cap and slipped a Browning automatic out of his right hand pocket. He held it in his lap, covered by the cap, without Rosa being aware of the fact and waited.

There was silence, the murmur of the priest's voice in the confessional mingling with the suppliant's. The door opened and steps approached, boots ringing on the flagstones.

"So, what have we got here?" the corporal said in bad Italian.

He paused at the old people before moving on to Rosa and Savage. He stood looking down at them and the other two moved up beside him. Tough, brutal men who looked as if they'd seen everything and experienced most things.

"What are you doing here?" he demanded.

"Waiting to see the priest," Rosa said.

"What for? To confess your sins." Their laughter had an ugly ring to it.

She smiled ingratiatingly. "We're getting married next week and need to see the good father to make the arrangements."

"Married, eh?" He moved round behind her. "Nice?" the corporal appealed to the other two and slipped a hand inside the bodice of her dress, cupping the left breast. "Virgin, are you?"

"Yes."

"We'll have to do something about that." He yanked her to her feet and pulled Savage's head back by the hair at the same time. "I'm doing you a favor, son, you do realize that?"

He took her by the arm and she twisted, pleading with Savage. "Please, no trouble. Is nothing. I can handle it."

As the corporal propelled her up the aisle one of the others called, "Don't forget your friends." He turned, grinning. "If I know him, he'll have her on the altar."

The other put one foot on the pew beside Savage and leaned over him. "You don't mind, do you? Like he says, he's doing you a favor. In fact, we're in such a generous mood today, we've all decided to do you a favor."

Savage fired through the cap, shooting him in the heart at point-blank range, killing him instantly. He shoved the body away, the Browning arching towards the other man who was frantically trying to unsling his Schmeisser. Savage's second bullet caught him in the left shoulder, spinning him around. The third shattered his spine, driving him headfirst across the back of one of the pews.

As Savage turned, the corporal already had Rosa in front of him and was jerking the Walther from his holster. He rammed it into her side.

"Drop it or she dies now."

But exactly this kind of situation had been a feature of OSS training. Savage's arm swung up and he shot him through the head instantly, the top of the corporal's skull fragmenting as he was hurled back against the altar rail.

Savage rushed for Rosa's hand. He pulled her away and, turning, found the old couple and the boy already making for the door followed quickly by another old woman who had just emerged from the confessional box with the priest.

He was about fifty, bearded, and wore the brown robes of the Franciscans. He came forward, his face strangely calm considering the circumstances. Without a word he proceeded to check the three Ukrainians.

"All dead. Who are you?"

"We were on our way to Crown of Thorns to see Padre Giovanni," Rosa said. "I am Vito Barbera's niece and this is an American officer, Captain Savage."

"I am Brother Lucio," the Franciscan said.

Savage retrieved his rucksack and M1 and moved to the door quickly. "The donkey is still there."

"Mine," said Lucio.

"Those people? What about them?"

"All they want to do is get home and forget this ever happened. They've too old and frightened to want to be involved." He turned to survey the carnage. "But we'll have to do something about this."

"What do you mean?" Savage asked.

"If the corpses are found here, it would mean heavy reprisals for Viterba. Much better they disappear all together. Help me and we'll take them out to the field car."

"I'll clean up in here," Rosa said.

She found a bucket in the vestry, filled it with water from the spring outside the door, went back inside, and started to mop the blood from the stone floor with a rag as Savage and Lucio returned for another body. When they came back for the corporal, she was cleaning the altar beside his body.

Savage said, "Are you okay?"

"You think I'm worried about a pig like that?"

She stirred the corpse with her toe and Savage said, "Okay, you needn't act so tough. We'll be back in a little while."

He and Lucio put the corporal in the rear of the *Kubelwagen* with the other two, then Savage and the Franciscan got into the front and Savage drove away, following his instructions.

They left the track further down the slope towards the village and turned into the forest, bumping over rough ground between trees. Finally, Lucio tapped Savage on the shoulder and he braked to a halt at the top of a short slope above a dark and stagnant pond.

"Here, I think."

They got out and together put their shoulders to the field car. It ran forward, gathering momentum, ploughed through a screen of young firs, and plunged into the pond. One of the bodies was pitched out and the field car turned over on top of him, the other two still inside. It didn't take long to disappear.

"Good," Savage said.

"A moment, Captain, please."

Lucio folded his hands and recited in a firm voice the prayers for the dying. "Go, Christian Soul, from this world, in the name of God the Father Almighty who created thee." By the time he was finished, the surface mud had settled.

He crossed himself and said gravely, "And now we go, I think."

They hurried back up the slope through the trees and along the track to the church. Rosa was waiting outside by the donkey.

Brother Lucio said, "You've cleaned up thoroughly?"

"Of course."

He swung a leg over the donkey, adjusted his robe, and set off. Savage and Rosa followed behind.

"Are you all right?" he asked her.

"Sure." She took out her old tobacco can and lit a cigarette, inhaled a couple of times, and passed it to him. "There was no need. I could have handled it.''

"No," he said violently. "Never again. You understand me?"

"Sure I do. I think maybe you like me, Savage."

"I think maybe you're right."

"Good," she said calmly. "Perhaps I make you a little bit crazy again tonight."

Savage, hopelessly and genuinely in love for the first time in his life, pulled her into his arms and kissed her, then they hurried after Brother Lucio.

Maria knelt in prayer in front of the altar of the Chapel at Crown of Thorns, at peace again for the first time in days, once more a part of a calm and ordered world that she understood. Luciano and Padre Giovanni stood in the shadows by the door.

"Have you heard from Don Antonio yet?" Luciano asked.

"Not a word."

"What do you think he'll make of her?" Luciano nodded down towards Maria.

The old man smiled faintly. "A very remarkable young woman. A whiff of holiness would not come amiss in Don Antonio's life, but frankly, I think the fact that Maria is a nun will have little effect on him. He is a strange, stubborn man. Quite unique. Himself alone."

The door opened, a young brother entered and whispered in his ear. Padre Giovanni said to Luciano, "It appears that your friends have arrived."

He turned and led the way out to the terraced cloisters.

Luciano looked over the rail and saw Savage and Rosa crossing the courtyard.

"Heh, you two," he called. "What kept you?"

FOURTEEN

Padre Giovanni led the way down the winding stone stair to the crypt of the monastery. He was preceded by a young monk carrying a couple of lanterns on a pole. Savage and Luciano followed behind.

"These cellars, more than anything else, have made Crown of Thorns famous all over Sicily," Padre Giovanni told them.

The young monk raised the pole high and Savage saw that the place was a charnel house, the bones of the dead visible on every side. Ribs, pelvises, hands, feet, femurs, tibulas, all cemented into the architecture. There were skulls piled everywhere.

The most horrifying aspect was the bodies, some lying down, some seated, others hanging from pegs. Many were total skeletons, but others retained skin and hair, even eyes and tattered vestiges of clothing.

"What in hell goes on here?" Savage asked in horror. "Who were these people?"

"Only the best, Captain Savage, I assure you," Padre Giovanni told him. "Sicilian aristocrats over the ages have taken it as a privilege to make this their final resting place. You will find much the same thing in the catacombs of Capuchin Zita Church in Palermo."

The remains of a child in a tattered velvet suit hung from a peg nearby and Savage shuddered and turned away.

Luciano said, "To the Sicilian, death is ever present and always important. In some villages on All Souls' Day, families make pilgrimages to the graves of the departed, taking their favorite food. They sit around the graves at midnight by candle-light. They leave presents for the dead in church."

"And why not?" Padre Giovanni said. "It reminds us that we all come to the same end. But I didn't bring you down here to find a suitable setting for a sermon. Over here, gentlemen."

In one corner of the crypt was an ancient wooden throne in black oak, shaped as a Norman arch and set into the stone. A decaying figure was enthroned in the seat, attired in a Franciscan robe, the hood drawn over the skull.

"Padre Leonardo, prior of the monastery at the end of the last century."

He turned a carved wooden rose in the top right hand corner and pushed and the throne swung back with its macaber burden, revealing a dark tunnel.

"This dates from Saracen times," Padre Giovanni said. "A way of retreat if things became too hopeless. For you also, I think, which is why it seemed sensible I show it to you."

"Have the Germans given you much trouble here at the monastery, Father?" Savage asked.

"On occasion. Colonel Koenig and his paratroopers were here three weeks ago. They searched the monastery most thoroughly."

"Were they looking for somebody?"

"No, I think Koenig merely wished to familiarize himself with the situation here. A strange young man. Courteous and decent in the extreme. Not like those Ukrainians of Major Meyer. We've had them here too."

Luciano said, "So this tunnel emerges

263

somewhere outside the walls?''

"About a quarter of a mile down the slope. Too far for my old legs to walk, but Filippo will show you the way.'' He reached up and took one of the lanterns from the pole. ''I'll see you later.''

He turned and walked back through the crypt. Brother Filippo started into the tunnel. Savage glanced sideways at the ghoul in the hooded robe on the wooden throne and hesitated, unwilling to pass him.

Luciano said cheerfully, ''Reminds me of a judge I once knew, but that's another story. Come on, let's get moving.''

He gave Savage a push and they moved on into the tunnel, following Brother Filippo.

Detweiler leaned against the wall in a daze. He had never been so tired in his life and every limb, every muscle in his body, seemed to ache. Conditions in the cell were appalling. The place stank like a sewer and he was weak and light-headed.

He had no idea how long he had been there, just as he had lost count of the number of times he had attempted to slump down to the ground and had been kicked and beaten back on to his feet. A man could only take so much, training or no training, that was apparent. There was a rattle of bolts, the door opened, and a shaft of yellow light flooded in.

He stood under a warm shower washing himself, watched by one of the Ukrainian guards. Standing in the passage outside, Meyer and Suslov peered in through the small glass window in the door.

Meyer said, "I've just received word that Koenig's been detained in Palermo by General Guzzoni. He won't be returning until tomorrow."

"An interesting situation," Suslov said. "Fraught with possibilities, especially where our friend in there is concerned."

"Exactly."

Meyer opened the door and went in followed by Suslov. Detweiler turned, instinctively covering his private parts with his hands.

Meyer said, "I've considered your case and I've now decided you can go."

Detweiler said stupidly, "Go?"

Meyer ignored him and said to Suslov, "Give him his clothes, see he gets something to eat, then kick him out."

He walked out. Suslov said, "You're bloody lucky, my friend. If I had my way. Still. . . ." He nodded to the guard. "Get him dressed, then take him to the canteen."

He went out and the guard threw Detweiler a towel. Detweiler dried himself quickly, then dressed in his clothes which had been piled neatly on the bench. It was incredible. His story had actually worked. The bastards were going to let him go.

In the canteen, he worked his way through a large plateful of some kind of spaghetti. There was black bread, cheese in plenty, real coffee. He was beginning to feel almost human again.

There was no one else in the canteen. The guard said, "Had enough?"

"Sure," Detweiler told him.

"Okay, follow me."

They went out and along the corridor and the guard opened a door leading into a small whitewashed cell with a bunk bed with a mattress on it. He gave Detweiler a cigarette and lit it for him.

"Wait here. I'll tell Lieutenant Suslov you're ready to go."

He went out, closing the door behind him and Detweiler relaxed, inhaling deeply on the cigarette. The next stage was the important one now. How to make contact with Carter and the others. And with Suslov out of the way. . . .

There was a sudden hideous clamor. He looked up and saw that an electric bell jangled above the door. Then the door burst open and they rushed in, four of them, and flung themselves on him.

He was kicked and beaten all the way along the passage, dragged by the ankles down a flight of stone steps, ending up in a corner, arms raised against the flailing truncheons. When they finally stopped he looked up fearfully and found Meyer and Suslov looking down at him.

Meyer said, "Now you know exactly where you stand. Have you anything to say to me?"

To Detweiler, in spite of his weakened state, one thing was obvious. The slightest hint of his true identity and God alone knew what they might do to him. So, he stayed in character.

"Please, Major, I'm a poor man," he whined. "I know nothing."

Meyer turned to Suslov. "He's all yours."

As he walked away, Suslov nodded to his men. They pulled Detweiler to his feet and made him stand against the wall braced on his fingertips, legs apart. One of them placed a bag of some black material over his head leaving him in total darkness. The pain in his fingers was already intense. He groaned, moving slightly, and a truncheon flailed across his kidneys.

Maria leaned on the battlements, staring out across the mountains to the Cammarata rising almost six thousand feet into the sky. The side of the valley was carpeted with flowers, fresh because of the rain. Red poppies, anemones, blue iris, spreading in the distance.

Padre Giovanni came up the steps to join her. "So, here you are." He nodded out over the land. "Well, what do you think?"

"Nothing changes," she said.

He nodded. "There are caves up there that used to hide Roman slaves two thousand years ago." He sat down. "Are you glad to be home?"

"Home?" she said. "This isn't home, Father. Not to me. We are taught that to hate is a mortal sin and yet I believe, with all my heart, that I hate this place."

"And your grandfather?"

"Antonio Luca," she said. *"Capo mafia*

in all Sicily. Lord of Life and Death. Does the church permit me to love such a man?''

"My child," Giovanni said, "it was not your grandfather who killed your mother. It was evil men who plotted his death.''

"He was responsible," she said, "because of what he was. If you defend him, you defend the Mafia. How can you, a priest, defend that?''

"I don't," he said tranquilly. "I defend no one. I deal in human souls as instructed by our Lord Jesus Christ in the Gospels.''

The gate opened and before she could reply Carter and Barbera entered the courtyard below, riding on mules.

Barbera said, "As far as we know, Detweiler was arrested and taken to the barracks at Agrigento.''

"How did they find him?" Savage demanded.

"An informer. He'll be taken care of.''

They were seated at one of the refectory tables where meals were eaten; Savage and Rosa and Barbera on one side, Luciano, Carter, and Maria on the other. Padre Giovanni was at the head of the table. He poured red wine into his glass and passed the bottle to Luciano.

"Even if Major Meyer is unaware of Sergeant Detweiler's true identity, he will still, I fear, be subjected to considerable brutality." He turned to Savage. "How strong would you say he is, Captain?"

"Oh, he's tough enough," Savage said. "Once during a commando raid on the French coast, he walked twenty miles to our rendezvous with a bullet in the foot."

Barbera said, "Most men have their breaking point. Once Detweiler opens his mouth, they'll be looking for us."

"Which means we must see Luca as soon as possible," Carter said.

Brother Filippo entered, holding a pigeon in his hand. He stroked it soothingly while Padre Giovanni unfastened the tiny capsule from its left leg. He pried it open with a finger nail, took out the paper it contained and unrolled it. He examined it, looked up, and smiled.

"In the morning, my friends. He will see you in the morning."

There were two additional members of the district committee replacing Mori and Russo. They were waiting in the living room at the back of the mortuary when Barbera entered with Harry Carter and Luciano.

270

Barbera made the introductions.

"Father Collura, you know, Harry, representing the Christian Democrats; Mario Verga who runs the inn here speaks for the Separatist movement."

"Father." Carter shook hands. "Signor Verga. Good to see you again." He turned to the other two men. "And these gentlemen?"

"Zizzo and Valachi," Barbera said, "Of the Communist Party. There have been changes in that respect."

Zizzo, a small, dark man in gamekeeper's leggings and corduroy suit, said angrily, "Stuff the pretty talk, Barbera. Pietro Mori murdered in his own home and Ettore Russo, our leader, vanished off the face of the earth. A direct attack on the whole Communist movement and we know who is responsible."

"You make me sick," Carter said. "All of you. Nearly two years since I first came to Sicily and you haven't changed a bit, like boys, stoning each other on the way home from school for no good reason. I couldn't care less who rules Sicily after the war. You can sort that out amongst yourselves. For the moment, the question isn't, do you want rid of Mussolini and the Fascist Party.

It's do you want rid of the Germans?"

Father Collura said mildly, "I agree with Colonel Carter. First, we get rid of our enemies. Afterwards, when Sicily is free again, we discuss our future democratically among the ourselves."

The two Communists reacted angrily, Valachi said, "Fine words which mean nothing. Why should we listen to Carter anyway? Is he one of us? No—a stranger, interested only in the needs of his own people. The English and Americans don't give a damn for Sicily or its people. We're just another pawn in the capitalist imperalist struggle."

Carter was tired. There was that pain in his lung again. When he breathed it hurt. More than that, he was weary. Tired of the scheming, the feuds, the personal vendettas. He was about to turn away in disgust when suddenly, Luciano was beside him.

"Why should you listen? I'll tell you why, you stupid bastards." He tore open Carter's shirt with one quick movement, exposing the livid, raised scars left by his chest wounds. "He's made his bones, the Professor. Two months ago, they carried him out of here in a coffin with a bullet in the lung. How much has that taken off his life at the other end? Why do you think he's come back—for the good of his health?''

Carter said, "You're talking into the wind, my friend, and the words blow back unheard."

He went out. There was a heavy silence. Zizzo said, "What in the hell has it got to do with you, anyway." He turned on Barbera. "Who is this guy?"

Luciano took his time over lighting a cigarette. "An interesting point," he said. "To the priest who baptized me I'm Salvatore Lucania, but to most people I'm simply Luciano." His smile was terrible to see. "Lucky Luciano. Would you like me to tell you why?"

Both Zizzo and Valachi recoiled in horror and Father Collura moved in quickly. "Please, Don Salvatore, no harm was intended, no offense, I'm sure."

There was a wooden, hand-painted icon of Our Lady and the Holy Infant on the far wall. Luciano's hand came out of his pocket holding the ivory Madonna. There was a click; he swung underhand and the point of the stiletto buried itself in the icon.

"You see, Father, the knife in the heart of the Virgin, something we Sicilians

273

understand."

There was a dreadful silence. He dominated the room now. "Cards on the table. Come with me, all of you."

He nodded to Barbera, who led the way through the waiting mortuary into the preparation room. Two bodies lay side by side covered by sheets. Barbera pulled back the first one to disclose the thin aesthetic features of Pietro Mori. The face had been carefully made up, the lips touched with carmine. He even wore his glasses.

"And here?" Barbera uncovered the other corpse and exposed Ettore Russo.

"We came at great personal risk to help the cause," Luciano said, "but these two used the occasion to work off some personal grudge against the Mafia. Russo was the instrument. He and the misguided youth with him paid the price, but it was Mori who stood behind the deed. He made the worst mistake of his life, not in attacking· me, but in exposing to danger of her life the granddaughter of Don Antonio Luca. who was with me at the Villa Bellona at the time."

"Holy Mother of God!" Zizzo whispered.

"Please, Don Salvatore," Valachi had his cap off now. "Such a thing was *infamita*

274

and never intended. You must believe this."
He turned to Barbera. "Vito, you can
surely make plain to the good Don Antonio
that this was none of our doing."

"Of course," Barbera said. "Although in
Don Antonio's eyes, deeds speak louder
than words. The fact that the district committee speaks with one voice in the future;
that we work together against the common
enemy in the coming invasion, would
impress him as an earnest of your good
faith."

"That goes without saying," Zizzo said
eagerly. "You may rely on us of the
Communist Party."

"Politics are politics," Valachi said. "But
we're all Sicilians first."

Luciano moved to the window and lit
another cigarette. Barbera said, "So, the
invasion will come and very soon now. You
and your people must hold yourselves ready
with all weapons at your command, and
when the time comes, you take your orders
from Colonal Carter. You understand
this?"

"Yes," Zizzo said.

Father Collura said, "The cooperation of
the Christian Democrat Party goes without
saying."

Luciano turned. "All in order now?"

Barbera nodded. "So it would appear."

"Good. So long as we understand each other."

He stood there waiting, left hand on hip, head thrown back. Zizzo and Valachi shuffled forward in turn and kissed his right hand.

Savage couldn't sleep. There wasn't much room in the small bed with Rosa squeezed in beside him. The old shirt she wore instead of a night shift had rucked up so that her breasts were warm against him and her hand had fallen across his stomach. In sleep she looked not so much young as vulnerable.

Lying there with an arm about her seemed the most natural thing in the world. He felt warm, secure, and content. He managed to turn up the lamp with one hand, lit a cigarette and reached for a small tattered volume on the bedside locker. It was the poetry anthology his grandfather had given him on his thirteenth birthday. He had read it a thousand times and the contents never bored him.

Rosa stirred and opened her eyes. She said sleepily, "What are you doing?"

"Reading."

"But what?"

"Poetry."

She touched his ear with her tongue and her hand slid down his stomach to hold him. "Is it better than me, this poetry?"

"You can't compare the two things."

"So?" she pouted. "This is how much you love me?"

"No," he said. "Sometimes the poetry can say how much, far better than I can."

"I don't believe you. Show me what you're reading now."

"I don't need to. I know it by heart. It was written a long time ago by a very great Englishman. Sir Walter Raleigh. He was just about everything a man could be. A gentleman in the true sense of the word, a fine soldier, musician, writer, poet."

"What happened to him?"

"They chopped off his head. The king was jealous of him."

She said, "The poem? What about this poem?"

He said aloud in English, quietly and softly,

"But true love is durable fire
In the mind ever burning:

Never sick, never old, never dead,
From itself never turning.''

She hardly understood the meaning of the words, but the poignancy was there. She started to weep, deeply and bitterly, as if mourning that lost innocence and everything that had ever happened to her. Savage, out of some strange perception, knew exactly what was taking place here.

He held her close, thinking about Boston and his mother and the whole Savage clan and Rosa. Suddenly he felt unaccountably cheerful. If they don't like it, he thought, they can do the other thing. She was asleep again now and he held her close, listening to the rain outside the open window.

In the cubbyhole at the back of the coffin room, Barbera sat at the radio while Carter and Luciano drank coffee and waited. Finally, Barbera took off his headphones and turned, his face suffused with excitement.

''They come,'' he said. ''The day after tomorrow.''

Carter got to his feet and paced nervously across the room. ''It doesn't give us much time.''

"Come on, Harry," Luciano said. "We see Luca tomorrow. One meeting is all it takes. Afterwards, he sends messages all over western Sicily and how long does that take? A few hours only."

Barbera had already taken a bottle and three glasses from a cupboard. He filled them quickly.

"A drink, I think, would be in order." He turned and twiddled the dial on the receiver. "Let's see what the British Forces Radio has to offer from Cairo."

The music was distant and far away and the voice of the man singing was strangely compelling, something of the night in it.

"I like that," Luciano said. "Who is it?"

"Al Bowlly," Carter told him. "One of my weaknesses. Did I ever tell you I play a very fair jazz piano? He was an English crooner, South African originally. Number One on the hit parade for years. He was killed in the Blitz in forty-one. That's 'Moonlight on the Highway,' probably the best thing he ever did. Recorded with the Lew Stone orchestra in March 1938."

The haunting melody filled the room. Luciano said, "What a way to go."

"His own choice. He was walking down Brewer Street when a bomb fell and the blast went the other way. From then on he believed in his luck, so when the siren sounded and other people went to the shelters, he stayed in bed."

"And paid for it with his life?" Barbera said.

"Exactly." Carter smiled. "But this is getting morbid. A toast, gentlemen. Now, what shall we drink to?"

"Why, to all three of us," Luciano smiled. "And to Luciano's luck. May it hold."

FIFTEEN

They left just after nine the following morning in Barbera's old truck, Luciano, Carter and Savage in the rear while Maria sat up front with Barbera.

It had stopped raining and it was already apparent that it was going to be a hot day. The truck climbed the dusty road into the mountains, passing through a medieval landscape, one wretched village after another, most of the houses windowless, the doors opening into dark caverns which in most cases housed livestock as well as people.

Luciano said, "What a bloody country. My people took us to America in 1907 to get away from this, and thirty-six years later nothing's changed."

"Was the east side of New York any better?" Carter asked.

They passed a long line of gaunt women, baskets on their heads, dressed in black as if mourning their daily existence, shoulders bowed as they struggled up the steep road.

"Professor," Luciano said with deep conviction, "anything would be better than this, even the backside of hell."

After an hour and a half of traveling they came into a small decaying village and Barbera pulled up outside the wine shop. He climbed down and a small, fat man came out, wiping his hands on a soiled white apron.

"Heh, Rafael," Vito hailed him. "How goes it?"

"Fine—everything's ready for you. Leave the truck here. I'll take care of it."

"Okay," Barbera called. "All out!"

He followed Rafael round to the rear of the wine shop. Half a dozen mules waited in a small corral, saddled and bridled, and a dark haired youth with a shotgun slung across his back leaned against the rail.

"This is Nino. He'll take you the rest of the way. A couple of hours' ride up into the mountains, that's all."

Luciano turned to Carter. "You really think of everything, don't you, Professor?"

"Better than walking," Carter said.

Luciano moved across to Maria and helped her up onto the broad wooden saddle of the lead mule. She sat sidesaddle and he took his time over adjusting her stirrup.

"Are you worried?" he said. "About meeting your grandfather?"

"Should I be?"

His inquiry had been one of genuine concern and the coldness of her reply angered him.

"What is it with you?" he said. "What happened to the Christian charity bit, the human concern? Did you peel it off along with the robes?"

Nino, the young muleteer, had passed her a riding switch and, in a sudden reflex action, she raised it as if to cut Luciano across the face.

"Now you're talking," he said. "Now I know there's some Luca blood in those veins."

"Damn you!" she said in a low voice.

"Harsh words," he said. "Three Hail Marys and two Our Fathers."

She slashed the mule across the rump and it cantered away.

Detweiler was almost completely disorientated. The pain in his fingers and arms was not so terrible anymore because he had passed through some sort of pain threshold, but every so often the Ukrainians took turns to belabor the bucket they had placed over his head with truncheons. It was a technique Suslov had picked up during a spell of duty at Auschwitz. The constant clangor had such an effect on the brain and eardrums that it usually produced total alienation within a matter of hours.

Detweiler had lost control of his bladder and his trousers were soaked with urine. Suslov, standing there watching, calmly said, "Hose him down, then throw him in a cell. I'll deal with him when I've eaten."

They took Detweiler out between them, feet trailing, and Suslov walked after them.

Maria guided her mule through a stream following Nino. As she started up the slope on the other side, Luciano rode up alongside her. They were moving through trees now, cork-oak and holly-oak, and above them the ridge was scattered with pines.

Luciano said, "I've decided to forgive you."

She smiled in spite of herself. "You have the Devil's insolence, Mr. Luciano."

"Oh, there's a lot to be said for the Devil," he said. "He was, after all, a fallen angel."

"A debatable point."

"True, but if the Bible is to be believed, still a force to be reckoned with. Has it ever occurred to you that perhaps people turn to God when the Devil no longer has a use for them?"

"No," she said, pain on her face. "I can't accept that. I could never accept such a thing."

They came through the pine trees and Nino reined in on the ridge. On the slope below was an old and rambling farmhouse among olive trees. There was a man seated at a table on the terrace, and, when Nino whistled, he stood and looked up towards them, tall with broad shoulders, grey hair.

"Don Antonio," the boy said simply.

Luciano waited, but she said nothing, simply sat there for a moment, her face very calm, then urged her mule forward and down the slope.

Luciano turned to Carter and Savage who crowded up behind him. "Professor," he said. "You know how Luciano's survived all these years?"

"No, but I'm sure you'll tell me," Carter said.

"It's simple." Luciano patted his stomach. "I get this feeling in my gut and it's never wrong."

"And what does it tell you now?"

"That this is all one hell of a waste of time. Five gets you ten that old buzzard down there isn't going to play."

In Palermo at command headquarters, General Guzzoni was in conference with his staff officers when Koenig knocked on the door and entered.

Guzzoni said, "Ah, there you are. The weather forecast couldn't be worse, but reconnaissance planes have located a considerable armada of allied ships south of Pantellaria."

"The feint which Intelligence has been expecting?" Koenig said.

"So it would appear. One would expect the bulk of the force to move on to Sardinia." He nodded to the Italian staff officers. "That will be all for now, gentlemen. I'll call you if I need you."

He waited until the last one had gone before offering Koenig a cigarette, then poured cognac into two glasses.

"Suddenly we have the Allied air forces back in strength. Messina bombed twice in twenty-four hours. Harbor installations, air bases, all under attack once more. I don't like it and neither does Field Marshal Kesselring. I've just spoken to him in Rome."

"General?" Koenig was guarded.

"The Field Marshal never did really buy this idea that Sicily would be only a sideshow and Sardinia the main target. And then there's the weather."

"I must confess I was wondering about that myself. A strange time to choose."

"The forecast for tomorrow is terrible and the same for the day after. Storms, gales, rain. The only reason for coming in such weather would be because it was not expected."

"And why go to all that trouble if the attack on the Sicilian shore is only a feint, is that what you're thinking, General?"

"Exactly."

Koenig sipped his cognac thoughtfully. "If it wasn't a feint. . . . If it was the real thing after all, then coming in the weather that has been forecast would make excellent sense."

Guzzoni put down his glass. "You intend

to return to Agrigento this afternoon?"

"Yes, General."

"I think I'll come with you. See for myself what the situation is on the coast."

Luca sat at the table on the terrace, leaning on his stick, the unmistakable aura of the regal about him, Katerina at his side. He waited as they dismounted and came up the steps to the terrace. He had eyes for no one but Maria. Katerina, with both hands resting lightly on his shoulder, could feel that he was trembling slightly.

Barbera kissed his hand. "Don Antonio. This is Colonel Carter and Captain Savage, an American officer. Don Salvatore, you know."

Luca ignored him, ignored all of them. "Leave us," he said hoarsely. "All of you. Katerina, see they get fed."

She squeezed his shoulders, then smiled at the others. "Gentlemen, if you'd come this way."

Carter was reluctant to go, but Barbera pulled at his sleeve and they followed Katerina inside.

Maria stood there, very tired, her hands folded in front of her. Her black dress was covered with dust and she took off her headscarf and ran her fingers through the cropped hair.

"So, it is true," Luca said. "You are a nun."

"For four years now."

"Wandering the mountain like a lost soul delivering babies that by all the laws should have died. To Solazzo and his friends you are a saint already."

"Is there nothing you don't know?"

"Nothing that happens in these mountains," he said flatly.

There was lemonade in a jug on the table and she helped herself and sat down. "Nothing changes. Antonio Luca is still Lord of Life and Death in all Sicily."

"I am of the Society," he said. "I have no shame in that. The Mafia made me. It is what I am."

"It also killed my mother."

"It was meant for me, that day. Those responsible paid the bill."

"Does that make the dead walk?"

He sat there, frowning, hands on the handle of his walking stick. "For a servant of God, you are singularly lacking in charity. I know what I am, but what are you, Maria? The nun in white robes, struggling with the sick in the hospital or on your knees in the candlelight praying to the Virgin to save the soul of Antonio Luca?''

Her face was pale, her hands gripping the arms of the chair so tightly that the knuckles gleamed white.

He said softly, ''Or could it be that your prayer is to the Devil to take me straight to hell?''

She jumped to her feet, upsetting the jug of lemonade, turned, and hurried down the steps into the garden. Katerina came out through the open window and joined him.

''Does it give you satisfaction, this thing? Are you happy now?''

''No,'' Luca said. ''But then I never expected to be.''

He went down the steps and walked along a path that finally brought him out on one of the terraces of olive trees above the valley, where he found her sitting on a stone wall.

He sat down beside her and took a cigar from his pocket. ''Remember the summer house at Trevese? What times we had there. How old were you when I bought your first pony? Nine?''

''I broke my left arm in two places trying to jump the boundary wall,'' she said.

''And we had to shoot the pony.'' He

sighed. "Life walks towards death. The human condition." There was silence for a while and then he said. "You're happy? As a nun, I mean?"

"Perfectly. I'm a trained nurse. I spend most of my time in hospitals."

"A strange life," he said. "Celibacy, for example. I could never understand that."

She laughed, unable to help herself. "The vow of chastity is a contract with God entered into voluntarily. Because I gave up any thoughts of a sexual life doesn't mean I don't feel any desire for it. We are human beings, flesh and blood like anyone else."

"True enough if you're my grand-daughter," he said. "So, the line ends here. No more Lucas when I'm dead and gone."

"So it would appear."

And then he saw it or thought he did. "Was that it, girl? Was that the intention? To cut off the flow of tainted blood?"

"Perhaps. I don't know." She was confused and struggled against it. "The woman?"

"Katerina? What about her?"

"Is she your wife?"

"No."

There was another awkward silence. He said, "Spit it out, whatever it is they wanted you to say. You didn't come all this way for love of your grandfather.''

She folded her hands in her lap. ''It's simple enough. The invasion will come soon now and the Americans need your help. One word from you and all over Sicily. . . .''

''No,'' he said. ''I will not do it.''

''Because you hate Americans?''

''I will not do it because you have asked me.'' He got to his feet. ''Even Christ only had to carry his cross so far,'' and he turned and walked back along the terrace through the olive trees.

Meyer was working over some papers in his office when there was a knock and Suslov entered.

''Well, what is it?'' Meyer demanded impatiently. ''I'm busy.''

''Several interesting new developments as regards this present case,'' Suslov said. ''I thought you might be interested.''

Meyer sat back. ''Go on.''

''Well, the old villain who sold him out to us was discovered on a dung heap outside the local village this morning.''

''Dead?''

''And his tongue had been cut out.''

"The traditional way the Mafia deal with an informer," Meyer said.

"And one of our patrols has found a parachute caught in a tree not a mile from the farm where we picked up our friend yesterday."

"A supply chute?"

Suslov shook his head. "No, very definitely the other variety. British. The kind their paratroopers use."

Meyer's eyes glittered. "This could be important, Suslov. He must be made to talk. He must."

"What would the Major suggest?"

"I give you one more chance your way. If that doesn't work, then we'll try scopolamine."

"Very well." Suslov turned to the door and opened it. "One other thing. We've a patrol very much overdue."

"The same area?"

"Yes."

Meyer nodded. "Then get to work. It would appear there are a great many questions to be answered and our friend may provide the key to all of them."

Luca sat at the table on the terrace drinking Zibibbo, an anise-flavored wine from the island of Pantellaria that was a particular favorite of his. Carter and Luciano sat opposite him and Savage watched from the other end of the terrace.

Carter said, "The invasion comes tomorrow or the day after, depending on the weather. I make no secret of this. I trust you as a man of honor."

"Colonel, I salute you as a soldier and as a scholar, but you're a rotten salesman."

"Don Antonio, if you give the word, the whole of the Cammarata will rise as one man. There's a fair chance that most Italian troops in the mountains will surrender without firing a shot. They're brave men, but they've had enough of Mussolini."

"I'm not interested in Italy, only in Sicily," Luca said.

"Then help us kick the Germans out."

"Colonel—Professor—whatever you are. The Nazis have lost the war. They lost it in 1940 when Hitler stood back and let the British Army go at Dunkirk. All we need to do is sit back and wait."

"And see thousands of young Americans die needlessly fighting their way through the Cammarata?"

"Not my affair."

"Why, because they sent your brother to

the electric chair? Must all Americans suffer?''

Luciano spoke up, turning to Carter. ''Tell him the numbers.''

Carter hesitated. ''My orders didn't cover that.''

''Fuck your orders, Professor. Tell him.''

Carter was silent for a moment. Then he leaned forward. ''Don Antonio,'' he said softly, ''in the initial assault there will be nearly three thousand ships and landing craft. They will carry 180,000 men, fourteen thousand cars and trucks, six hundred tanks, eighteen hundred guns of major caliber. If they land successfully and gain control of the island quickly, the next step is Italy. What more do the Sicilian and Italian people want now than to be rid of the German plague that keeps food from the mouths of their children? And SS all over the place telling Sicilians what to do and what not to do.''

Luciano put up a hand. ''You hear the numbers, Don Antonio. An army of that size working with us, that cannot work without us.''

Luca shook his head, a line of weariness tightening around his mouth. Then, without a word, he stood and left the patio.

Luciano said, "You're wasting your time, Major." He stood up. "I'm going to take a walk." Quickly he moved through the garden and found Maria walking along the terrace between the olive trees towards him.

"What's happening?" she asked.

"Carter's ramming his head against a stone wall called Antonio Luca."

"He won't help?"

"Wouldn't lift a finger. Obviously, you didn't get anywhere either."

"Why should I?" There was a curious edge of bitterness to her voice. "I came here for one reason only and it certainly wasn't for love. How stupid, when you think about it. I've avoided him for years, made my feelings absolutely plain. And now, to turn up in such circumstances, expecting him to come running, like snapping one's fingers to a dog."

She walked up through the trees towards the house, head bowed, and Luciano turned and moved down towards the valley.

It was shortly after noon when they dragged Detweiler out into the courtyard at the rear of the police barracks. There were two posts in the center and a thin, hollow-faced man in ragged clothes was strapped to one of them. He had obviously been terribly beaten, Detweiler was aware of that as they strapped him to the next pillar.

Suslov said, "Right, this is it, then. No last cigarette. They're in short supply."

Detweiler was aware of the firing squad on the other side of the square as the Ukrainian pulled a black bag over his head. His brain refused to function and his mouth was so dry that he couldn't cry out. There was a pause that seemed to go on for ever, a shouted command, a sudden volley.

Detweiler hadn't even braced himself for death, simply hung there in the straps, aware of steps moving towards him.

The bag was wrenched from his head and Suslov said, "Still with us, I see."

Detweiler turned and saw that the man next to him hung there, saturated in blood, head lolling to one side.

"Always like to make sure," Suslov said.

He took his Walther from his pocket and fired at point-blank range. Pieces of bone and blood sprayed, the body sagged, and Detweiler cried out.

Suslov nodded to the guards. "Bring him along."

Detweiler was half conscious as they took him upstairs between them. He was aware of being dumped in a chair and opened his eyes to find himself in Meyer's office.

The Major came around the desk. "Still nothing to say. Well, we'll soon remedy that." He picked up a hypodermic. "Scopolamine, otherwise known as the truth drug."

Detweiler tried to struggle, but Suslov and the guards held him firmly and Meyer moved in close and rolled up his sleeve.

It was very hot, very still on the olive terraces, and thunder rolled on the horizon as Luciano produced a pack of cards he had found up at the house. He took out six of the cards and lined them up in a crack in a large rock. Then he walked away.

There had been a time when he could draw, turn, and hit a playing card six times at that distance inside a second, but that had been long ago. His hand went under his jacket, found the butt of the Smith and Wesson. He drew, turned, crouched, arm extended, and fired very fast.

He went forward to examine the cards, reloading as he did so. *Three out of six.* Not bad, considering.

Luca said, "So the hand *has* lost its cunning."

Luciano turned and found him standing a few yards away leaning on his stick.

"You want to try?"

Luciano offered him the gun. Luca balanced it in his hand, then emptied it very deliberately, taking his time, hitting four of the cards.

"Not bad," he said. "A tendency to pull to the right. Maybe you could lighten the trigger."

Luciano took the gun back and reloaded. "Anyway, it's good to see you again."

"And you, Salvatore, even on a fool's errand like this. What possessed you to do such a thing? The promise of a pardon?"

"Only a possibility," Luciano said. "Nothing on paper."

Luca was astonished. "Then why did you come?"

"You've been to prison. You know how it is. Can you imagine how a thirty-to-fifty-year sentence feels for something you didn't do?"

Luca nodded. "Yes, I can see that almost anything would be preferable to that."

Luciano said, "Anyway, what about Maria?"

"Maria and I have nothing to say to each other," Luca said. "Salvatore, what has this nonsense to do with us? Whatever happens, the Mafia will survive. Mussolini couldn't crush us. Neither could the Germans. The wise man keeps his own counsel and lives a hundred years. You know the saying."

Luciano hesitated, then bowed his head formally. "If that is your decision, then I accept it, Don Antonio."

Luca put a hand on his shoulder. "Then you will stay here with us. We can talk of old times, old friends. . . . Stay, Salvatore." He reached for Luciano's arm. "Together, there is nothing we can't accomplish. Eventually, you would take my place, that goes without saying."

"*Capo di Tutti Capi* in all Sicily." Luciano smiled, remembering Maria's words. "Lord of Life and Death."

"Look what's happened to the Mafia in New York," Luca said urgently. "For some of the families, whores have become big business. They tell me there are even those who deal in children. I ask you. Can you believe that of a true Sicilian. And this drug thing. *Infamita.* And not for a man like you. Stay here in Sicily, where you belong.

Where you have respect.''

His fingers had hooked into Luciano's arm and there was a strange kind of pleading on his face. Luciano detached himself gently.

"I'm sorry, Don Antonio," he said, "but I can't be the son you never had. I go back with Carter and take my chances with that parole board. If it works, I'll be free again—really free—for the rest of my life."

"And if it doesn't?"

Luciano shrugged. "I'll deal with that when it happens. And there's Maria to consider. She certainly won't stay here, you must see that."

He turned and fired left-handed so fast that it sounded like one continuous roll and he knew what he would find even before he reached the cards. Six hits, each card drilled cleanly.

"Remarkable," Luca said.

"I know," Luciano smiled. "It's this weather, you see." He looked up into the sky as heavy drops of rain spotted the dry earth.

General Eisenhower was due to go to Malta with Field Marshal Alexander and Admiral Cunningham. Waiting for his staff car he had a final cup of coffee, standing in front of the map of Sicily on the wall of his office at dar el Ouad. There was a knock at the door and Cusak entered.

"A signal from Admiral Ramsay with the fleet, General."

"Anything important?"

"Everything is going well except for the deteriorating weather. Force four to five winds over the sea."

Eisenhower nodded. "Any word from Colonel Carter?"

"I'm afraid not."

Eisenhower put down his cup and reached for his cap, "There are 2,500 ships out there. Chief Air Marshal Tedder's promised us blanket air cover of five thousand planes when the right moment comes, the sole aim being to put 115,000 British and Canadians at one end of the island and 66,000 of our boys at the other to drive the enemy out of Sicily."

Cusak helped him on with his field coat. "Quite a responsibility, General."

"One hell of a job of organizing," Eisenhower said. "Months of research, planning, arguments, sleepless nights, and the irony is that the whole damn thing could quite easily stand or fall on Carter's negotiations with this—this mountain brigand or whatever he is.''

''Carter could still bring it off, General.''

''Well, all I can say is he's running it damn close,'' Eisenhower said and he picked up his briefcase and went out.

At the farm it had started to rain. Katerina sat at the table at the end of the terrace with a pack of cards, laying them before her one by one. Maria came out of the living room and stood watching her.

Katerina said, ''You have wasted your time, I think.''

''So it would appear.'' Maria sat down opposite her. ''I should never have allowed them to persuade me to come. He is the same man I ran from so long ago.''

''Not true,'' Katerina said. ''Everything changes.''

''Even Antonio Luca?''

''He is not the man today that he was yesterday. Are you the same woman you were when they came to you back there in your convent? Has nothing changed?''

Maria smiled sadly. ''You're right, of course. There I had certainty, the days had a pattern. Now, there is only doubt.'' She hesitated, and when she spoke it was from the depths of her being. "I even doubt my vocation now. I thought I sought God, now it would appear I was only fleeing Antonio Luca."

"You hate him so much?"

Maria touched her breast. "It is like a stone in here, a constant pain that won't go away!" She sat back. "But for you it is different, I think. You love him."

"Oh, yes, for me that is the only certainty."

They sat there in silence. Luciano and Savage appeared in the doorway. Katerina shuffled the cards and laid them out again.

Maria said, "The tarot?"

"Yes."

"I haven't seen that done since I was a child. My mother constantly sought news of the future."

"It is there for those who would see."

"Irrevocably?"

"I'm not certain. Perhaps a warning only. An opportunity to take another road."

Maria watched her for a while and then said, "Let's see what the cards have to say for me."

Katerina shrugged. "If you like. Your future on one card, although I don't think the Vatican would approve."

She counted quickly and flipped over the seventh card. It was an ornate, brightly colored picture of a young man hanging by his ankles from a tree.

"The Hanged Man," she said. "Interesting. No such symbol exists in orthodox Christianity. Equal for man or woman. The individual is torn between two selves, the same and yet not the same. Symbol of a sacrificial victim since pagan times. You suffer for others, that is your destiny."

Maria stood up. "Goodbye, Katerina Scorza. I don't think we shall see each other again."

She went inside and Luciano and Savage moved to the table. Luciano took the cards from her and said to Savage, "A very superstitious people, we Sicilians."

He counted out seven cards and turned the last one over. It was a six-spoked wooden wheel, a crudely drawn dragon above it.

"The Wheel of Fortune," she said. "The symbol of inner order. You have cast yourself free from the bonds of society."

"Seen through the bars of a prison cell, of course," he said.

"But not for long."

Luciano turned to Savage. "If I was paying Gypsy Rose in a tent at Coney Island, I'd really think I'd had my money's worth."

Savage said, "What about me?"

Looking up at him, Katerina's eyes clouded, and there was an unwillingness that Luciano sensed, if Savage did not.

"I'm tired," she said. "One can give only so much."

"Just tell me whether I'm lucky in love," he said. "That will do."

She hesitated, then took the pack and counted, turning over the seventh card long enough to glance at it. She put it back on top of the pack.

"Great happiness results from a marriage or birth. The Three of Cups in an upright position."

"Here, let me look."

He reached for the card and turned it over. Two ornate birds perched on the rim of a golden goblet, each holding a smaller cup in a claw.

He laughed excitedly. "Well, what do you know? Can I keep this? There's someone I'd very much like to show it to." He slipped it into his breast pocket and said to Luciano, "If it's in the cards, it's in the cards, isn't that so?''

He was smiling excitedly as he went back inside. Katerina reached for the pack and Luciano grabbed her wrist, twisting until she opened her hand disclosing the card she had palmed. It fell to the table between them.

Death stared up, crudely depicted, a skeleton, scything no field of corn, but a crop of human bodies.

In the living room, Carter stood by the fire confronting Luca. ''Is there no way I can persuade you, Don Antonio?''

''Those friends of yours in Cairo or wherever it is, must be stupid. Did they really think that the sight of my grand-daughter coming in through the door would make me change my opinion in this matter?'' He poured himself a glass of Zibibbo with great care. ''Why, that in itself would be enough to make me say no, even if I had not intended to in the first place.''

''Don Antonio, men will die,'' Carter said urgently.

''A habit they have,'' Luca told him.

Carter turned angrily to Luciano, who lounged in the window. ''A waste of bloody time, the whole thing, just like you said. We might as well get going. The sooner we return to Bellona, the better."

He went out and Luciano helped himself to wine. He sniffed the bouquet approvingly. "Hate and love—it's a thin line. You should remember that."

"Not for her."

"A remarkable girl. I thought that when I first met her in that convent in Liverpool. Since then, she's parachuted into enemy territory by night, faced death many times, been hunted through the mountains. . . ."

Don Antonio said, "So she's my granddaughter. Half a Luca, whether she likes it or not. Blood of my blood and she can't escape that, whatever she thinks of me. But I will not do what Carter's people want. This war is not my war. It will pass as the wind passes. Sicily will be free again and things will be as they were."

Maria said from the doorway, "We're ready to move, Mr. Luciano."

Luca sat there, no expression on his face, no emotion. Luciano put down his glass and moved to the door. She started to turn and he said softly, "He's an old man. He may think otherwise, but without you, there is nothing."

She stared up at him for a moment, then something moved in the eyes. She turned and crossed to Luca and knelt in front of him. Her words, when they came, were pure Sicilian, a ritual as old as time itself.

"I go on a long journey, grandfather. I seek your blessing."

Luca was transfixed, his iron features dissolving. Almost as a reflex, he placed a hand on her head and replied with the same ritual words. "Go with God, go in peace, go with my love, and return in safety."

She stood up, leaned forward, and kissed him gently on both cheeks, then turned and walked out, brushing past Luciano. Luca sat there, staring blindly into space, tears in his eyes.

Luciano went forward and kissed his right hand as a mark of respect. Luca whispered, "Can it be that she still loves me in spite of everything?"

Luciano put a hand on his shoulder. "Old friend, she never stopped."

SIXTEEN

Detweiler's body was racked by convulsions as he bucked and twisted, heaving against the chair to which he was tied. It took three of the Ukrainians to hold him still.

Meyer said, "I'll ask you again. Where did you get the American weapons from?"

Detweiler's eyes bulged and there was froth on his lips. He tried to speak, wanted to tell them everything, but the words wouldn't come.

Meyer said, "Give him another ten cc's."

"I'm not sure if he can stand it, Major," Suslov said. "I've seen them like this before. It's like a dam building up. The heart. . . ."

"Get on with it," Meyer said impatiently.

Suslov jabbed in the needle. Detweiler went into another convulsion, lost his balance, and fell over, still strapped to the chair.

"For Christ's sake!" Suslov said angrily and kicked him in the body.

And the dam finally burst inside Detweiler in a great aching scream and he cried out in English, "No more! No more!"

Meyer turned from the window, thunderstruck. "He's American."

Suslov and his men had Detweiler upright in the chair again and Meyer leaned over him, shaking him by the shoulders. "Who are you?"

Detweiler sat there, eyes glazed, and Meyer turned to the desk and quickly refilled the hypodermic.

Suslov said, "Another shot will kill him, Major. I've never known anyone to survive such a massive dosage."

Detweiler seemed to calm down after the final injection. He sat there in the chair, head slumped on his chest and Meyer waited. Finally, he leaned forward and tilted Detweiler's chin up.

"Now then, who are you?" Meyer said in English.

Detweiler tried hard, something moving in the eyes. The mouth parted and he said hoarsely, "Sergeant Joseph Detweiler, Ranger Division, on detachment from the

Twenty-First Specialist Raiding Force."

Meyer pulled up a chair and sat in front of him. His voice, when he next spoke, was soft and gentle.

"I see, Sergeant. That's very interesting. Tell me more."

Twice on the way to Agrigento, Koenig and Guzzoni, traveling in the general's staff car, had to take shelter in trees at the side of the road when military convoys, en route for the coast, were strafed by RAF Hawker Typhoons, whose cannon inflicted severe damage.

Before reaching Agrigento, they called at the coastal defense command post for the section of the coast bordering the Sicilian Channel. Koenig waited in the car. When Guzzoni returned, he looked glum.

"Not good," he said as they drove on into Agrigento. "They're hitting harbors and airports hard and Messina has taken a real pasting. They estimate five thousand tons of bombs at least. Something's up, that's obvious."

They were driving along the coast road and Koenig looked out to sea. The waves were already lifting into white caps.

"Well, if they're coming, I don't envy

them. Hell in those landing craft in this weather."

"On the other hand, how far would you say you could see out to sea at the moment?" Guzzoni asked. "Six or seven hundred yards? There could be an armada out there now ready to pounce."

Koenig said delicately, "Do we assume that the enemy must succeed with his landing?"

Guzzoni said, "That is quite impossible, I assure you. Mussolini has ordered us to wipe out the invader before he can break through inland."

"Indeed?" Koenig said drily.

"Yes, I believe the phrase was, as he takes off his bathrobe and before he has time to get dressed."

"The enemy or the Duce?" Koenig enquired.

Guzzoni laughed heartily. "That's really very good. Have a cigarette," and he offered his carved ivory case.

It was long after lunch and the officer's mess at the Agrigento barracks was empty when General Guzzoni and Koenig went in. The barman hurried to serve them and they took a corner table and waited while he opened a bottle of Chianti.

Rudi Brandt came in, glanced around quickly, then approached and saluted smartly.

"My apologies, Colonel, but might I have a word?"

Guzzoni waved his hand. "Carry on, by all means."

Koenig walked to the window with Brandt. "I saw you come in, Colonel, and came straight over. There's something going on to do with that prisoner. The suspected partisan."

"I gave orders that he was to be left alone until I returned," Koenig said.

"I don't know what happened but he's dead. I was tipped off by one of the attendants from the infirmary mortuary. But more than that, Major Meyer's left instructions that I notify him the moment you arrive."

There was a quick step in the doorway and Meyer appeared. He carried a folder in one hand.

Koenig said, "I told you that the prisoner brought in the other day would be dealt with by me on my return. I now find he's lying in the infirmary, dead."

Meyer offered Guzzoni the folder. "Read

that, Herr General, and see who has behaved in the most responsible manner. Me or the Colonel.''

Guzzoni, frowning, opened the file. He scanned the first page and his eyes widened. He looked up. ''Is this true?''

''Most certainly.'' Meyer turned to Koenig. ''This ragged peasant who you treated with such consideration, Colonel. Do you know who he was? A sergeant in the American Ranger Division.''

Koenig turned to Guzzoni, who nodded. ''According to this, he parachuted in with a party two nights ago. He became separated from the others and landed in the wrong valley.''

''Read it, why don't you?'' Meyer said. ''Your old friend Carter, a Colonel now, it seems, whom you let slip through your fingers last time, and some interesting companions.''

Guzzoni passed the file to Koenig who moved to the window to read it. After a while, he turned.

''How did you obtain this information?''

Meyer shrugged. ''Does it matter?''

''To me it does. I'd be interested to see the condition of the body.''

Guzzoni said, ''Colonel, the morality of

what has occurred here is one thing, but the facts are something else again. To speak plainly, there is considerable merit in this plan to enlist Mafia aid on the side of the Americans in the coming invasion. From what Detweiler admitted in his interrogation, the man, Luciano, is dead, but Colonel Carter still has the daughter of Antonio Luca in his charge. Luca holds immense power in Sicily, believe me. If he falls in with their wishes, then anything is possible."

"Perhaps he already has," Koenig said.

Guzzoni spread his hands. "On the other hand, they have not had a great deal of time to operate. I suggest we proceed on the assumption that they haven't. This monastery they are using as a base, Crown of Thorns near Bellona. Do you know it?"

"Yes," Koenig told him.

"The Franciscans of Crown of Thorns," Guzzoni said. "Now I remember. There was a considerable scandal several years ago. A trial in Palermo. The Mafia monks, the newspapers called them. You could have trouble there."

"With respect, Herr General. I really don't think so," Meyer said. "I can be up there in four hours. We'll be through the front gate before they know what's hit them. If Carter and his people are still here, we'll root them out, believe me."

Koenig laughed harshly. "You wouldn't get within ten miles of the place before they knew you were coming. Every shepherd on the mountain, every goatherd, is in some way involved with the Resistance movement. They have a signaling system from crag to crag. A normal approach would be quite impossible."

Meyer started to protest and Guzzoni cut him off impatiently. "Colonel Koenig, in this kind of soldiering you are second to none, that is a known fact. Is there any way at all, in your opinion, in which Colonel Carter and his party might be apprehended, particularly the lady in question, Luca's granddaughter, this Sister Maria Vaughan. Her capture is of primary importance." He smiled gently. "I need also, I trust, hardly stress the necessity for delicate treatment in her case. We don't wish to offend the Vatican if it can be avoided."

"But General," Meyer protested, "the woman is a spy and, as such, liable to be shot under the rules of the Geneva Convention."

"A question of attitude, I suppose,"

Guzzoni said. "We Italians perhaps take a different view of these matters, but then, we are an old race." He selected a cigarette from his ivory case. "Well, Colonel?"

Brandt, who had stood by silently at this time, stepped smartly forward and gave him a light. Koenig said, "There is a way, General. A parachute drop."

"Could it be done?"

"I'm not sure. I'd need some advice on that. With your permission?" Guzzoni nodded and Koenig said to Brandt. "Get a message through to Colonel Nagel at Otranto Luftwaffe base. Present General Guzzoni's compliments and ask him to get here as quickly as he can."

Brandt turned smartly on his heel and went out on the double.

"Excellent," Guzzoni said. "Now, as we last ate in Palermo, I suggest some late lunch." He turned to Meyer. "And you, Major, must be about your duties, I'm sure."

"Herr General—Colonel." Meyer turned and marched out stiffly.

Wolf Nagel was twenty-five, and already a full colonel, *Gruppenkommandant* at Otranto and responsible for three *Staffeln*.

He had seen combat service in Poland and Norway, had shot down sixty-nine enemy aircraft over the Channel and England by the end of 1941. In Russia, he had achieved even greater distinction, adding another eighty-four, his total until a bad crash had necessitated the amputation of his left leg. Not that this had deterred him; he had returned to combat flying within six weeks until he had been relegated to a desk job on Goering's personal order.

He had very fair hair, a handsome, rather dashing young man in an old, black leather Luftwaffe flying jacket, who wore the Knight's Cross with oak leaves, swords, and diamonds at his throat.

He leaned over the large-scale map in Koenig's office, a frown on his face. "Lousy flying country."

"Could it be done?" Guzzoni demanded.

"Getting there is no problem—no more than fifteen minutes flying time from Otranto—but it's getting this madman and his men on target that worries me. I mean, you want someone to fly up that valley at four hundred feet and drop your men inside the walls of this damn monastery." He shook his head. "As good a way of committing suicide as I've heard of."

Koenig said to Guzzoni. "General, my men are a special breed. Six jumps earns the paratrooper his qualification badge and, after that he must never make less than six a year if he wishes to keep it. We make a specialty of jumping from under four hundred feet. Is this not so, Sergeant?" he said to Brandt.

Guzzoni said to Nagel, "Are you saying it can't be done?"

"Not at all, Herr General. A Junkers 52, doing no more than a hundred miles an hour, would be the thing, but they'd have to get out damn fast."

"A dawn drop to catch them wholly by surprise," Koenig said. "Not the best time for flying in the mountains."

Nagel rubbed his chin. "Which means you're going to need the best pilot I've got." He grinned. "Not that I mind. I could do with a little action."

"Twenty men including myself," Koenig said. "No time for more than that number to jump over the target, but it should suffice."

"And what of my command?" asked Meyer, who had been standing silently by.

"Leave here in the early hours of the morning, approach under cover of darkness.

No more than twenty men. You wait here at the head of the valley." He indicated the place with his finger. "Make your move when you see the Junkers pass overhead. By the time you reach the monastery, we should be in control and the gates open!"

"An excellent plan," Guzzoni said. "Which seems to cover all contingencies. Wouldn't you agree, Major?"

"So it would appear, General," Meyer said.

"Good." Guzzoni slapped his thigh. "Well, I've got things to attend to. I'll try and see you off in the morning, Koenig. Until then."

Meyer moved to the door. Koenig said, "A moment, Major."

Meyer turned. "Well?"

"I am in command of this operation. I use you and your men with considerable reluctance, but for good or ill, they will follow my orders. Is that clear?"

"Perfectly, Colonel," Meyer said calmly. "May I go now?"

"Of course."

Meyer went out and Rudi Brandt said, "You've got trouble there."

"Never mind that now," Koenig said. "We've more important things to consider.

You and me, Rudi, which means selecting another eighteen. You can handle that dirty job for me. You won't be popular with the men who stay behind."

"That's what sergeant majors are for, Colonel."

Brandt saluted and went out.

In the cubbyhole behind the coffin room at the mortuary, Harry Carter sat at the radio. He finished transmitting and waited for a reply. After a while, he took off the headphones. As he lit a cigarette, the secret door opened and Vito Barbera came in.

"Well?" he asked.

"They're on their way."

"In this weather? It's blowing up a real storm out there."

"All the better when they hit the coast."

"What did you tell them?"

"About Luca? Mission a failure." He started to cough over the cigarette and there was that sudden sharp pain in his lung again.

Vito said, "Half a loaf's better than none, Harry. I'll call a meeting of the district committee for tonight. Father Collura, Verga, those two Reds. Warn every man to oil his gun and be ready to move tomorrow."

"And the Mafia?"

"In the Bellona valley, I speak for the Mafia," Vito said simply. "Luciano and Captain Savage have taken Maria up to Crown of Thorns. Better you spend the night up there, too, Harry. You're not looking too good. I'll come in the morning."

"All right." Carter got up and Vito Barbera led the way out through the coffin room. They passed through the waiting mortuary and Barbera opened the door to the street. It was pouring rain, everything out of focus, the houses, the mountain beyond. He went and untethered Carter's mule and led it to the door.

Carter was seized with a violent paroxysm of coughing. He leaned against the doorpost, holding a grimy handkerchief to his mouth. When he examined it, he saw that it was stained with blood.

He held it out to Barbera and tried to smile. "Ain't life grand?"

"Come on, Harry," Barbera said gently. "The sooner you're up there, the better. Maria will know what to do."

Carter clambered up, sitting sideways on the wooden saddle. He reached for the reins and managed a smile.

"Suddenly I feel tired, Vito, really tired. You know what I mean?"

"I know, old friend, I know," Barbera said sadly.

Carter kicked his feet against the mule's belly and moved away across the square.

Padre Giovanni, a large black umbrella protecting him from the rain, was feeding the pigeons on the battlements when Luciano came up the steps.

"How is Colonel Carter?" the old man asked.

Luciano stood under the overhanging eaves of the hut to avoid the worst of the rain and offered him a cigarette.

"Not good. High fever, something close to pneumonia. Maria says he probably needs surgery and he certainly isn't going to get that here."

"Remember the Americans will get here soon. He'll have the best of treatment then. The finest doctors."

"If he lives that long." Luciano looked out at the mountains, shrouded in rain. "Crazy when you think of it. It's only a few weeks since the guy took a bullet in the lung. He should have been invalided out, back to that university of his."

"He is an exceptional man, I think." Padre Giovanni said. "For some people, moral decisions come out of a personal evaluation of what is right against what is wrong. Frequently, circumstances modify their actions."

"What you mean, Father, is they won't do what's right if it looks as if it might prove unhealthy for them."

Padre Giovanni nodded. "Colonel Carter, on the other hand, does what he does because he can do no other."

"Here I stand," Luciano said. "Isn't that what Martin Luther said? People like that can make life damned uncomfortable for the rest of us."

The door opened in the small courtyard below and Maria came out. She had on an old raincoat over her shoulders and looked tired as she came up the steps.

"How is he?" Luciano asked.

"Not good. Medical supplies in the emergency kits we carried are limited. I've given him morphine for the pain and the monastery clinic was able to supply me with quinine. I've given him a heavy dose of that. It should help to reduce the fever."

"Will that be enough?"

"No. In my opinion, the lung is ulcerated. I suspect the original wound didn't get a chance to heal properly, mainly because of a lack of any kind of convalescence."

"I'll go and sit with him for a while," Padre Giovanni said.

"That would be a kindness, Father."

The old man went down the steps and Maria and Luciano stood there under the eaves, looking out across the the valley as evening fell.

"So here we are," Luciano said. "A hell of a lot of effort that seems to have added up to a considerable waste of time."

"Perhaps," she said.

The wind dashed rain across the pantiled roofs. Luciano said, "A long way from Liverpool and that convent of yours."

"Oh, yes," she said. "Too far to go back." There was an expression of infinite sadness on her face when she looked up at him. "I know that now."

Luciano couldn't think of a thing to say. He stood there, watching her go back down the steps to the courtyard and disappear through the door.

By four o'clock in the morning, under cover

of darkness, Meyer and his men in an armored troop carrier and three *Kubelwagens* had taken up positions in the pine forest at the south end of the valley some five miles from Crown of Thorns.

Suslov joined Meyer beside the front vehicle, glancing at his watch. "They should be taking off in one hour exactly at five o'clock."

There was a paleness in the sky beyond the mountains and Meyer looked up at the monastery through Zeiss nightglasses.

"Is this going to work, Major?" Suslov asked.

"Of course it is," Meyer said. "I don't like Koenig, I make no secret of the fact. I don't think he's a good German and I have heard him make remarks which indicate a certain contempt for the Führer, but he is also a soldier of genius. If anyone can pull this off, he can."

"And afterwards?"

Mayer turned and smiled coldly. "Oh, that, of course, is quite another matter."

At the Otranto Luftwaffe base, rain swept across the tarmac in solid sheets, but the three engines of the Junkers 52 were already ticking over. Nagel leaned out of the cockpit window and raised a thumb.

The men, in Brandt's charge, were already on board and Koenig stood beside the open hatch with Guzzoni. He wore a paratrooper's camouflage smock in the SS pattern, a machine pistol was suspended across his chest.

Guzzoni said, "It would appear he thinks it's still on in spite of this wretched weather. You really think you can jump in conditions like this?"

"They jumped at Maleme, they dropped into Stalingrad. They'd jump into hell if I told them to." Koenig saluted. "And now, I think, Nagel is getting impatient."

Guzzoni grasped his hand warmly. "What can I say?"

"Nothing, I suspect, would be perfectly adequate in the circumstances." Koenig placed the end of his static line between his teeth and climbed into the Junkers. The hatch was closed and Guzzoni stepped back.

Nagel increased engine revs and the Junkers moved away into the rain and darkness. The flare path had not been lit due to the ever-present chance of an Allied airstrike. The lights switched on now for the final run only. The roaring of the engines filled the morning as Nagel boosted power and the Junkers skimmed along the runway, rain spraying up in great waves on either side.

Guzzoni watched it lift above the trees and fade into the grey morning. He shivered, pulling his cloak around him, and turned away.

At the monastery, Carter slept fitfully, his hands clutching sheets that were drenched in his own sweat. Maria, on the chair beside him, slept the sleep of total exhaustion. The blanket she had wrapped around herself had slipped to the floor. Luciano, sitting in the window seat, crossed to her side, picked up the blanket, and covered her. The wind moaned eerily around the battlements. He lit a cigarette and stood, peering out through the window, suddenly uneasy.

Savage was so tired he hadn't bothered to undress, simply lay on the small bed in one of the monks' cells and was instantly asleep.

He couldn't remember when Rosa joined him, but when he awakened, just before dawn, he found her lying in the crook of his arm.

She stirred sleepily, "Savage, is that you?"

"Who else would it be?"

She smiled, still half asleep, then raised her head. "What's that? I thought I heard something."

"The wind," he said. "Just the wind. Go back to sleep."

She closed her eyes again and turned her face into his shoulder, smiling.

SEVENTEEN

Flying at one thousand feet the view was spectacular in the dawn light in spite of the heavy rain. Chains of mountains, peaks and ridges on every hand, the valleys dark with shadow.

Sitting beside the hatch, Koenig looked down the line of his men, anonymous in the dim light in helmets and camouflaged jump jackets and parachutes. No bulky equipment this time, no supply bags. Each man carried a Schmeisser across his chest, ammunition pouches, grenades.

"How many times have we done this, Rudi?" he asked Brandt, who sat next to him.

"God knows," Brandt said. "Narvik was the first, I know that, but in between is a blur. Too many good men gone."

"Yes," Koenig said. "Sometimes I think

that's all we have, our dead."

"No, Colonel," Brandt said firmly. "We have each other. We have the Regiment. We have you."

My God, Koenig thought. Is that all we're left with after so much suffering? Is that what it was really all about? He looked out of the window and saw the jagged peak of Monte Commarata, the western slope. They started to descend rapidly. A jagged ridge seemed to bar their way, the Junkers lifted as Nagel eased back the stick, the spine of rock no more than fifty feet beneath them as they slipped over it.

And there was the Bellona valley below them, the river running through pine trees, the rain and mist so heavy that it was impossible to see Bellona itself or Crown of Thorns at the other end of the valley.

Nagel swung into the wind, the tip of his starboard wing breath-takingly close to the rock face. Koenig got up, moved along the fuselage, and leaned in the cockpit.

"What do you think?"

"I think it stinks. If you want to go through with it, I'll play along, but you only get one chance, remember that, and when you go, go together and very fast or you'll miss the target altogether."

"Understood."

"Right—you've got approximately two minutes."

Koenig moved back along the line. "On your feet and let's get ready."

Brandt opened the hatch as they stood and clipped on their static lines, each man checking his neighbor. The Junkers descended even further and then everything happened at once.

As the light flared above the hatch, they roared across the village and Wolf Nagel banked to starboard.

There was Crown of Thorns, the road snaking up the side of the valley to the great gate.

"Now!" Koenig cried, even before they'd reached the outer wall, and Brandt went out through the door, the others following him so fast that they seemed to be falling on top of each other.

Then it was Koenig's turn. He plunged out, aware of the courtyard directly below him, the red pantiles of the roofs, and then his parachute open. He glanced up to see the Junkers fading into the rain, looked the other way and saw his men to the left and beneath him, drifting in over the wall.

The essential difference between the parachutes used by the Germans and the English and Americans was that the German variety carried no shroud lines which made any kind of manoeuvring by the parachutist impossible. This explained the popularity of drops at a very low level by German forces. But the system had its disadvantages, especially in a case like this. Koenig saw two of his men vanish on the other side of the wall, a third land badly on the battlements above the gate, then fall headfirst to the courtyard below.

Others had already landed in the courtyard itself, parachutes billowing, and then the red pantiles at one of the higher levels were rushing up to meet him. He braced himself for the shock, folding his arms and landed hard, smashing right through the roof.

From the pine trees, Meyer watched through field glasses as the parachutes drifted down.

"He's done it!"

"Fifteen, by my count," Suslov said. "The rest are somewhere outside."

But Meyer didn't seem to hear him. "Mount up!" he cried. "And let's get out of here."

He nodded to the driver of his *Kubel-wagen* and they drove away rapidly.

Luciano, unable to sleep, went out on the battlements just after dawn and found Padre Giovanni standing there under his old black umbrella, enjoying the first cigarette of the day.

"So, you couldn't sleep either?" he said.

"No, I guess not," Luciano replied.

"Holy Mother of God!" Padre Giovanni said, the smile wiped clean from his face.

Luciano swung round as the Junkers appeared from the rain like a grey ghost and roared down the valley towards them at four-hundred feet. And as the first para-trooper plunged into space, all became horrifyingly clear.

Padre Giovanni pushed him towards the door. "You must leave, you and the others, as quickly as possible and take Carter with you. There is nothing to be gained by trying to stand and fight here."

Carter, half dazed, was struggling to sit up in bed, and Maria was on her feet as they entered the room.

"We're in trouble," Luciano said. "Para-troopers. We've got to get out of here."

The door opened and Savage appeared,

pulling on his rucksack. Rosa was behind him holding his M1 and she passed it to him.

"What's happening?"

"Detweiler, or I miss my guess," Luciano said.

They moved to the window in time to see Koenig crash through the red pantile roof to the left of them and disappear. The men in the courtyard, under Brandt's direction, were already discarding their parachutes.

Savage raised his rifle to fire and Luciano knocked it up. "No need for that. We're getting out of here. That way we leave it clean for the Franciscans."

"How?"

"The catacombs," Padre Giovanni said. "Follow me, please, but we must hurry. There isn't much time."

Luciano said to Savage, "Sling Carter over your shoulder and you bring clothes, Maria. We'll dress him later."

They hurried along the passage outside. Padre Giovanni produced a key and opened on oak door at the far end disclosing a stone spiral staircase.

"This goes all the way down to the chapel. The entrance to the crypt, I showed you the other day. I can only wish you luck,

336

my friends. Now hurry, I beg you."

Luciano led the way and Savage followed, Carter over his shoulder, Rosa and Maria behind. Padre Giovanni closed the door and locked it. As he turned, one of the SS paratroopers appeared from the stairhead at the other end of the passageway and covered him with his Schmeisser.

Koenig's left arm was badly broken and he sat on one of the benches in the monastery refectory while a young Brother bandaged it. There was also a gash in his left cheek and Koenig held a handkerchief against it to stem the flow of blood.

Padre Giovanni said, "It will need stitches, I fear, Colonel, and the arm is not good. Broken in two places. You will need a skillful surgeon if you are not be left with permanent injury."

There was a quick step and Brandt came in. "We've searched the place thoroughly, Colonel. Not a sign of anyone except the Fathers."

"Should there be?" Padre Giovanni inquired.

"My information was that there were enemy agents here, Father, led by a British Officer—a Colonel Carter."

"Then I can only say you have gone to considerable trouble to no good purpose. There is no one of that description here." He raised the crucifix around his neck to his lips and kissed it. "I give you my word."

Koenig stood up wearily, grimacing with pain. "What about the men?"

"Three dead, Colonel. Two in the ravine outside and Vogel broke his neck falling off the wall. Hartman has a broken leg."

"And all to no purpose," Koenig turned to Padre Giovanni. "You were right, Father."

There was a sudden burst of firing from outside. Koenig hurried out followed by Brandt and Padre Giovanni and stood at the top of the steps. There was a young paratrooper on the battlement above the gate and Koenig called up to him.

"What is it?"

"It looks as if there are people down there in the forest, Colonel, moving towards Bellona. Major Meyer and his column have turned off the road to go after them."

There was a renewed burst of heavy firing. Koenig turned to Padre Giovanni. "I see now, Father. You told the truth because they'd already gone." He didn't wait for a reply, simply turned to Brandt and said,

"Right, Sergeant Major, round up the men and follow me at the double."

For the first time in their long association, Brandt queried an order. "Look, sir, I don't think in your present state that you're fit to go anywhere."

"Your opinion is duly noted," Koenig said. "Now let's get moving," and he went down the steps and hurried across the courtyard.

Padre Giovanni watched the last paratrooper double through the gate after him, then turned, hurried to the chapel and started to toll the bell, one deep solemn stroke after another. The sound echoed all the way down the valley to Bellona to where Vito Barbera, already alerted by the gunfire from the forest, stood listening.

Verga and Father Collura hurried across the square to join him. "What does it mean?" Verga demanded.

"I don't know, but I've just been on the radio and the Americans have landed at Licata. Spread the word. Tell everyone to have what weapons they have ready."

"It will take time," Verga said.

"Do the best you can."

They hurried away and Barbera went back inside, climbed up to the coffin room and entered the cubbyhole through the secret entrance. He got down on his knees, pried up a floorboard in one corner and took out a machine pistol and several clips of ammunition, then he went back downstairs.

On emerging from the tunnel on the hillside, Luciano and the others had stopped to dress Carter. They got him into pants and a jacket and Maria and Rosa hurriedly forced his feet into boots. Carter was still in a high fever, but reasonably articulate.

"What's happening?"

"We've been rumbled," Luciano said. "We're going to try to make our way down to the village to see what Barbera can do for us. Don't try to talk. Just save your strength and let's get going."

Savage passed his M1 and his rucksack to Rosa. Then he hoisted Carter on his back and they started down the slope. There was a small clearing to cross where the olive terraces ended and the pine trees began. It was when they were halfway across that the firing started.

It was Meyer, in the lead field car as his column raced up the zigzag road to the monastery, who saw them first and cried to his driver to halt.

Suslov in the *Kubelwagen* at the rear of the small column, stood up, reaching for the heavy machine gun mounted on its swivel and started to fire. The bullets kicked up fountains of dirt, chasing the fugitives into the trees and Maria stumbled and fell. Luciano reached down, dragging her to her feet, and they staggered into the shelter of the trees.

"After them!" Meyer cried, urging his driver on, and the *Kubelwagen* left the road and hurtled over the rough ground between the olive terraces.

Miraculously, it was only the heel of Maria's shoe that had been hit and they hurried along the track through the pine trees, following Savage and Rosa.

The trees at that part grew closely together, making it impossible terrain for the vehicles to operate in. After a while, Luciano, pausing to listen, heard voices.

"They're coming on foot," he said, and a burst of machine gun fire cut through the branches overhead.

He fired back quickly, emptying his M1, then rammed in another clip as he ran after the others. There was a crashing in the bushes to the right and one of the Ukrainians appeared, running very fast, his rifle held waist high. He fired twice, kicking up dirt to one side of Savage. Luciano went headlong down the hill and jumped, giving him both feet in the back. The Ukrainian rolled over twice. As he tried to scramble to his feet, Luciano shot him through the head.

Savage was gasping for breath now, lurching from side to side as he ran on, borne down by Carter's weight. He lost his balance and went headlong, Carter sprawling on top of him.

He managed to get to his feet. Carter said weakly, "Leave me. Save yourselves."

Luciano passed his M1 to Maria and pulled Carter to his feet. "Lean on me, Professor. One step in front of the other, that's all it takes. Aren't you the guy who went four miles with a bullet in the lung?"

"Keep moving," Savage said. "I'll guard your back."

He took a couple of hand grenades from the rucksack Rosa was holding and put one in each pocket. Then he reloaded his M1.

"Okay," he said. "Get going. They may need you. I'll follow on."

She shook her head stubbornly. "No, Savage, I won't leave you."

There was a rustle in the bushes behind, he turned and fired from the hip and a Ukrainian pitched forward on to his face. Savage gave her a push.

"Get out of it!"

He rammed in another clip, ducking as someone fired over to his left. He fired in reply and there was a cry of pain.

She crouched beside him. "Please, Savage, we go now."

He slapped her backhanded across the face. "Get out of here, you stupid little bitch!"

She recoiled in dismay, genuine hurt on her face, then turned and started to crawl away. He reached out, catching her left hand.

"Heh, I love you, don't forget that. Honeymoon in New York, that's a promise."

He turned, raising the M1, and received a burst of machine gun fire full in the chest that lifted him back off his feet.

There was blood in his mouth and he was choking on it, aware of Rosa screaming; then she was crouching over him, her face the last thing he saw as he died.

She knelt there, holding him in her arms, his blood staining her clothes and they came out of the bushes, four of them, and stood watching her.

One of them laughed harshly. "Let's see if you know your manners."

They were all laughing now as they lowered their weapons and moved in on her, and Rosa was laughing too as she laid Savage gently on the ground. She reached in his pockets and turned, still laughing, a grenade in each hand. The Ukrainians recoiled in horror, turned to run, already too late.

Luciano and Maria, Carter supported between them, emerged from the pine trees and started across the patch of broken ground leading up to the village. Vito Barbera, from the upper window of the mortuary, saw the Russians moving down through the trees, higher up the slope.

There was sporadic firing and, to his dismay, he heard Luciano cry out and saw him go down. Carter reeled against Maria and Barbera leaned out the window and fired a long burst from his Schmeisser across the open ground. Miraculously, Luciano was on his feet and helping Maria with Carter again. As they reached the edge of the village, two or three Ukrainians ran out of the forest and started across the open ground.

The streets were deserted, everyone was indoors, as Luciano and Maria staggered across the square with their burden. They could hear vehicles coming along the road, very close now. Luciano was bleeding profusely from the right leg, limping badly as they turned into the side street leading to the mortuary. Barbera opened the door and hastened to meet him.

Meyer stood in one of the troop carriers in the middle of the square and watched as the Ukrainians went from house to house turning everyone out. It was Suslov, pausing casually on the corner of the street leading to Barbera's premises to light a cigarette, who noticed blood on the cobbles, a clearly defined trail. He followed it to the steps leading up to the mortuary door. The door was unlocked. He pushed it open, drew the Walther from his holster, and moved inside cautiously.

There was more blood on the stone flags of the passage leading to the door at the end. He opened that and found himself in the waiting mortuary. It was totally silent and very still in the dim light, and he recoiled at the sight of the corpse of a gnarled old woman in the first coffin on his left.

There was a spot of blood on the floor, another. He carried on, passing several open coffins containing corpses, each one holding the end of the bell pull in stiff fingers.

There was another patch of blood beside an ornate black coffin. He crouched down to examine it and then the hair lifted on the back of his neck as a bell tinkled faintly.

He stood up and peered over the edge of the coffin. The corpse of the man inside seemed peaceful enough, hands folded around an ivory Madonna. It was really very beautiful. Suslov leaned closer to examine it and the corpse's eyes opened. There was a click as the Madonna swung upward in the right hand.

Father Collura stood against the wall of the church facing half a dozen Ukrainians forming a firing squad while the people of Bellona watched. Meyer, standing in one of the *Kubelwagens,* nodded, there was a sharp volley and the old priest fell to the ground.

"That's just to show you I mean

346

business," Meyer called. "You all know who I'm looking for. I'll give you five minutes to come up with some answers. If you haven't, I'll select two more. Then four and so on. It's your choice."

Watching from the upper window of the mortuary, Maria said, "We must do something."

Barbera said, "There isn't much we can do. Most of the young men are in the hills. We didn't have time to organize. The whole thing caught us by surprise."

"What about the American troops?" Luciano said. "How long before they get here?"

"I don't know what's happening."

"Then let's try the radio."

They went out, Luciano limping badly, his left leg bandaged, and Maria opened the window in time to hear Meyer say, "The Englishman, Carter, and the woman, Maria Vaughan."

The people stood there, quiet in the steady rain. He gave an order and two of the Ukrainians moved into the crowd and grabbed a couple of old men.

She didn't really think about it, simply went downstairs, opened the front door and went along the side street into the

347

square. There was a murmur in the crowd as she appeared. She stopped and looked up at Meyer standing there in the *Kubelwagen*.

"I am Maria Vaughan, Major," she said simply. "You may release these people."

Meyer gazed down at her. "And your friends?"

"I cannot help you there. I speak only for myself."

He looked around him. "Where is Lieutenant Suslov?"

"I don't know, Major," one of the sergeants told him. "Still searching house to house, I think."

"Very well," Meyer said. "Put this woman against the wall." He looked down at her again. "Unless, of course, you have changed your mind."

"I have nothing to say," she said tranquilly.

Two of the Ukrainians seized her and hustled her across to the wall. They left her there beside the body of Father Collura and another firing squad was hastily formed. She crossed herself, closing her eyes to pray, and was not aware of Koenig appearing on the other side of the square, a handful of his paratroopers behind him.

"No!" he called.

They had come from the monastery on foot and he was tired. The pain in his arm was almost unbearable and his face was coated with dried blood. He moved forward, the paratroopers strung out behind him led by Brandt, and halted beside the troop carrier.

"Who is this lady?"

"The Vaughan woman. She refused to tell me where the rest of her people are."

Koenig called, "Fräulein Vaughan, would you come here, please."

"No!" Meyer said violently. "I will not have it."

Koenig didn't even bother to look at him. "I command here, Meyer. What you wish is of little importance."

"Damn you, Koenig!" Meyer cried, all the pent-up hatred finally overflowing. He pulled out his Walther and shot him twice in the back.

Koenig staggered forward and Maria tried to catch him, half twisting round in an attempt to hold him up. Meyer kept on firing in a kind of insane rage, bullets smashing into her, driving her and Koenig down together to lie like lovers, limbs entwined.

The people scattered, running for their homes in panic. Brandt dropped on his knee beside Koenig and gently turned him over. He looked up at Meyer, his face hard, and Meyer reached for the handles of the heavy machine gun on its swivel and swung it to cover Brandt and the paratroopers.

"He was a traitor to the Reich and to the Führer," he said. "You hear me? Now stand back, all of you!" He called to his men, "Mount up and let's get out of here."

The rest of them scrambled into the other *Kubelwagen* and drove quickly away.

EIGHTEEN

Luciano and Vito Barbera came out of the mortuary and ran across the square. Luciano dropped on his knees beside Maria. Brandt said, "She's dead. They're both dead."

Her face was peaceful, her wounds in the chest and heart. He knelt there for a long moment looking down at her, then gently touched her breast. The blood stained his fingers and he raised them to his mouth.

He stood up, wholly Sicilian now, and whispered the ancient formula. "In this way may I drink the blood of the one who killed you."

Men had appeared in the square, old and young, armed with everything from shotguns to automatic weapons and Brandt and the remaining paratroopers moved in on each other, faces grim, ready for anything.

A teenage boy came running across the

square and stopped before Barbera. "They've taken the north road."

"Then that means the monastery. It leads nowhere else."

Two old women knelt beside Maria to straighten her limbs and one of them took off her shawl to cover the pale face. Luciano was filled with a sense of total despair.

He turned. "Okay, let's go and get him." He nodded to the troop carrier. "Can anyone drive this thing?"

"I can," Rudi Brandt said.

There was a moment's silence. Luciano said, "I thought we were supposed to be at war?"

"This is personal."

Luciano looked at Barbera, who nodded. "I'll get my truck."

"Fine." Luciano turned to Brandt. "I'll go with you boys. Now let's get moving."

They braked to a halt just before the crest of the hill below the main gate. Barbera, who was carrying more than twenty armed men in his old truck, got out and hurried to the troop carrier.

"How are we going to handle it?"

"The troop carrier goes first," Luciano told him. "It's the only way we'll get through those gates. If it works, you come straight in after us and remember Padre Giovanni and the Franciscans are on our side."

"Okay." Barbera grinned. "Do I wish you luck?"

"When did I ever need it?" Luciano slapped Brandt on the shoulder and they drove away.

When Meyer got out of his field car in the courtyard at Crown of Thorns, there was no one in sight, the whole place unnaturally quiet in the heavy rain. The only visible signs of the action that had taken place were the parachutes which were draped untidily on the walls or in the courtyard and were lifting uneasily in the slight breeze.

At that moment in the catacombs below, Father Giovanni was supervising the departure of the last of the Franciscans into the tunnel, taking with them the young paratrooper with the broken leg. He gave one last glance around, then followed them in. The wooden throne swung back into its place with its macabre burden.

Meyer was unable to think clearly. It had

all happened so quickly, the rage in him, something that could not be denied. Now he was faced with the appalling consequences.

A sergeant came out of the entrance, ran down the steps, and hurried towards him. "Not a soul in the place. Quiet as the grave, Major."

"Impossible," Meyer said.

One of the men on the gate called out, "Someone's coming, Major."

Meyer ran out and paused on the bridge over the ditch. From that vantage point the approach road could be seen in its entirety. The half-track troop carrier was coming up fast followed by an old truck. Way behind, a considerable crowd of people were following on foot.

The Ukrainians crowded around him and one of them held a pair of field glasses to his eyes. He lowered them and turned to Meyer, bewildered.

"I don't understand. Koenig's paratroopers in the troop carrier and the truck's crammed full of peasants."

Meyer took the glasses from him and raised them, and the troop carrier jumped into focus. It was Brandt, who he recognized instantly, the rest of his men, and Luciano. Barbera was at the wheel of the truck behind and the men with him were armed.

"They've joined forces," Meyer said. "They're coming up together. Inside quickly and get the gates closed." He turned and ran for the courtyard.

Meyer was no soldier, never had been, and the Ukrainians ignored him now. Someone closed the gates and slid the retaining bar through its sockets and the rest of them took the two heavy machine guns from the *Kubelwagen* and carried them up to the battlements above the gate.

They were all up there now and Meyer stood in the center of the courtyard among the billowing parachutes quite alone. There was a Schmeisser in one of the *Kubelwagens*. He picked it up, turned, walked away from the gate, and mounted the stone steps to the east rampart.

Brandt, peering out through the open visor of the troop carrier, said to Luciano, "Get down here. This could be a hot one."

Luciano did as he was told. Above them, two of the paratroopers crouched over the heavy machine gun, hanging on as Brandt increased speed, turning into the last stretch, the half-tracks kicking up mud and filth from the road.

The machine guns above the gate started to fire when they had still a hundred yards to go. The armoured plating of the troop carrier took most of the brunt and their own machine gun was returning the fire now, raking the battlements above the gate.

One of the Ukrainians was hit and came over the parapet, dragging a machine gun with him, falling on to the bridge as Brandt roared on, bouncing over the body, the machine gun, hitting the gates at close to sixty miles an hour, tearing them from their hinges.

The troop carrier kept on going, smashing into one of the *Kubelwagens,* drifting broadside past another. One of the paratroopers tossed a stick grenade, there was a tremendous explosion as the *Kubelwagen's* gas tank exploded.

The Ukrainians up on the wall were firing down into the yard, working their Schmeissers furiously, and two of them tried to turn the heavy machine gun round. Rudi Brandt ran forward, hurling another stick grenade. It curled lazily through the air exploding above the gate. Two of the Ukrainians fell into the yard and the machine gun followed them.

The second *Kubelwagen* exploded, showering burning gasoline over a wide area. A dense pall of black smoke drifted across the courtyard.

Luciano, crouched at the side of the troop carrier, snatched up a Schmeisser from a fallen paratrooper. Bullets bounced from the armor plating and he turned and fired instinctively at the battlements on the other side of the courtyard, at the figure crouched up there beside the wall.

"That's the man who killed Maria." He emptied the Schmeisser in another long burst, pulled out his Smith and Wesson and ran for the steps leading to the east rampart. He paused at the bottom, peering up through the smoke, fired three times very fast at what might have been a shadow and went up the steps on the run.

Below in the courtyard, Barbera and his friends had arrived in strength and there was a confused mêlée of hand-to-hand fighting in the smoke and rain.

Up there on the ramparts, it was quiet. Smoke drifted eerily and the noise of the battle in the courtyard seemed far away, as if it were happening in another time, another place.

Luciano removed his shoes and went forward cautiously on silent feet, the Smith and Wesson ready. He was at the highest point in the monastery, he knew that, smoke billowing around him. He was aware of the pigeons in their loft, fluttering in alarm, and paused. Then, quite suddenly, a gust of wind lifted across the battlements, dissolving the pall of smoke.

Meyer was standing only a few feet away, covering him with the Schmeisser. "Drop it!" he said. "Now!"

"Whatever you say." Luciano put the Smith and Wesson down carefully on the battlements.

Meyer was surprisingly calm. "Who are you?"

"Salvatore Lucania, but most people call me Luciano."

Meyer was shocked. The dead had come to life. His surprise showed in his eyes and his finger slackened on the trigger. A gunshot rang out to their left and Meyer turned instinctively. The Madonna was ready in Luciano's left hand. As he swung, the blade jumped, catching Meyer under the chin, shearing through the roof of the mouth into the brain.

It took all Luciano's strength to pull the knife free. Meyer staggered back, still alive, a look of astonishment on his face, then he fell backwards over the low parapet.

The pigeons in the loft thrashed around in panic. Luciano lifted the latch and opened the screen door and they flocked out, launching into space, climbing above the smoke into the clear rain.

He watched them go, then realized that he was still holding the ivory Madonna. For a moment, he was tempted to throw it out into space, but that would not have been Salvatore Lucania's way, or Lucky Luciano's.

He kissed the blade, still wet with Meyer's blood, the ritual completion of the oath he had taken in the square, then wiped it clean, closed it, and slipped the Madonna into his pocket.

Life for life, blood for blood and no satisfaction in it at all, but then Maria could have told him that, and he turned and went down the steps to the courtyard.

Maria Vaughan lay in a coffin before the altar of the little church at Bellona, her features relaxed and at peace in death, her wounds covered by a shroud.

Candles flared around her, placed there by the villagers, but now the place was empty, except for Katerina sitting in the front pew and Don Antonio Luca beside the coffin.

Luciano and Mario Sciara standing in the shadows at the back of the church watched as Luca leaned down to kiss the pale face. Katerina stood up and put an arm around him. They started up the aisle. Sciara opened the door and he and Luciano waited. When Luca reached them, he paused.

"You know what to do, Mario," he said to Sciara.

"Yes, *Capo.*"

"Good."

He turned and looked at Luciano, eyes dark. Luciano waited, but there was, after all, nothing to say. Katerina tightened her arm around him and they went out. Sciara followed them.

It was very quiet in the church and his footsteps echoed between the walls as Luciano walked down the aisle to the coffin. He stood there looking down at her, suddenly tired. He touched her hand gently. It was cold, hard, no life there at all.

Maybe people come to God when the

Devil has no further use for them.

His words to her echoed in his mind and her reply: *No, Mr. Luciano. I could never accept that. Never.*

He turned and walked away quickly.

Harry Carter lay in Vito Barbera's bed at the mortuary, propped up against pillows, still very weak as he sipped the brandy Barbera held for him.

"So, in the end, we got exactly what we wanted."

Luciano, standing at the window looking down into the square, nodded. "All over the Cammarata, in every village, every town in western Sicily, all the way up to Palermo, the word is already passing. That Don Antonio Luca is for the Americans."

"Because a German killed his grand-daughter?"

"Exactly," Luciano said. "Blood for blood, an old Sicilian custom. I'd have thought you'd have realized that by now."

Carter nodded. "And the paratroopers?"

"We let them clear off in the troop carrier, what's left of them, to take their chances. They took Koenig with them."

Carter frowned, "I don't understand."

"It turned out he was still alive. Badly

361

wounded, but in there with a chance if they can get him to a decent surgeon in time. I should imagine the sergeant major of his will ride over the devil himself to get him to Palermo."

Barbera said to Carter, "You need to eat now. I'll get you some soup."

He went out. There was a small silence. Carter said to Luciano, "You could take to the mountains. We could say you were killed in the fighting."

Luciano grinned. "Heh, don't tell me I've succeeded in corrupting you completely?" He shook his head. "No, I'll go back."

"Why, because the President said that was the way it had to be? He made no promises remember. You could be back inside for years."

"Well, you take a chance every day of your life."

Luciano walked to the window, opened it, and leaned out into the rain, breathing in its freshness.

Across the valley from Crown of Thorns high up on its crag, the bells started to peal.

NINETEEN

And so, the Mafia card was played and played to the full. In a single night, two thirds of the Italian soldiers defending the vital positions overlooking the main road through the Commarata to Palermo deserted. Even their commander was detained by Mafia trickery and handed over to Allied forces.

German units in the area, left in a hopelessly vulnerable position, had no other choice but to pull out. American forces raced north, reached Palermo in only seven days from the initial landing in what General George Patton was to describe as the fastest *Blitzkrieg* in history.

Mussolini was toppled from power by a war-weary nation on July 24, and in spite of spirited resistance by German forces, the whole of Sicily was in Allied hands by the seventeenth of August.

Charles Lucky Luciano returned to Great Meadow Penitentiary and appeared before a State Parole Board in 1946. The circumstances of the proceedings are still shrouded in controversy, but in February, of that year, Governor Dewey commuted his sentence and Luciano was sent to Ellis Island and deported.

Nearly sixteen years later, on January 25th, 1962, he died of a heart attack at Capodichino airport near Naples. The body was held at the chapel of the English Cemetery until arrangements could be made to have it transported to America.

For a while, there was considerable interest and many visitors. By the third day it had slackened off a little and the young reporter and photographer from Associated Press were beginning to think about packing it in when a small tour bus appeared. Fourteen or fifteen people got out and went to the entrance of the chapel, mainly American women chattering among themselves.

"More tourists," the young reporter said sourly. "Five hundred lire a time to gaze at a corpse. I reckon that's about it. Put your gear in the car and let's get out of here."

He went to the porch where the door stood open and looked inside. The women were gathered at the rail peering over at the coffin, and the reporter noticed a grey-haired man in his sixties wearing a black overcoat, standing at the back of them.

They turned and came down the aisle. The grey-haired man paused, raising his collar against the cold, suddenly breaking into a paroxysm of coughing.

"Are you all right?" the reporter asked, concerned.

"Smoker's cough, that's all. Been trying to stop for years."

"You didn't know him?"

"Who, Luciano?" Professor Harry Carter smiled. "Did anybody?" and he turned and went down the path to where the rest of the tourists were boarding the coach.

The publishers hope that this Large
Print Book has brought you pleasurable
reading. Each title is designed to make
the text as easy to see as possible.
G. K. Hall Large Print Books are
available from your library and
your local bookstore. Or you can
receive information on upcoming
and current Large Print Books by
mail and order directly from the
publisher. Just send your name
and address to:

G. K. Hall & Co.
70 Lincoln Street
Boston, Mass. 02111

A note on the text
Large print edition designed by
Cindy Schrom, and produced in cooperation
with Lyda Kuth and Lynn Harmet.
Composed in 18 pt English Times on a
Compugraphic Compuwriter II by Adhanet Elias
of G. K. Hall Corp.
Printed on Potsdam Opaque paper, and
bound by Fairfield Graphics.